Praise for

Sharon Ward's IN DEEP is a stellar, pulse-pounding debut novel featuring a female underwater photographer. A heady mix of underwater adventure, mystery, and romance.

— Hallie Ephron, New York Times bestselling author

Pack your SCUBA fins for a wild trip to the Cayman Islands. *In Deep* delivers on twists and turns while introducing a phenomenal new protagonist in underwater photographer Fin Fleming, tough, perceptive and fearless.

— Edwin Hill, author of *The Secrets We Share*

How much did I love In Deep? Let me count the ways. Fin Fleming, underwater photographer, is a courageous yet vulnerable protagonist I want to sip Margaritas with. The Cayman Islands are exotic and alluring, yet tinged with danger. The underwater scenes and SCUBA diving details are rendered in stunning detail. Wrap that all into a thrilling mystery and you'll be left as breathless as - well, no spoilers here. You must read it to find out!

— C. Michele Dorsey, Author of the Sabrina Salter Mysteries: No Virgin Island, Permanent Sunset, and Tropical Depression

Breathtaking on two levels, Sharon Ward's debut novel IN DEEP will captivate experienced divers as well as those who've only dreamed of exploring the beauty beneath the sea. The underwater world off the Cayman Islands is stunningly rendered, and the complex mystery involving underwater photographer Fin Fleming, especially the electrifying dive scenes, will have readers holding their breath. Brava!

— Brenda Buchanan Author of the Joe Gale Mystery Series

In Deep is a smart and original story that sucks you in from page one. Edge-of-your-seat suspense, a hauntingly realistic villain, and a jaw-dropping twist make this pacy read unputdownable until the very last word.

— Stephanie Scott-Snyder, Author of When Women Offend: Crime and the Female Perpetrator

Rip Current

Copyright © 2024 by Sharon Ward

All rights reserved.

All rights reserved. No part of this book may be reproduced in any form or by any electronic or mechanical means, including information storage and retrieval systems, without written permission from the author, except for the use of brief quotations in a book review as permitted by U.S. copyright law. For permissions contact: Editor@PensterPress.com

No part of this book may be used for the training of artificial systems, including systems based on artificial intelligence (AI), without the author's prior permission. This prohibition shall be in force even on platforms and systems which claim to have such rights based on an implied contract for hosting the book.

Covers by Cover2Book.com

ISBN eBook: 978-1-958478-15-8

ISBN Trade Paper: 978-1-958478-17-2

ISBN hardcover: 978-1-958478-18-9

Printed in USA

First Edition

Rip Current

A Fin Fleming Scuba Diving Mystery

Sharon Ward

Rip Current

A Fin Fleming Scuba Diving Mystery

Sharon Ward

For the world's best husband, Jack, and the world's best dog, Molly.

Contents

Part One
Stella
1. Earlier — 3

Part Two
Fin
2. A New Order at RIO — 11
3. Kayaks — 17
4. Identification? — 23
5. Another — 25
6. Search — 31
7. Second Search and the Station — 33
8. Gary Graydon — 39
9. Swimming With Turtles — 43
10. Diving on Enviroman — 47
11. Benjamin Returns — 57
12. Mermaid Diver Training — 59
13. Day Two of Mermaid Diver Training — 65
14. Open Water Mermaid Diving — 69
15. After the Party — 73
16. Boating and Secrets — 75
17. Bump — 83
18. Search — 89
19. The New Methodology — 95
20. A Struggle — 101
21. Important Realizations — 107
22. Planning — 113
23. An Announcement — 117
24. Davy Jones — 123
25. First Commercial Mermaid Class Graduates — 127
26. A Mermaid Struggles — 133
27. Bari Arrives — 139
28. Shark Feeding — 147
29. Liam — 157

Part Three
Bari

30. Bari — 163

Part Four
Fin

31. Rescue — 171
32. Recovery — 181
33. The Face of a Charity — 185
34. Puppy Love — 189
35. Morning — 195
36. Dive at Three Sisters — 199
37. Missing — 205
38. Dane Arrives — 213
39. Austin — 219
40. The Return — 223
41. Mixed Identity — 229
42. Bari Meets Austin — 235
43. Diving — 241
44. A Wedding — 245
45. Little Cayman — 259
46. Final Dive — 263

A Sneak Peek at In Deep

1. Freedive Training — 269
2. Dive on Rum Point — 279
   - Links to my Books — 281
   - Also by Sharon Ward — 282
   - Acknowledgments — 285
   - About the Author — 287

Part One
Stella

Chapter 1
Earlier

THE SUN here was so hot. It never got this hot back home. All day she'd been alternating lying on her blanket and then parading up and down the famous Seven Mile Beach on Grand Cayman, hoping to attract the attention of one of the Hollywood stars she'd heard was in town. She was in full makeup, and she'd carefully styled her long blonde hair to look perfectly, artfully, windblown, then sprayed it into place so heavily that not a single strand could move even with the stiff wind coming off the ocean.

She'd expected gentle trade winds like it said on the travel sites, but this wind was a howling gale. The winds came out of nowhere, blew like crazy for a while, and then suddenly stopped with no warning. "Global warming," the concierge at her hotel had said in explanation, adding that she'd lived here all her life and never seen anything like it.

Well no matter about the wind. She'd curated every aspect of her appearance to make her look like she'd been born this way. Naturally gorgeous. She knew she looked her best, and if she could just cross paths with one of those Hollywood moguls, her future would be set.

But no matter how she sashayed up and down the sand, nobody paid her any mind. The beach was practically littered with exquisite women in tiny bikinis—some of which were even smaller and more revealing than the one she wore.

Truth be told, in her mind her tiny white crochet bathing suit was so skimpy it was embarrassing. But she was willing to suffer a little embarrassment if it led to her big break. All her life she'd planned to be a star, and she'd do whatever it took to achieve her goal.

It was hot out here on the sand. So hot. The ocean looked inviting, but she couldn't go for a swim. It would spoil her hair and makeup, and she needed to look perfect.

Just in case.

She'd walked all the way to the far end of the beach and was just about to pack it in for the day and go back to her hotel for a cool drink when a man approached her. He was young, but not too young. Brown hair with a few streaks bleached gold by the sun. Nice looking, dressed in stretchy sleek fitting shorts and a blue t-shirt with some kind of logo on the chest and an expensive looking black and gold chronograph watch on his left wrist.

He smiled at her before removing his designer sunglasses and putting them on the top of his head. His blue eyes twinkled at her. "Don't I know you?" he said.

She shook her head. "I don't think so."

"I'm sure we've met. Weren't you at that party at Rafe Cummings' place last week?"

"You were at a party at Rafe Cummings' house?" she said, impressed despite herself. "You know him?"

"Know him? Of course, I know him. We work together a lot. In fact, we just finished up a project together. We'll be starting our next film soon." The man looked over her shoulder, out toward the horizon where the blue sky met the even bluer sea.

She took in the man's well-muscled physique. His expensive looking watch. Trendy sunglasses. High cheekbones and enormous blue eyes. He was attractive, and if this man knew Rafe Cummings, he had to be well connected.

She bit her lip, desperate to have him continue to pay attention to her. "What do you do on Rafe's movies? Are you his assistant, or his bodyguard or something?"

The man smiled. "I do all the casting on his films. I know the look he likes in his costars, and I have to say that you have the right look in spades. You'd be perfect for a role in his next flick."

Her heart began to pound. This was it. "Really? What do I have to do to get an audition?" She didn't want to get her hopes up too high yet. Men had approached her before, and she routinely discovered that the promised audition was dependent on the sexual favors she was willing to dispense.

But this must be her lucky day because the usual leer wasn't forthcoming.

"Can you swim? This role will require a lot of ocean swimming. You'll need to be able to keep up with Rafe."

She gulped. She could swim, sure, but she'd done most of her swimming in a pool. Mostly just paddling a few strokes to get from her pool float to the ladder. She was from the mid-west of the US, far from the ocean. If she went into the sea now, it would be her first time swimming in an actual ocean.

She knew Rafe Cummings was a phenomenal swimmer. Or at least it looked that way in his movies. She swallowed hard and lied. "I'm a great swimmer."

He looked skeptical. "Wanna show me? Let's go for a swim right now. That way you'll get the most important part of the audition process out of the way right up front. There's lots of beautiful girls in the world, but very few of them can swim the way Rafe needs his costar to swim."

She looked into his eyes but didn't see any subterfuge. "How will Rafe know I can keep up? Doesn't he have to be here to watch me swim?"

He raised an eyebrow. "No, he doesn't have to be here. If you pass the swim test with me, I send you on to Rafe. We don't waste his time unless a candidate has a serious shot at the part."

She looked down at the sand. "That makes sense. I bet he's a very busy man." She raised her gaze to his face and searched his eyes again. "Do you have a business card?"

He waved a hand down along his body, taking in his skimpy garb. "Nope, not on me. I have a stack of them in my car. I can get you one later if you pass the first test. But for now, you want to swim or not?"

What did she have to lose? It was hot, and a dip in the ocean would feel good no matter what. "Okay, sure."

"Good," he said. "I'm excited about your audition. Let's go."

He hurried across the beach to the water, and she followed him as fast as she could go. She didn't pay any attention to the warning signs posted every few feet along the tide line. Even if she had read the signs, it wouldn't have mattered.

She didn't actually know what a rip current was.

And even if she did know, it might not have made a difference in her decision. This was her shot, and she was going for it.

No matter what.

They waded out a little way, and then the man dove headfirst under the waves. He swam straight out for several yards, then turned to face her where she stood in the shallows. "You coming or what?" He sounded annoyed.

She didn't want to blow her big chance, so she took a deep breath and dove under the waves. With just a few strokes, she'd reached him. "See, I can swim."

"You call that swimming? That's not even one scene's worth." He turned and faced out to sea. "Let's go." He swam straight out, away from the shore.

He didn't look back at her to see what she was doing, so if she wanted the role, she had no choice but to follow. The cool water did feel good after the heat of the beach, and even though she wasn't a great swimmer, she was easily able to keep up with him. That boosted her confidence.

They'd gone quite a distance when he stopped swimming and started treading water. "Okay, I guess you can swim. But now I need to see your form." He flicked a thumb over his shoulder. "Swim that way until I tell you to stop. I'll wait here and watch."

She nodded and started swimming parallel to the shore. After a few strokes, she felt the ocean grab hold of her and begin to push her farther out. She tried to swim back toward shore, but the current was too strong.

She was scared. She needed help and she didn't care if it cost her the role. "Help me," she yelled. "This current's too much for me."

"Yep," he said softly. He smiled, then he turned and swam parallel to the beach in the opposite direction until he was well away from the rip current still dragging her away from safety. Without a twinge of feeling, he left her to fend for herself.

When he reached the sand, he turned and looked out to sea. The beautiful woman wasn't even a speck on the horizon.

Part Two
Fin

Chapter 2
A New Order at RIO

AT THE END of the short film, the credits frame stayed on the monitor, glowing softly in the dim light. My name, Fin Fleming, was all over them. The credits read: "Produced by T-8/Lawton Films. Narration by Rafe Cummings and Fin Fleming. Videography by Fin Fleming and Rafe Cummings. Script by Fin Fleming. Music by Douglas Samuels. Promotional consideration provided by the Madelyn Anderson Russo Institute for Oceanography (RIO)."

The other viewers in the conference room were silent for a moment, then they broke into cheers and clapping. Tate Crusoe issued a loud whistle, and my sometimes fiancé, Liam Lawton, laughed out loud.

Rafe Cummings stood next to me in the front of the room. He'd been an invaluable partner through every step of this project. Thrilled with our success, we gave each other a high five. Then we turned back to face the group seated in front of us and playfully took a bow. Our small audience laughed and cheered even harder.

I was sure the smile on Rafe's face was a duplicate of the one on mine. After the release of the full-length theatrical film Tate "T-8" Crusoe and Liam Lawton had produced a few months ago, Rafe had been free to go on to another project until he decided on his next Hollywood action hero role.

So he and I had started working on this documentary on stingrays, which coincidentally we both loved. We'd worked hard on the production for months, and it showed. The film was flawless.

My friend Genevra Blackthorne, the newly promoted COO of RIO, threaded her way through the maze of chairs crowding my office and gave me a hug. "Good job," she whispered. "If this is what you can do when we free up your time from administrative work, we should have made it happen long ago."

She stepped aside for my mother, Maddy Russo. "It's brilliant, Fin. I'm so proud of you, and I know Ray would have been as well." Mentioning my late stepfather Ray Russo brought me a pang of missing him, but her words warmed my heart. Nobody had known Ray better than Maddy, and if she believed he'd have been proud of me, I was happy. She gave me a massive bear hug, then stepped over to Rafe.

I have no idea what she whispered to him, but he threw back his head and laughed joyfully before lifting her into a hug and swinging her around, her dainty feet flying behind her.

Liam crushed me to his chest and kissed me, long and thoroughly. "Brilliant, as always," he said before stepping aside for my father, Newton Fleming.

Newton gave me a hug and patted my back. "That's my girl," he said. The pride I saw shining on his face nearly brought me to tears.

Joely Wentworth, who was Newton's significant other in addition to being one of my best friends, gave me a hug. "There's nobody better at this than you. I am in awe," she said. "Every time."

Tate Crusoe, or T-8 as he was also known, removed his posh sunglasses from the top of his head so they wouldn't fall to the floor when he leaned down to kiss my cheek. "Good job," he said in his California drawl. He clapped my shoulder and bobbed his head before moving away to talk to his best friend Rafe.

I blinked hard and held up a hand. "Thank you all for your

congratulations. I'm sure Rafe appreciates it as much as I do, but now let's get back to the real purpose of this meeting."

My friend Benjamin Brooks, RIO's newly appointed VP of business development laughed. "I agree. We have to decide what our next money raising venture will be, and we also need to come up with the next documentary topic. Will you guys all take your seats so we can get back on the agenda, please?"

I smiled happily at Benjamin, Genevra, and Maddy. They'd all been concerned when I said I wanted to step down from my former COO responsibilities to focus on my creative pursuits, but already, the results spoke for themselves.

Of course, Maddy had been the CEO of RIO since its founding, so it was easy enough for her to move back into the role once her health allowed, but Genevra and Benjamin were new at their jobs. They'd each taken on their responsibilities with energy and enthusiasm, and I, for one, was much happier without worrying about the routine business of RIO.

We took turns running the board meetings, and today was Benjamin's turn. "Fin, do you have any ideas for the next documentary?"

"I do. I was thinking I'd like to focus on spawning grounds for endangered species and the environmental threats they face. I'm thinking octopus nurseries, shark mating locations, turtle migrations, whales…you get the idea." Everyone nodded along as I spoke.

"I love it," said Maddy. "It's a very timely topic."

Newton added, "It's certainly something Fleming Environmental Investments can get behind, and we're happy to contribute to the budget." He paused a moment. "Rafe, can we count on you for another stellar narration job? Your name carries a lot of weight with viewers and the networks. Your participation will definitely boost the take from the film."

Rafe looked at me with a wink and a smile. "I love working with this team, and I've discovered I love narrating even more than I love making movies. I'm in."

Liam had grown used to Rafe's flirting, so he ignored it. "Will

Dougie be able to do the music again? His work on this one is fantastic."

Douglas Samuels was Rafe's older brother, currently residing in a home for the criminally insane. But while there, he'd discovered a heretofore unknown musical ability, and he quickly learned to play multiple instruments. In addition to playing some of those instruments on the soundtrack, he'd composed the entire score for this film.

Knowing about the difficult life he'd had when he was younger, this made me sad for him. What might he have become if he'd had the opportunity to explore his musical talents as a child?

Rafe's pensive expression told me his thoughts were traveling along the same path as mine, but he shook off the melancholy before he answered. "I'm sure Dougie would be thrilled to participate."

Benjamin nodded. "Excellent. Anybody object to the topic?" he asked. After a moment of silence, he said. "Okay. Fin, will you please start on the script and a list of places where we might want to submit the finished film? Also, make a list of any travel and crew requirements. I'll work up the budget for you once I get it."

"Will do," I said. I was excited about the idea, and equally excited by Benjamin's offer to take on the dreaded budget work. Everybody in the room knew how much I hate numbers and working with spreadsheets.

He looked down at his computer screen. "Next on the agenda, new business ideas. Anyone?"

We all looked down at the floor. RIO's research was still heavily dependent on donations, and despite the revenue from sales of our documentaries, it grew harder every year to meet our goals. We'd recently started several new businesses to provide funding for our research, but there was still a large shortfall between our income and our financial requirements. We'd all been confident we'd be able to close the gap with the addition of a few new businesses.

But our latest business, personal submarine rides, had totally tanked after the recent highly publicized implosion of a homemade sub. There was a huge difference between that homegrown sub and our multi-million dollar custom made commercial sub, and an equally massive disparity in the depths that we planned to take our guests to and those the doomed sub had attempted.

But the public knew what it wanted, and right now, most of the public didn't want to go for a submarine ride under any circumstances. We were on the verge of shutting down that business, since with the necessary spending on personnel, maintenance, and insurance, it was costing us much more than it earned.

Nobody spoke. It seemed that none of us had any idea what other business we should start up next. And nobody wanted to be responsible for a repeat of the submarine ride fiasco.

The original idea for opening peripheral businesses to support RIO's research effort had been mine, and it looked like my plan to make RIO less financially dependent on donations was in jeopardy. The team clearly didn't want to hurt my feelings by pointing out the obvious. It wasn't working, and now we might have to redouble our fundraising efforts to make up for the losses.

Just as the silence in the room bordered on uncomfortable, Benjamin said, "Well, if nobody else has anything they want to talk about, I have an idea."

"Spill it," said Maddy.

Benjamin grinned. "Mermaid school."

There was a moment of stunned silence before I responded with a straight face. "Sorry. I don't think that idea has legs."

It took a second for the laughter and groaning to stop.

Genevra was still giggling. "That has to be the worst pun ever, even for you."

"Could be. But I am still the pun master," I replied. "I'm intrigued by the idea. Benjamin, can you show us the business plan?" He was always so organized that I knew he'd have the whole plan already worked out, complete with research reports, projected budgets, and an extensive slide deck with a complete list of pros and cons.

He put the presentation up on the big screen and started outlining his idea. "Mermaid training is one of the hottest specialties in dive training right now. Even PADI offers multiple mermaid certifications, and some dive shops now totally specialize in it. It's kind of an offshoot of freediving, so our staff and our facilities here are perfect for us to take on mermaid training."

"The only thing we'd need to add is maybe a small grotto or fountain somewhere on the grounds because we'll want to offer our students the opportunity to have their photos taken with our resident mermaids." He looked pointedly at Genevra and me.

"And maybe mermen?" His gaze swiveled between Liam and Rafe.

Liam laughed. "If I'm around, sure. You can take my picture."

Rafe nodded. "Me too. I've been photographed in enough crazy getups that one more won't make any difference."

Benjamin smiled." Good. I made a list of items we'll want to add to the dive shop inventory for Stewie and obtained a quote on building the grotto. Meantime, I've already investigated mermaid diving training school, so once I complete the course I'll be able to certify new mermaids and new mermaid instructors. I'll be gone a week when that starts. That'll give Stewie some time to order the inventory for the dive shop, and we can launch an advertising plan when I get back. I'll email the entire proposal to all of you, and we can vote on it at next week's staff meeting. Deal?"

I stood up. "No deal. I say we vote right now. It's a brilliant idea. Arms up if you support Benjamin's plan."

Everybody in the room raised their hand.

Benjamin grinned. "Excellent." He laughed. "I knew you'd do that, Fin. My flight leaves in the morning. Next time you see me, I'll be a certified mermaid trainer."

Chapter 3
Kayaks

THE MEETING BROKE UP, and Liam and I walked out of the conference room hand in hand. "Fancy a kayak ride?" he asked.

I smiled. "Don't mind if I do."

We strolled across the lawn to the boathouse, where Liam stored his kayaks while his boat, *Enviroman*, underwent repairs. We each lifted our favorite kayak off the hooks where they hung on the wall and hoisted the lightweight boats up to shoulder level to carry them to a shallow sandy area on the far side of the dock where it was easy to put in.

I lowered my kayak into the warm clear water and handed the line to Liam. "Be right back," I said. "I want to get some snacks and drinks from Ray's Place to take with us."

My eyes were still adjusting to the dim lighting inside the nearby tiki bar when I saw Austin Gibb standing at the sink washing dishes with his back to me. He was wearing ear pods and swaying in time to music only he could hear. I couldn't see his face, but I recognized him by his light brown hair and the sleek, stretchy shorts he'd recently started wearing in place of the cargo shorts almost everybody at RIO wore. I walked over and tapped him on the shoulder, and he jumped before he turned to face me.

I was surprised to see the person facing me wasn't Austin

Gibb as I'd expected, but Davy Jones, manager of the failing submarine ride business. I'd never realized their builds and hair were so similar. Dressed like Davy was, in styles similar to Austin's usual clothing, it was easy to mistake them for each other.

I apologized to Davy for startling him. "Sorry," I said. "I didn't realize you were pitching in at Ray's Place. That's great."

He nodded. "Yeah, I hate being idle, and I don't have any submarine ride reservations for today." He looked pensive. "Or even this week. So I asked Noah if he could use some help."

It was high season for tourism right now, and Ray's Place was one of the most popular bars or restaurants on the island. It was always packed, so of course Noah jumped at the chance to add another pair of hands.

"Wonderful, Davy," I said. "Much better than just hanging around. And maybe things will pick up soon for the submarine rides." Even I didn't believe that. Since the initial rush of interest after we opened it, the new enterprise had very quickly dwindled down to nothing.

I asked Davy to pack up a box of snacks and soft drinks. When he'd finished, I carried it back to the shore, where Liam was waiting. I stored the box of goodies in the dry compartment of my kayak. Once it was secure, I got in and quickly pushed off, with Liam following close behind me in his own kayak.

We paddled gently through the crystalline water, side by side. Liam gazed out toward the horizon while I looked under the surface to see what I could see. We weren't planning to go far because of the dangerous rip currents that were unexpectedly springing up at various points around the island due to the recent unusual weather patterns. We paddled slowly around RIO's protected cove rather than exploring the coastline as we usually did.

We'd only gone a short distance when I jumped back and dropped my paddle, nearly overturning my kayak with the sudden violent move. "There's someone in the water," I shouted to Liam, who was several feet away and looking in the opposite direction.

Without thinking, I rolled out of my kayak and dove down to try to rescue the person I'd seen.

When I reached her, I could tell by her open mouth and staring eyes that I was too late, but I pulled her into a rescue hold and shot to the surface. I began performing in-water CPR, a complicated and difficult procedure, while Liam paddled toward me. He dropped a marker buoy in the water with one hand and threw me a line with the other. He tied my kayak to his and then paddled rapidly back to shore while I held on tight to the line, doing my best to resuscitate the woman.

As soon as we reached the shallows, he stepped out of his kayak. Easily lifting the drowned woman, he rushed toward the dive shop. I ran along with him, shouting out for Stewie, RIO's dive shop manager, to call Doc.

Liam placed the woman on the lawn near the shop and rolled her onto her left side to clear any water or debris in her mouth. I threw myself to the ground near her, and as soon as the trickle of water slowed, I flipped her onto her back and resumed chest compressions. Stewie dashed out of the dive shop with a small rescue canister of oxygen, which he fitted over her nose.

Liam rose to call DS Dane Scott of the RCIP to let him know about our gruesome discovery. He'd just disconnected the call when Doc and a couple of EMTs from her team raced up to where we huddled around the woman.

One of the EMTs took over the compressions while Doc knelt beside me to check the woman's vitals. I could tell by her expression she thought there was little hope, but she let the EMT continue. The doctors at Cayman Islands Hospital would call time of death when the woman arrived in the ER, and in the meantime, there could always be a miracle.

Dane Scott and the ambulance arrived at the same time. The hospital EMTs ran across RIO's recreation area, pushing a portable gurney ahead of them. Dane loped along beside them, easily keeping pace with the younger people.

One EMT quickly swapped places with the RIO medic and smoothly took over the compressions. The hospital team raised the gurney and pushed it along as they raced back to the ambulance, waiting in the parking lot with its bay doors wide open.

Dane watched them go. "Any reason for optimism?"

Doc sighed deeply and lifted her shoulders in a frustrated shrug. "Don't think so, but you never know."

Dane nodded his agreement and turned to me. "Tell me how you found the woman. Where were you and what were you doing? Did you see anything suspicious?"

I told Dane the story and mentioned that Liam had the foresight to drop a marker buoy where we'd found the woman. "When you're through questioning us, we'll take some tanks out and do a search pattern. See if we can find anything to help with the ID."

"Thanks," said Dane. "Someone must be missing her. I'll get Morey checking for missing person reports while you do the dives."

Liam and I went to the employee storage area near the dive shop and picked up our gear and a couple of tanks from the stack on the cement pad outside the shop. We geared up on the small beach near where we'd launched the kayaks and waded in.

We'd done enough grid searches in this area over the years that we didn't need any discussion to know the landmarks and number of kicks that marked the grid's boundaries, or even who would handle which quadrant. We gave each other the okay sign and dove under.

It took two tanks a piece and about two and a half hours to cover the entire site. Neither of us had seen anything that might have been a clue to the woman's identity or how she ended up in our cove.

When we waded out of the water after the completing the search, Dane was waiting at a picnic table outside the dive shop. He raised his eyebrows in a question, and I shook my head. His face fell. An unknown victim makes his job even harder, and I gathered that so far at least, he had no way to identify the woman.

I sat beside Dane and filled him in on our dives while Stewie and Liam took care of our empty tanks and salty gear, but he'd known as soon as he saw us emerge after our last dive that we'd found nothing because the catch bags hanging from our BCDs were empty.

I finished the recap. "Any news from the hospital?"

His face was troubled. "Nothing good. She didn't make it."

"And still no idea who she is?"

His face looked grim. "Morey's canvassing the hotels and guest houses, but so far we've got nothing."

Chapter 4
Identification?

IN ONE OF those coincidences that feels like the universe is throwing your words back at you, Dane's phone rang. The caller ID showed Morey.

"Whatcha got?" Dane said when he answered. He listened for a moment, then stood up. "On my way."

There was a deep sorrow in his eyes as he spoke to me. "One of the guest houses near the beach reported a woman missing. The woman arrived a week ago, and they have no idea how long she's been gone because she opted out of daily housekeeping. The only reason they noticed she's missing at all is that she was supposed to check out today and she never did. All her stuff, including her passport, is still in her room."

I tried to sound positive. "That's a big break. Now at least you'll know who the woman we found is. That should make it easier to track her. What's her name anyway?"

"Stella St. Francis. I'll call you later and let you know what we find out. We don't know yet that it's the same woman." He started to walk away, but he hadn't gone two steps when his phone rang again. "Hey, Roland. I'm just finishing with Fin. What's up?"

His face turned grey. "When?" A pause. "We'll be right there. She may be able to help us determine the entry point."

Dane hurried off across the lawn toward the parking lot. After a few steps, he turned back. "Aren't you coming? I said I need your help."

He was in full investigator mode, so this was not the time to point out that he hadn't said any such thing to me. How was I supposed to know that 'she' meant me? Since I couldn't hear the other end of his phone conversation, I'd had no idea what was happening.

But on the other hand, I was happy he'd automatically included me in his investigation. "Coming," I said. "I'll just run inside to let someone know where I'm going."

Liam stepped forward. "No worries. I'll let them know. You don't want to hold Dane up."

We both laughed. Dane wasn't waiting—he was already halfway to his car. I scurried to catch up. "Thank you," I shouted over my shoulder to Liam.

He blew me a kiss and smiled that beautiful smile of his.

Chapter 5
Another

I'd no sooner buckled my seat belt when Dane slammed his unmarked police car into gear and took off, leaving the parking lot on two wheels. Dane was normally a very safe and sane driver, so this was surprising.

I reached up and gripped the handle above my head. "What's the hurry?" I hoped the rush meant we didn't have another body on our hands and that this time the victim had made it through.

He drew in a deep breath and slowed down to his usual pace. "I'm sorry. There's no reason to hurry." He rolled to a full stop at the intersection of South Church Street and Harbour Drive, tapping on the steering wheel impatiently while he waited for the light to change. "Another drowning. Those rip currents are deadly this year."

"Wait. I'm confused. Are we up to three drownings now, or is the woman missing from the guest house one of the victims?"

"Two drowned; one missing," he said. "No match on the ID from the guest house to either of the drowning victims." He bit his lip. "She could be anywhere. We don't know that she drowned. So far, she's just missing. Just missing."

I could hear how upset he was by the tone of his voice and the repetition of those last few words. His speech was usually very concise, and he seemed distracted.

"Got it," I said.

I knew Dane took it personally when people on the island went missing or when murders took place. It made him feel like he and his team weren't doing their jobs. I gazed out the car window to give him a moment of privacy. Dane was a good cop, and part of what made him so good was that he never lost sight of his own humanity—or the humanity of the crime victims he worked so hard to find justice for.

But this sequence of events seemed to be hitting him hard. I'd never known him to be anything but cool and composed, always in control.

I wasn't sure what to do, so I waited a minute before saying anything. "Everything okay with you?" I finally blurted out.

He looked at me, the pain in his eyes so searing I felt my own eyes tear up.

"My daughter. Sydney." He drew in a shuddering breath. "She'd have been about your age now."

My mouth gaped open. I knew Dane pretty well. We'd worked together on several cases, and he'd been seeing my mother for a long time. But this was the first time I'd ever heard he had a child.

"I didn't know you had a daughter. Where is she?" I asked softly.

He gulped. "She was five when I lost her. Last time I saw her a rip current just like the ones we have this season swept her away."

He blinked back tears. "And as you know, back then I couldn't swim a stroke. I tried to save her. God knows I tried. But I couldn't get to her. The last time I heard her voice she was screaming, "Daddy, help me." I hear it every night in my dreams."

My voice was no more than a whisper. "I'm so sorry. I didn't even know you'd been married."

His bitter laugh sounded strained. "I've never been married, but that doesn't mean I couldn't father a child. I lost Sydney's mother that day too when she tried to save our daughter. Current took them both. I never saw either of them again. I like to think that maybe Sydney wasn't as scared once her mother was out there with her, but I don't know. They never found the bodies..." His voice trailed off.

We drove in silence for a few minutes until Dane turned into a small parking area that serviced a tiny beach in the West Bay district. The beach was next to a cemetery, and the eerie location sent a chill down my spine.

As soon as Dane parked, we both jumped out of the car and hustled over to where Roland and Morey stood next to a sheet-covered mound in the sand. They'd closed the beach to outsiders, but that didn't stop a handful of curious bystanders from huddling near the crime scene tape, craning their necks to see what they could see.

Dane held the tape up so I could duck under, then he followed me into the marked off area. Our arrival set off murmurs through the crowd. Most islanders knew DS Scott by name if not by sight, and his presence announced the possibility of a juicy crime.

Dane ignored them and pulled out his notebook. "What have you got?" he asked Roland.

"Young woman, mid-to-late twenties. About five foot six, 120 pounds. Blond hair. Blue eyes. No ID. No identifying characteristics. Likely drowning victim. No evidence of foul play." Both Roland and Morey were always professional when relating the facts about a crime, but this time they were almost robotically so. Morey stared off down the beach. Roland's voice was a monotone, and he avoided Dane's eyes while he gave his report. I realized they both knew about Dane's daughter and how hard this must be for him.

Dane had scribbled the details they gave him in his notebook. When he finished writing, he snapped it shut and returned it to his pocket. "Let's take a look," he said.

Roland leaned forward and lifted the sheet, holding it at such an angle that Dane and I could see the victim's entire body, but the onlookers couldn't see anything.

I took a quick scan. I didn't see any signs of deliberate drowning. I did notice that the sea hadn't held her long enough to have its way with her, so she couldn't have been in the water very long before she'd washed up on shore.

"Is this where she was found? Right here?" I asked. "In this position?" The body was pretty far up on the sand, even accounting for the change in the tide level, so I assumed she'd been moved. The sand around her had been churned up by multiple bystanders, so any drag marks showing how she'd arrived in the specific location and position had been eliminated.

Roland shrugged and gestured toward a man standing alone off to the side. "I don't know exactly. That gentleman there found her. Said he dragged her up a little way. Rolled her over to see if she was okay. Then he called us." He gestured at the churned up sand along the edge of the beach. "It seems he drew a crowd."

Dane and I both looked at the man Roland had indicated. He was small. Nondescript. Badly sun burned. An off islander then, most likely.

"Name?" Dane barked.

Morey looked at his notebook. "Smith. Joseph Smith. From Boston, Massachusetts. A big part of the crowd over there is his family. They were with him when he found her."

Dane and I both turned to scan the crowd. Most of the people were craning their necks trying to catch a glimpse of the body or to see what we were doing. One person in the back of the crowd raised a hand with an obviously expensive black and gold watch on his wrist pulled the brim of his hat low over his forehead. He walked away at a brisk pace before jumping into a nearby car and quickly driving away. Dane and I were closest to the road, but neither of us was in a good position to see the license plate.

Dane scowled and looked at me. "Did you see anything? What kind of car was he in?"

"No idea," I said lamely. "You know I can't tell one model from another. It was black though. Or maybe dark blue."

I ignored Morey and Roland's eye rolls. I can't even pretend to be interested in cars. They all look the same to me.

Fish—now that's a different story. I know them all.

Dane turned to the members of his team. "Did you guys get contact info for everyone in the crowd?'

They shuffled their feet and looked down at the sand. "No. Not yet. So far, just the guy who found her," Morey finally said.

Dane rolled his eyes and didn't say anything for a few seconds. Then he sighed and said, "Okay then. I'll go talk to him while you two canvas the crowd. Fin, please come with me."

We walked the few paces across the sand to where the man—Joseph Smith—was standing alone, wringing his hands, and looking like he might vomit at any moment.

Dane smiled and introduced himself. He gestured to me. "This is Doctor Fleming, a member of my team."

Smith looked up sharply. "Are you related to Fin Fleming? Can you get me her autograph? I'm a big admirer of hers," he said.

Dane held up a hand and shook his head. "She's not related to Fin Fleming," he said, which was sort of the truth.

Smith looked crestfallen. "Okay, then. What do you want to know?"

Dane had Smith walk through exactly where the woman was when he found her. The position of the body. What he'd been doing on the beach, and had he noticed anyone hanging around. When Dane finished his questions, he turned to me. "Anything else you'd like to know?"

I nodded. "How high up was the tide when you found her?" By now the waves had erased any signs of the body's original position, as well as most of the marks from when Smith had dragged her and the gawking crowd had surrounded her.

Smith gazed out at the tranquil surf. "I guess I pulled her about ten feet," he said. "I knew the tide was coming in and I didn't want to lose her. Was that the wrong thing to do?"

"No, that was exactly the right thing to do," I said without looking at Dane to check if that was actually the truth. I didn't want Smith to clam up if he thought he'd be in trouble for making a mistake when he was only trying to help. "Did you see her while she was still in the water, or was she already on the shore when you found her?"

He thought a moment. "I think she was still out a little ways, because I remember wondering what it was I saw floating out there in the water."

"Good. Can you show me where she was when you first saw her?'

He pointed. "About there. Maybe twenty feet out and off to the side. But the water wasn't even up to my waist when I got her."

"Perfect. Thank you." I looked at Dane. "I don't have any other questions."

Morey and Roland rejoined us then. "Nobody saw anything until the body was already on the beach."

Dane sighed. "Looks like we've got another one."

I put my hand on his arm. "I want to dive the area to search the bottom for any clues. Clues don't last long in the ocean, so it makes sense for me to start right away."

Dane nodded. "Go for it."

I pulled out my phone and called Stewie to ask him to bring me what I needed for the search.

Chapter 6
Search

WHILE I WAITED FOR STEWIE, I used my cellphone to check the tide tables for this beach, so I'd know how much the tideline had changed since Smith first saw the body. When Stewie hadn't arrived after five minutes—admittedly that would have been a near impossibility given the distance—I kicked off my flip-flops and walked down the beach in the opposite direction from the one the body would have come from. I waded in a few feet, then dove. I knew I should be able to easily conduct the first part of my search from the surface since the water here was shallow until quite far out.

I kicked along slowly and searched the bottom below me, ignoring the stinging of the salt water in my open eyes, and hoping Stewie would get here quickly with the gear I'd requested. My bare feet didn't provide anywhere near the propulsion of a pair of fins, so the going was slow. A short time later, I popped my head up to take another breath and noticed Stewie finally standing on the sand with my snorkel vest, mask, and fins in his hands. I quickly changed direction and headed toward the beach.

A flash of bright red caught my eye as I made the turn toward shore, and it was so out of place amid the dull green and beige colors around it that I stopped to check it out. My eyes were stinging so badly from the salt water that I couldn't tell what it was, so I reached out to pick up the object.

It was a small leather ID card case enclosed in a zip lock plastic bag. My heart started beating faster as I realized this could have belonged to the drowned woman. If it did, it might help Dane solve his case. At least he'd know who the victim was.

I was only a short distance from shore, so I quickly kicked twice toward the shallows and then stood up. The water still came up to my midriff, but it would be faster to walk than to swim without fins. I took a few giant steps and then waded onto shore. I raced across the damp sand, holding the zip lock bag delicately by one corner.

Dane looked astonished that I had found anything at all, and I could sense he and his team were trying to hold back their excitement in case whatever I'd found turned out to be irrelevant.

Only Stewie looked confident, his face beaming with pride. "I knew if there was anything to find, you'd find it," he said with a big smile.

I handed the plastic bag to Roland, who had hastily donned a clean pair of latex gloves. He flipped the bag over to look at the other side of the red leather case, which had a clear window meant to hold an ID so the owner could show the card without having to remove it from the case.

The EMT team was bundling the woman's body on a gurney for transport to the morgue, but they quickly stopped their work when Roland held up a hand to stop them.

He walked over to the gurney and lifted the sheet that covered her, holding the ID card near her face. "It's a match," he said.

Then he let out a whistle. "Name's Dora Smith. Lives in Boston. Maybe this case won't be so hard to solve after all."

Chapter 7
Second Search and the Station

DANE TURNED TO ME. "I won't need you for this next part. Would you and Stewie do another sweep of the underwater area while we question the witnesses? You heard what Smith said and you understand the currents better than I do. You don't need any advice from me to know the area you should cover. If you're curious about what we find out about Ms. Smith, you can come by the station when you're done. Or if you don't have time, I'll call you later and let you know what we find out."

I nodded. "Will do."

He smiled. "Thanks. And if you find anything else of interest, please call me right away."

"Got it." Stewie and I started gearing up while Roland and Morey went back into the crowd to collect the members of the Smith family.

The water here was as clear as glass and relatively shallow even a long distance from shore, so Stewie and I planned to do our search using snorkels rather than scuba gear to minimize the number of times we'd have to exit the water to change tanks.

We'd split the area we planned to search into three sections. The outer two were of equal size, each about eighteen feet wide, while the center section was about twenty-four feet wide. We waded a few feet into the water and started swimming, both of us about six feet from the outermost edge of our assigned area. I took the left hand third while Stewie took the right.

We each scanned the bottom on both sides of our centerlines as we kicked slowly along the surface. Periodically, one or the other of us would dive down to the bottom to investigate anything that looked like it might be of interest.

Whatever we found, we placed in a catch bag clipped to a D-ring on our vests. Most of what we found looked like discarded junk, but even if it turned out not to be a clue, it wouldn't hurt to get any trash we found out of the water.

When we'd swum out as far as we'd planned to, we repositioned ourselves in the center section. Now we swam back toward shore, staying about twelve feet apart. We were still scanning the bottom for about six feet on either side of the imaginary line we were following. When we finished, we'd have covered an area that was about sixty feet wide and 200 feet long.

We were exhausted when we ended our search, and even more so than usual because we'd found nothing but trash since the ID wallet. It was disheartening.

Stewie stood up in the shallows and pulled off his mask. "Guess you found the only thing here to find. And you were barely even trying. Figures."

I shrugged. "You know it's better to be lucky than smart." I was known for doing some crazy things, occasionally relying on luck to get me through the tight spots.

He wiggled his eyebrows. "You've got really good luck, but I have to admit you're pretty smart too." He sighed. "And thank goodness for that. Otherwise who knows what kind of messes you'd get yourself into."

I gave him an exasperated look. Stewie always worried about me, and it was completely unnecessary. At least in my opinion.

"Let's get going," I said.

We packed our gear into Stewie's open air SUV and drove to the police station. The desk sergeant sent us right to Dane's office as soon as we walked in. Dane was behind his desk, and Morey was sitting in one of his visitor chairs. They both had glum faces and slumped shoulders.

As soon as we walked in, Stewie took up a position leaning against the back wall of the office. I dropped into the other guest chair. "You guys look pretty down. What's going on? Smith not talking?" I asked.

Dane sighed deeply. "No, he's talking. In fact, he won't shut up. Neither will his wife or their two oldest kids. If only at least one of them had something useful to say."

I looked at him quizzically, and Morey took up the story. "They all claim they don't know Dora Smith. Apparently, Smith is the most common name in the states. Did you know there are more than 500,000 people with the last name of Smith in that country? It ranks number one out of all last names in the US."

Stewie broke in. "Kinda like here in the Caymans. But unlike the family here, I'm guessing the members of the US-based Smith clan don't all know each other, right? Hence your glum faces?"

Dane nodded. "Apparently Mr. and Mrs. Smith are very proud of their name. Even the youngest of their kids can recite all manner of statistics about the origins of the Smith name, but nobody in the family has ever heard of a Dora Smith. So far, the ID is a dead end."

"But there must have been an address on the ID card. A landlord or rental company might be able to give you some insight into her life. Or maybe the mortgage holder could if she has a house or a condo…"

Roland interrupted me when he walked in. "That man never stops talking. I think my ears are bleeding from the abuse."

Dane gave a ghost of a smile. "Thanks for listening to him." He turned to me. "We've already sent inquiries to the Boston police. They'll check into the address, see if there's anyone who knows anything about her. Meanwhile, you guys find anything else of use?"

I shook my head. "Nope. Just trash. But it's all here in case you want to check it out."

Stewie and I both put our catch bags on his desk.

Morey looked at the small cache of soggy detritus. "Shouldn't we have found a purse, or a beach bag or something? How would her ID wallet get in the water? It's not something you women take in swimming, is it?"

I thought about that for a minute. "Was there any cash in it? A credit card?"

Roland stood up straight. "There was one credit card. Why? Does that make a difference?"

I shrugged. "It might. She may have gone to the beach planning to go swimming, so she just took the little case with her so she wouldn't have to leave her purse unattended on the beach. The case is small enough that it would be easy to carry, and she'd be able to use the credit card for any emergencies that came up. She might have had it tucked in her bathing suit somewhere just in case she needed it. Maybe it slipped out while she was paddling around in the shallows, and then maybe a rip current took her by surprise and dragged her out. It's possible there was no foul play here at all."

"Hmmm," grunted Dane. "Maybe." He didn't sound convinced.

I hated not being able to help. "If you really believe somebody murdered the poor woman, we can expand the search area. But I don't think it's very likely we'll find anything."

Because he took all his cases personally, he sighed like the weight of the world was on his shoulders. It very well might have been.

But then he shook his head. "No. You're right. We have two women drowned, but no signs of foul play. No marks on either of the bodies. Tox screens are still out, but I don't think they'll show anything. We have another woman missing, but she may or may not be in the water. I think these ladies we found ignored the rip warnings and went into the ocean, never realizing what they'd be up against. I just hate it, that's all."

I agreed with him. When you live all your life on land, never venturing beyond the shallows, it's hard to realize the awesome might and majesty of the ocean. There's no room for mistakes. And it looked as though these victims had made a mistake and then simply lost their fight with the rip current.

When the ocean wants you, it takes you unless you know exactly what you're doing. Sometimes it takes you even then. The sea has no mercy, and it never makes allowances for innocent errors.

I stood up. "I'm sorry we didn't find anything, but let me know if you change your mind about expanding the search area. If you don't need me right now, I'm going to head back to RIO to get some work done. Ready, Stewie?"

Chapter 8
Gary Graydon

It wasn't until we got back to RIO and I smelled the aroma of grilled meat from Ray's Place that I realized how hungry I was. I hadn't eaten anything all day except a muffin this morning while we were screening the movie. It was only mid-afternoon, but being in the water uses a lot of calories. I was famished.

I veered off to see what I could scrounge up from Noah Gibb, the manager of Ray's Place. Noah was taking orders from a group at a four-top when I reached the bar, so I waited patiently for him to be free, helping myself to a handful of mixed nuts from a dish on the bar while I waited.

Candy, the Cayman parrot who lives in Ray's Place, gave a loud squawk when she saw me. "Look. It's Fin Fleming," she screeched.

I was annoyed at whoever had taught her to say that, because now she announced my arrival every time I walked into the tiki bar. I was working on teaching her to say it when anyone came in, not just me, so people would stop looking for me. And also, since I suspected Stewie was the culprit who had taught her the phrase, I'd been teaching her to say, "Look. It's Stewie Belcher."

I repeated the phrase I wanted her to learn, and I was surprised when she said it immediately after I did.

I heard a laugh from behind me. "She's not quite right," said

Gary Graydon, my boss at *Ecosphere*, the premier nature magazine focused on environmental issues. "It's only me. Got a few minutes? I want to talk to you."

After Candy's arrival announcements, heads had popped up all over the restaurant to try to spot Stewie or me. I turned to Gary. "Let's go aboard the *Tranquility*. Otherwise, pretty soon they'll mob us, and we won't be able to talk."

Already I could see people fumbling for paper and pen to ask for autographs, so I smiled and waved to the room. If this went as it usually did, I could end up signing autographs for hours. I didn't have the time right now.

I took Gary's arm and steered him across the lawn and down the dock to the *Tranquility*. As soon as we climbed aboard, we walked along the gunwale to soak up some sunshine on the bow of my boat. We sat there in silence for a minute, leaning back against the transom. Gary removed the expensive designer sunglasses from his head and put them on, covering his expressive brown eyes.

"So…," I said. "What's up?" Gary and I were friendly business associates. Maybe a little more than that because he was Liam's best friend. But he rarely came to see me. My deal with *Ecosphere* was that I had complete autonomy over my column, and Gary had always scrupulously honored the deal.

Gary looked down, twisted the dial on his titanium and gold Tag Heuer dive watch and paused a moment before answering.

I could tell he was trying to think of the best way to tell me whatever it was he wanted to say. "Just say it, Gary. Whatever it is."

He frowned slightly. "Okay. It's just that I had an idea for a column."

Now I frowned. Of course, I'd listen to his idea, but I didn't want to set a precedent of him getting involved in vetting my topics or even editing my copy. It was going to have to be a wowzer of an idea to earn my buy in.

Slowly, he started speaking. "Whatever your topic is for next month…"

I frowned. "…Has already been on the editorial calendar for

months. You can't change it or veto it. That's in my contract." I folded my arms stubbornly.

He gave a quick laugh. "Relax. I don't want to veto it, adjust it, or make any changes to whatever you have planned. Your column is the most popular one we have, and I'm not stupid enough to mess with success, even if I hadn't given you my word and put the deal in your contract. Plus I trust you completely, and just as importantly, Liam—who you may remember is my boss—also trusts you completely. There will be no attempts from me to change your plans. Now or ever. You have my word on that."

I consciously relaxed my shoulders. "So what is it then?"

"I want to tag along and film you as you go about finding what to shoot. Then I want to interview you to find out how you decide what to focus on each month. Talk about how often you have to dive to get the incredible photos you deliver, month after month. I'm thinking of creating another column to explain how you do what you do. Sort of a companion column."

"A companion column? Every month?" I asked. "That's a lot of extra time for us both."

He smiled. "I agree. So maybe not every month. Maybe just a couple of times a year. I've already got some ideas. Like one column focused on how you choose your locations. One on your models. Your topics. Even your gear."

He gave me a moment to think about what he'd said before he asked, "What do you think? Are you willing to try it?"

I nodded. "Sure, I'm willing to try almost anything. But let's not announce it as a recurring feature until we see how the first one turns out, okay?'

"Agreed," he said. "So what's on the agenda this month?"

I thought for a minute. "Rafe and I were going to do a feature on the Turtle Centre. We wanted to talk about all the good work they've done supporting the threatened turtle population and helping scientists understand turtle movements and behavior. And it's right here on Grand Cayman."

He laughed. "No exotic travel for me, I guess. The Turtle Centre it is."

"Great. That's settled then. I'm starving. I haven't eaten all day. Want to join me for a late lunch? We can discuss the timing of the new column."

Gary nodded, so we climbed down from the *Tranquility*'s bow and strolled back to Ray's Place. As we walked in, Candy screeched, "Look. It's Stewie Belcher." Gary and I both burst out laughing as we made our way to a small table in the far corner.

Chapter 9
Swimming With Turtles

THE NEXT MORNING, Gary picked me up at RIO for our trip to the Turtle Centre. Rafe Cummings, the world's most popular superstar action hero, was going to meet us there. His best friend Tate Crusoe would be dropping him off.

We weren't planning any filming today, although we were going to meet the Centre's management team and develop a plan. They'd already accepted my proposal, so it was just a matter of working out timing and a few small details.

The Centre's manager first took us on a tour of the facilities. In my proposal I'd requested that they allow me to shoot inside the predator tank during the shark feeding, and they'd told me that I could do it, but it would have to be at my own risk. Usually nobody was in the tank during feeding time, which could get a little wild. Most of the time, feedings were viewable by the Centre's patrons through clear portals that provided visibility to the spectacle, but we wanted to do our shoot during a closed feeding session.

According to the Turtle Centre's response to my proposal, if I went into the tank I had to supply my own insurance for the shark feeding. At the end of the meeting, Gary told them that *Ecosphere* would be providing the policy. He and the manager left us to discuss the details, so Rafe and I walked down the trail to the onsite café for a coffee. I added a couple of the house special cookies to our order even though I knew Rafe would only eat a single bite of his. Then we sat at a table in the corner to enjoy our break.

I finished my coffee while Rafe was still savoring the tiny bite of his cookie. People always talked about how Rafe must have either undergone surgery or have unbelievably great genes to maintain his good looks and perfect build. There's no doubt his face is a genetic blessing, but I knew he worked extremely hard to stay in shape. He spent hours in the gym lifting weights, and lots of additional time every day running or swimming. He always ate sparingly, and the results of his discipline were impressive.

Me, on the other hand, well, I'd reached over and taken the rest of his cookie after he'd broken off the small piece that I knew was all he'd allow himself.

Luckily, I had a super-fast metabolism. If it wasn't for that, I wouldn't be able to fit into my dive suits for long.

I'd just swallowed the last of Rafe's cookie when Gary rejoined us. "The manager invited you to swim in the lagoon with the turtles before the Centre opens to the public this morning. Interested?"

"Yes," I replied.

Rafe nodded, and we both stood up to head over to the lagoon.

I usually wear an athletic-cut two-piece bathing suit under my cargo shorts and t-shirts, so whenever it's time for a dive, all I have to do is pull off my outer layer of clothes. Instead of his usual cargo shorts, Rafe was wearing a pair of those stretchy, form-fitting shorts the guys on the RIO team had recently adopted. He just kept his shorts on instead of changing into swim trunks and slipped his REO branded blue tee off over his head.

With that, we were both ready to swim with turtles. We sat on the lagoon's edge and eased into the water so we wouldn't startle the fish and turtles who lived in the lagoon. We weren't wearing any fins or other gear, because unlike for those creatures who still lived in the ocean, seeing people in their pool was a common occurrence here. We didn't want to take a chance that we might accidentally injure any of the lagoon's inhabitants by brushing a fin against them if they came too close.

The water in the lagoon—actually a giant swimming pool—was clean, clear, and cool. The turtles living here were comfortable with visitors, so they swam up close to us and even let us touch their shells gently with one or two fingers. Rafe and I were grinning like fools around our snorkels.

We stayed with the turtles for about fifteen minutes, but we were mindful of not wanting to wear out our welcome with the turtle farm's management before we even started shooting film for our feature. Reluctantly, we climbed out and padded barefoot over to where Gary and the manager were sitting at a table in the shade. After thanking the manager for his time and for letting us swim in the turtle lagoon, we set off for the return trip to RIO.

Gary dropped us off at RIO's front entrance and drove on to park his car, while Rafe and I ambled across the front of the building to the back lawn and then on toward Ray's Place. We picked up a couple of lemonades on our way past the bar, then continued down the pier toward *Tranquility*.

Chapter 10
Diving on Enviroman

As we neared my boat, I noticed Liam sitting on the deck of his own boat, *Enviroman*, which was back in its usual slip across from mine. Ever since the boat had been extensively damaged a while ago, it suffered frequent problems and it spent more time in the boatyard than on the water. They just couldn't seem to get it back into prime condition.

I hurried down the pier to greet him. "Your boat's back," I said, happy that the boatyard had finally finished the latest round of repairs and returned his boat again. "That's great."

Liam closed the lid on his computer and smiled at me. "Yes. They dropped it off just a few minutes ago. I've been waiting for you to get back so we can test it out. Maybe we can get in a dive or two if all goes well." He turned to Rafe. "You're welcome to come along too if you want to."

I was pleased by Liam's gesture of friendship. He and Rafe had not started out destined to be friends, because the first time they'd met, Rafe had been kissing me. But my wonderful fiancé soon realized that there was nothing going on between Rafe and me—at least there wasn't anything on my part—so he'd let it go with a stern warning to Rafe not to let anything like that happen again. As they'd worked together on the movie and then the more recent documentary, they'd become actual friends. The fact that Rafe had kept his word about not kissing me again had probably helped a lot with that.

Rafe smiled at Liam's invitation. "Thanks. I'd love to come along."

Gary walked up to the boat behind Rafe. "Can I tag along too?"

I knew Gary dove occasionally, but I didn't think he was an especially avid diver. That's one reason it had surprised me when his article idea turned out to involve following me around on my dives.

But I smiled a welcome. "Good idea." I wanted a chance to see how skilled a diver he was before we started diving together for his article, and this was a perfect low-stakes opportunity.

Rafe and Gary walked back to the dive shop to pick up their gear, looking almost like twins from behind. Same height, similar builds. They both had sunglasses perched atop their heads and wore heavy dive watches on their left wrists. Rafe's hair was a sun-streaked sandy blonde just a shade lighter than Gary's medium brown.

I turned back to the task at hand and grabbed my gear bag from the *Tranquility*, which was moored just across the dock. Liam had already stocked *Enviroman* with four tanks for us to use, and Rafe and Gary each carried two more when they returned from the dive shop a few minutes later.

"Where to?" Liam asked when everybody had stowed their gear and secured their tanks. "Just remember, we may not want to go too far. Consider this is a shakedown cruise as much as a dive excursion. I just got *Enviroman* back after another round of some pretty extensive repairs."

Rafe bit his lip and looked down. His brother Dougie had damaged Liam's boat, and Rafe felt so bad about it that Liam and I tried never to mention it in front of him.

I wanted to change the topic of conversation quickly, because as far as I was aware, Gary didn't know the cause of the damage to *Enviroman*. Rafe felt guilty enough about it as it was without having to sit through a lengthy conversation about his brother in front of a near stranger.

Liam was sensitive about it too. He prided himself on both his situational awareness and his physical stamina. Doug had gotten the drop on him, and that wounded his pride, not to mention that he'd nearly died from his injuries. I didn't want Gary to open a topic that would only bring pain to both Rafe and Liam, so I took the conversation in a totally different direction.

"Gary, do you have a dive locker at RIO, or are you using rental gear today? It didn't take you very long to gather your stuff."

"Rental gear," he said with a smile. "I don't have my own stuff with me today. I didn't realize outsiders could even have storage lockers at the dive shop."

"You're right. Usually they're not available to outsiders—just employees and special guests. But I think you qualify as a special guest. Remind me when we get back and I'll have Stewie set you up with one so you don't have to lug your gear around all the time while we're working on your column."

Before Gary could even say 'thank you,' Liam looked up sharply. "What column?" he asked.

Gary was *Ecosphere* magazine's publisher, but Liam owned the entire publishing company, Quokka Media. He knew how badly the false accusations of plagiarism early in my career had hurt me, so he was fiercely protective of the terms of my contract with *Ecosphere* to make sure there would be no question that I'd produced all the work that appeared under my byline.

I sat next to Liam on the gunwale. "Gary wants to follow Rafe and me when we do our Turtle Centre feature and then produce a column of his own showing how we work. It might be a good idea."

He stared into my eyes for a long moment, and I knew he was trying to figure out how I really felt about this. I gave a quick shrug, letting him know I was still undecided about it. At least for now.

He nodded back. "If it's okay with Fin, it'll be fine with me. But there will be no—and I mean absolutely no—commingling of work, no shared attribution of photos or text, and as always, Fin has the final say on how and when you use her work."

"Easy there, mate," said Gary, holding up his hands in a 'calm down' gesture. "I know the rules. It's just that Fin's column is so darn popular I thought the readers might enjoy a little 'behind the scenes' peek. No worries if she doesn't want to do it or if you don't approve. It was just an idea."

I put my hand on Liam's. "If we decide to move ahead with the idea, I'll be fine. Gary's your best friend, and he's not about to steal from either of us." I looked at Gary. "In fact, if you're up for it, why don't we start today. You can take some shots of Rafe and me scouting the dive area."

"Great idea," he said. "But I don't have any of my camera equipment with me."

"No problem. You can borrow some from the rental setups in the dive shop." I sent Stewie a text asking him to bring a full professional grade camera system to *Enviroman*.

Within a few minutes, Stewie had dropped off the photo equipment and showed Gary how to use it. Although most of Gary's best work had been with land-based nature photography, he was also pretty familiar with underwater photography. It didn't take long for him to get comfortable with the new setup.

Meanwhile, Liam, Rafe, and I discussed where we'd like to dive. Eventually, we settled on Turtle Reef, a relatively easy and very pleasant dive site on the West End.

"After all," said Rafe, "our goal is to find turtles, and this is a great spot for turtle sightings."

Stewie untied the line holding us to the dock and tossed the free end to Rafe while Liam backed his boat out of the slip. I relaxed, putting my feet up along the bench and tilting my head back to catch the sun—until I remembered Maddy's recent bout with skin cancer. I went below to grab a wide-brimmed hat and a long-sleeved shirt with built-in sun protection before going back to my perch on the gunwales.

It took only a few minutes to reach our destination. I hopped up and grabbed the long gaffe to catch the mooring ball and tie us off. I raised my arm so Liam would know we were secure, and he shut off the engines.

Liam, Rafe, and I quickly geared up, but we had to wait a moment for Gary to finish. He fumbled with his setup a little bit, but I was willing to give him the benefit of the doubt. It's hard to be smooth when you're using unfamiliar gear.

Liam went over to help him. Eventually, both Gary and Liam joined us near the dive platform in *Enviroman*'s stern.

I stepped off the platform first, then swam back to the boat so Rafe could hand me my camera. Once I'd backed away far enough to leave the area near the platform clear for his entry, Rafe joined me in the water. A few minutes later, first Gary, then Liam made their entries.

Rafe and I sank down along the mooring line and swam to the nearby mini wall. We swam slowly, checking out the nooks and crannies and exploring the overhangs near the sandy bottom. We found several green moray eels and then two spotted moray eels, all poking their heads out into the current and working their jaws to pump water over their gills.

I took a few photos of them before we quickly moved on. Everybody loves moray eel pictures, but we were on the hunt for turtles.

We kept moving, veering off toward deeper water and swimming across the sandy area heading toward the second drop off where it was much more likely we'd see turtles. As soon as we reached the crest of the wall, a green sea turtle popped up. He quickly took a sharp turn away from us, but I was still able to take several photos of him.

Rafe and I dropped over the wall and sank down to about eighty feet. We swam slowly, looking out into the blue for turtles or larger pelagic creatures. This reef was healthy and alive with several species of angelfish, including a large pair of queen angelfish, a few vibrant rock beauties, and a blue tang.

Feather duster worms swayed in the slight current, their delicate fronds wafting in a subtle dance. A sergeant major and a yellowtail damselfish swam a twining path around each other, while a queen triggerfish and a porcupine fish munched their way through a swarm of krill and a few unfortunate arrow crabs who'd been caught out in the open.

On our way back up the wall, we saw two lobsters, each secure in its own crevice, but peering out at the world side-by-side like two friends perched on adjacent bar stools. The sight made me smile.

I glanced behind me and saw Gary and Liam in the distance. Gary appeared to be having trouble with his buoyancy, and he was kicking hard to keep up with us. Liam was hovering patiently beside him.

He saw me glance their way, and he dropped behind Gary far enough that Gary couldn't see what he was doing before he flashed me the okay sign. I knew that meant he would be keeping an eye on Gary and that I should just do what I would normally do. Still, I motioned to Rafe to slow down a little bit. I wanted to avoid unnecessarily stressing Gary out, and we were in no hurry.

Rafe and I continued gradually rising in the water as we swam along the wall. It took only a few minutes until we crested the lip of the deepest part of the wall and moved back onto the sandy area. A few moments later Liam and Gary joined us on the plateau.

Gary pointed to his air gauge, so I knew it was time to return to the boat. We'd only been under for about twenty minutes, a much shorter dive than Rafe and I would normally have done. But I simply gave him the okay sign before we took off across the sand, heading back to the mooring line.

The four of us hung out at fifteen feet, letting our bodies off-gas the excess nitrogen we'd absorbed on the dive. When our three minute safety stop was up, I signaled for Gary to reboard first, followed by Rafe. Once they were both safely aboard, Liam and I hung out for a few extra minutes, enjoying being underwater, and loving the sense of peace and connection we always felt when we dove together.

Back at RIO's marina, Liam navigated *Enviroman* into his assigned slip, and then Rafe tied us off to the cleat on the dock. We all packed up our gear and stepped off the boat.

"I'm starving. Anybody else ready for some food?" I asked. "I bet there's an empty table waiting for us at Ray's Place if you're up for it."

There was a chorus of agreement to my plan.

Liam took my gear bag along with his own and gestured for Gary to follow him. "I'll clean our gear while you get us a table, okay?"

I nodded.

Gary said, "Rafe, I'll take your stuff. Then Fin won't have to sit in the restaurant alone."

Rafe thanked Gary and handed his bag to him. We all walked together along the dock, but Rafe and I veered off toward Ray's Place as soon as we set foot on land, while Liam and Gary headed in the other direction toward the dive shop to rinse and stow the gear.

It was the quiet hour between peak mealtimes, so although there was a healthy crowd at the bar, most of the tables were empty. Rafe and I selected a four-top in a shadowy back corner, but sharp eyed Candy saw us anyway. Luckily she didn't know Rafe's name, or she'd have set off a mob scene by announcing the arrival of the world's most beloved action hero movie star. "Look" she said. "It's Fin Fleming." Nobody so much as glanced away from the football game showing on the TV over the bar.

I guessed that Candy had been announcing my arrival so frequently that by now, nobody was paying her any attention. Rafe and I started laughing, but we kept walking toward our table.

Noah Gibb was behind the bar, and he looked up as we passed by. Within minutes, he'd brought two tall glasses of icy cold lemonade and two menus.

"There'll be four," I said when he set down the glasses. "Liam and Gary will be joining us."

"Got it," he said. "Do you know what Gary drinks?" Noah waited on Liam, Rafe, and me so often that he knew our usuals by heart.

"Nope. No idea. Sorry," I said. "But here he comes now, so he can tell you himself."

Liam slid into the seat next to mine, and Gary sat next to Rafe.

"Caybrew, please," Gary said.

"Lemonade for me," said Liam. "And thank you."

Noah winked at me and took off to get the drinks and two additional menus.

After we all scarfed down our juicy burgers and fries, we split up. Gary went back to the Quokka Media offices downtown, and Rafe wandered off to find Tate, his best friend and business partner.

Liam and I stayed at the table, sipping at the fresh round of lemonades Noah had just delivered. We spent a few minutes in silence, enjoying the momentary peace and avoiding the elephant sitting at the table with us.

Liam finally said, "Go ahead. Say it."

"Okay. You and Gary go way back to your college days, and you know him much better than I do. I assume you've been diving with him before. Was today a bad day for him, or will he have trouble keeping up with Rafe and me every time we dive together?"

Liam stirred his lemonade thoughtfully. "He's an okay diver, but he's definitely not in your league."

I sighed. "Why did he put himself forward as the new column's photographer then? He must know he won't be able to keep up with me. I don't have the time or the patience to babysit him, and I won't compromise the quality of my work to accommodate his ego."

Liam put his hand on mine. "Why did you agree to let him do the column without first making him prove he could keep up?"

"He's your best friend, and he's my boss at a job I love. I was in a tough situation."

Liam nodded thoughtfully. "I could squash the idea. All I'd have to do would be to tell Gary I don't like it."

I rolled my eyes. "He won't fall for that. He'll know you're doing it for me. And the truth is, I do think it's an interesting idea. I just don't think Gary's the right guy to do it. My columns will suffer if he can't keep up with me."

After taking a slow sip of his lemonade, Liam said, "Not too many people could keep up with you. You're an extraordinary diver."

I scowled at him. "You can. Rafe Cummings can. So can Oliver, Stewie, Maddy, Genevra, Doc…"

"Yes, we all can. But when you're with us, you're only asking us to keep up with you as a diver. To do what he proposed, Gary would not only have to keep up with you, but probably be even better than you. He'd need to anticipate your next move, photograph anything you do that's interesting, and catch you capturing those elusive underwater shots. It's a lot to ask of anyone."

I sighed. "His column idea's not going to work out, is it?"

"Probably not," he said. "The question is, do you want to tell him yourself or do you want me to?"

I shook my head ruefully. "I don't want to do anything too quickly, and if it finally comes down to it, I'll tell him myself. But first let me think about it. I already know it'll never work as a regular column, but maybe I'll decide it's okay for him to do this if it's just a one-time thing."

Chapter 11
Benjamin Returns

THE NEXT SEVERAL days were quiet. I rose early, worked hard, dove often, and ate way too many cookies while drinking way too much coffee. I spent hours training Rosie in the research lab. Typical days for me. I hadn't decided yet what to do about Gary's column idea, although the topic was constantly running through my mind.

I was at my desk early, eating the warm blueberry muffin I'd picked up at the cafe, when Benjamin popped his head in my door. His huge smile was joyous. "Guess who's a certified mermaid instructor trainer? And RIO is now a certified mermaid training facility."

I stood up and gave him a quick hug. "Congratulations. That's so exciting. What's our next step?"

He came in and sat at the table in the corner of my office. "We need to get some RIO mermaids certified. You and Genevra. Maddy. Doc probably won't go for it…"

I nodded. "Highly unlikely. But maybe Maddy can talk her into it. Who else?"

He looked sheepish. "I was hoping you could convince Liam and Rafe to become certified mermen…"

I raised my eyebrows at him. "Really?"

He took a quick sip of his own coffee. "It might help attract outside students if they thought they'd be able to have their picture taken with one or both of those guys."

"I can always ask, but I can't make them agree. And they're both pretty busy with their own interests. They don't have a lot of free time." I popped the last of my muffin in my mouth. "So other than that impossible task, what else do you need from me?"

He looked at the floor. "I need you to start your mermaid certification process."

"And?" I asked.

"We'll want to attract students right away, so I need you to let me do some publicity to raise our profile. You'll be heavily featured in it."

I groaned, and then an idea flashed into my mind like a great ball of light. "Would a no-fee column in *Ecosphere* meet your publicity requirements?"

"Sure," he scoffed, "But that's never going to happen. *Ecosphere* isn't like *Human* magazine. It's a serious platform."

"Let me see about that. I do know the publisher, after all."

He grinned. "That's right. You do. Okay, I'll see you in the pool house at ten for your first lesson. I'll let Genevra and Maddy know we're good to go. Maybe Maddy will be able to convince Doc to join us. And would you please ask Rafe and Liam? You're more likely to get a positive response than I am."

He walked out with a satisfied smile on his face.

The first thing I did was pick up the phone to call Gary. My latest idea might solve two problems at the same time.

Chapter 12
Mermaid Diver Training

I'D ALWAYS BEEN FASCINATED by mermaids, even as a kid. In fact, when I was very young I had an imaginary friend who was a mermaid. Her name was Kaimana, which means powerful sea. Ray and Maddy indulged my fantasy friendship, since I had so little opportunity to interact with other kids. My friend Kaimana had blue hair and a sparkling turquoise tail. She was very beautiful, at least in my mind.

I told Kaimana all my secrets, and we were best friends for years, until I finally outgrew the need for a fantasy friend. Despite leaving Kaimana behind, I never really got over my fascination with mermaids. So although I'd probably never admit it to anyone, I was secretly excited about the idea of mermaid training.

I was at the pool house at ten, just as Benjamin had requested. Liam and Rafe weren't there yet, but Genevra, Maddy, Doc, and Stewie were sitting on the pool deck, dangling their feet in the water. I was surprised to see Doc, but I figured Maddy must have been able to convince her. And the fact that Stewie was taking the class too probably didn't hurt.

My best friends Theresa Simmons and Joely Wentworth were in the bleachers next to my father. None of those three were comfortable enough in the water to join the class, but I appreciated their support.

Benjamin glanced at his watch, then gave me a pointed look.

I shrugged. I couldn't force Liam or Rafe to become mermen if they weren't interested.

Resigned to his inability to attract more mermen, Benjamin handed us waterproof tablets preloaded with the mermaid training course materials. He'd just given me mine when the door to the men's locker room banged open. Liam, Rafe, Tate, my brother Oliver, and Noah and Austin Gibb all walked out in their swimsuits.

They'd all recently switched from the baggy cargo shorts they'd used to wear as swim trunks. Now they wore sleeker, stretchy, more close fitting shorts with long legs and no pockets. I had to admit, they looked good. Liam gave me a wink and sat on the edge of the pool next to me.

Tate's blue eyes glowed in the sunlight that spilled from the skylights, and it took a moment for me to realize that the glow was because for once, he wasn't wearing his trendy and impenetrable sunglasses.

Austin was always very careful with his possessions and he took very good care of his things. He too wore his sunglasses on the top of his head, but he removed them and carefully placed them in their case and then put the case down on one of the benches, along with the Apple watch that did double duty as his dive computer.

A few seconds later, Gary Graydon entered the pool house, carrying an armload of underwater photo and video equipment along with a full scuba setup. He wore those same stretchy shorts all the male members of RIO's staff had adopted, along with a blue Quokka Media t-shirt. He pulled a small cart with several scuba tanks on it behind him.

I sighed with relief. Gary hadn't sounded convinced that filming the mermaid training class would be a better choice than filming something in the open ocean, but he'd agreed to think it over. Apparently he'd concluded, as had I, that this project might be more in line with his capabilities. He set up his video camera near the edge of the pool, hung an underwater camera around his neck, and waited to see what came next.

Benjamin smiled and gave waterproof tablets to the newcomers. He had us all sign the electronic release forms before going over the first few lessons. Then it was showtime.

He looked at me. "Fin, would you explain the mechanics of the dolphin kick and then demonstrate for us, please."

I'd become extremely adept at the dolphin kick while Christophe Poisson had been training me for a deep freedive a while ago, so it made sense for Benjamin to ask me.

"Sure," I said. "The dolphin kick gets its name because it resembles the way dolphins move through the water. And unlike most swimming kicks, both legs move in unison, and you initiate the movement mainly from your core muscles, not your legs. You get the best propulsion if you keep your legs extended and your feet together. Start by pushing your head and chest down, which should naturally cause your hips to rise. Let the force of that movement undulate through your legs and feet. Keep your hands together and your arms extended slightly up and out in front of you. Push your hips down again to start the next cycle."

"Don't try to move too quickly or to create too much speed or amplitude. This stroke takes a lot of effort. Work toward a wave size that allows you to make maximum forward progress without exhausting you too quickly. I'll show you."

Gary had been filming my little speech, while I tried to ignore the camera's presence. When I'd finished the explanation, he jumped into the water and swam to the center of the pool to be ready to take underwater shots as I did the demonstration. Once he was in position, I put down my tablet and dove into the water, using the dolphin kick to traverse the pool's entire length before coming up for air. "Any questions?"

There were no questions. Almost everybody in this class was a very accomplished diver, so we all knew at least the rudiments of the dolphin kick. After a beat, Benjamin said, "Good. Thank you. Now everybody into the pool. Dolphin kick up and back please."

We each chose a lane and obediently kicked our way along the length of RIO's massive pool and then back again. I knew this was a greater distance than the certification actually required, but why not? Most of us were water specialists. We could all handle it, and I knew Benjamin was hoping to certify at least a few of us to help out with teaching mermaid training classes. This way we could complete the in-water skills for both certifications in one go.

While we were doing our laps, Gary was on the pool deck taking video of us making our way up and back along the pool. After he'd caught at least a few seconds of video of each of us underwater, he jumped back in and took still photos of us while lying on the bottom shooting up at us as we passed over him.

We all laughed and smiled whenever we surfaced for air. The dolphin kick, although hard work, is a lot of fun to do. Austin and Noah were the last to finish their laps, and I noticed Austin was the only one of us breathing hard when he reached the shallow end.

I looked up and saw that Gary had set the video camera on automatic, so it was still filming us as we swam. He smiled and gave me the okay sign. I grinned at him, pleased that he seemed to be enjoying working on the topic I'd suggested for his column.

Benjamin checked something off on his clipboard. "Great. Everybody back to the deep end. We're going to float for ten minutes. I'll let you know when to start."

The basic mermaid course only required five minutes of floating and the ability to swim a single length of our enormous pool, so I realized that Benjamin was definitely saving time by setting us up for passing the advanced mermaid training at the same time as basic.

We all swam quickly toward the deep end and hung vertically waiting for Benjamin to give us the signal. "In case you're on your back and your ears are in the water, I'll blow a whistle to make sure you can hear me when you've hit the ten minute mark. Everybody ready? Start now." He clicked his stopwatch, and Gary started shooting photos.

A short time later, Benjamin blew his whistle, signaling we'd finished the floating requirement. Then he put us through some additional skills, including dolphin kicking on our backs, and doing multiple types of turns at the ends of the pools. It was a surprisingly rigorous workout, and Gary seemed to be everywhere, watching us through his deep brown eyes and taking shot after shot.

Professional mermaids looked so graceful, pretty, and serene, always smiling, blowing bubbles and kisses. I'd never realized how much hard work went into making it look so easy.

By now it was lunchtime, and we were all starving from the hours of effort we'd spent in the water. Benjamin thanked us for coming and told us he had lunch set up for us in the conference room. The pool was empty, and the locker room doors had slammed open before he'd even finished his sentence.

I took a quick shower, slicked back my hair, and changed into a dry bathing suit under some clean cargo shorts, flip-flops, and a RIO-branded tee, before hustling to the conference room for lunch.

Chapter 13
Day Two of Mermaid Diver Training

THE NEXT MORNING we'd all met for an early breakfast in RIO's café, so we walked into the pool house as a group. Everyone except Gary claimed one of the waterproof tablets and sat on the edge of the pool to complete the day's written tasks. While we worked, Gary set up his video equipment and picked up his camera to take some pics of us sitting shoulder-to-shoulder along the edge of the pool, each of us with our feet in the water, diligently working on the required curriculum.

Once he had the shots he needed, he took the steps down into the water so he would be ready to go as soon as the class started.

My fellow 'mer-people' and I made short work of the written material and waited for Benjamin to signal the start of the water portion of the training. I knew that today we would be covering rescue skills and problem management.

Since most of us were certified scuba course directors, we already had well-honed rescue skills. But as my late stepfather Ray Russo had drilled into me my entire life, you have to practice your skills diligently so when the time comes that you need them, your response is automatic. It would never hurt any of us to refresh our rescue skills.

Benjamin assigned the teams. I was buddied up with Stewie. Noah was with Liam, and Austin was with Genevra. Rafe was paired with Doc, and Tate with Maddy. When everyone was buddied up, Oliver was the odd man out. "Oliver, you're with me," said Benjamin.

Each member of a team took a turn at being the rescuer and the "patient." We had to swim to the patient, who was on the bottom at the other end of the pool. Ditch the patient's gear and bring them to the surface. Then we performed simulated in-water CPR while swimming toward the pool exit. Next we used a fireman's carry to get the patient out of the water and down on the pool deck. Afterward, we practiced CPR on mannequins. All the while, Gary was filming and shooting stills. I was happy to see that he seemed to be taking his assignment very seriously.

When we'd finished, Benjamin blew his infernal whistle again. "There's a box with your name on it for each of you near the locker room door. In it, you'll find a monofin, one or more mermaid tails—some of you may need several in your wardrobes—and some accessories. Grab your monofins and let's start with techniques for using them. Fin, will you demonstrate the use of a monofin please?"

"Sure thing." I searched the pile of boxes until I found the one with my name on it. Inside was a mermaid monofin, several stretchy mermaid tails in a variety of colors, and a couple of matching bikini tops with string ties.

I glared at Benjamin. He knew I never wore bikinis or any bathing suit with ties or ruffles. With suits like that, something always came untied or popped off at awkward moments. That made them much too fussy for me. Above all, my bathing suits needed to be functional.

Sure, I often wore two piece bathing suits, but they were bathing suits designed for athletes. I put the tiny bikini tops Benjamin had provided aside. We might sell them in the soon-to-open mermaid department in the dive shop, but I was absolutely certain I wouldn't be wearing them.

I walked back to the pool carrying my mermaid monofin. It was softer and more bendable than the monofin I'd worn for freediving, and it had flexible, rolled edges to help prevent snagging or tearing when worn inside a tail.

I sat on the edge of the pool and slipped my feet into the pocket of the monofin. Then I pushed myself into the water and dolphin kicked from one end of the pool to the other before coming up for air. As always when using any type of fins, it took less effort to cover the distance than swimming with bare feet. The monofin also made it easier to keep my feet together during the dolphin kick. I wouldn't lose any momentum by accidentally letting my feet drift apart—because they couldn't.

Benjamin smiled when I popped up for air. "Thank you. Now everybody, go ahead and try it for yourself."

The members of RIO's new mermaid team each extracted their monofin from the box marked with his or her name and sat on the side of the pool to put them on. One by one, they slipped into the pool and began the required swim.

When they'd completed all the laps, Benjamin requested that we each select a mermaid tail and put that on for the next exercise. He demonstrated how to insert the monofin into the tail before putting it on, and then how to gather the fabric of the tail, put our feet into the fin, and then carefully pull the stretchy tail up to our waists to avoid snags. It was sort of like putting on pantyhose—that most dreaded of garments.

When everyone had their tail on, Benjamin had us do another lap to get comfortable with the tails. Then he asked us to simulate a problem underwater and perform a self-rescue.

One member of each team held onto the buddy's tail from behind and down low near the foot area. The person in distress had to find the "snag" and attempt to free the tail. When that didn't work—and Benjamin had instructed us to make sure it didn't—the mermaid or merman in distress had to figure out how to get out of the tail and make it to the surface. We performed this skill in the pool's twenty-five foot deep end.

Tate, Noah, and Austin, the least experienced divers in the

group, had a little more trouble than the rest of us, but they managed to get out of the tail and reach the surface safely.

Benjamin smiled when we'd all finished the skill. "Lunch is available in the conference room."

He didn't have to tell us twice.

Chapter 14
Open Water Mermaid Diving

THE NEXT DAY our training moved outside, to the newly built lagoon and grotto we'd had constructed to be the centerpiece of our mermaid attraction. The hardest part of building it had been getting the permits, but Benjamin had been working on the process for months before he sprang the mermaid idea on the management team. Once Newton and Liam understood what we needed, they'd helped expedite the necessary permits.

With the combined efforts of the three powerhouse businessmen, we didn't have to wait too long. Permits in hand, we'd built an artificial reef that curved out from the ironshore behind the dive shop across the cove's sandy bottom toward the natural drop off to the wall. There was a small opening in the artificial reef to allow the cove's water to flow in and out with the tides.

Luckily, there was already a natural rise in the reef on the other side, so we now had a large, shallow, basin-like area inside our larger cove for our mermaids to cavort in. On shore, we'd also built a grotto, with recirculating seawater gently cascading down around rocky seating areas that could each accommodate anywhere from a single mermaid to groups of three—or even four if they were all children. We planned to use the grotto for class photos and publicity stills.

Although the new artificial reef had only been in place for a little over a week, it had already started to show signs of acceptance by the mighty ocean. Small stands of coral were starting to sprout along the scaffolding, and tiny sea creatures darted about. Their presence would attract larger specimens, and soon we'd have a healthy functioning reef ecosystem to delight our mermaid students and visitors.

But today, it was just us. Benjamin put us through a rehash of the skills we'd practiced in the pool. Once we'd all satisfactorily completed our assignments, we'd be ready to receive our mermaid C-cards.

Liam had taken Gary diving in the cove yesterday after class so he could get some underwater shots of the artificial reef, and today, Gary was on hand to photograph the skills display.

When we'd completed our skills demonstrations, we all climbed up into the grotto for our formal photos. Benjamin walked around to each of us and handed out seashell necklaces and bracelets, and colorful flowers for our hair. Maddy had a pearl tiara that looked stunning with her white-blonde hair. The men all received torcs and amulets. Liam had a trident, which made us laugh.

Later, Gary shot a series of more formal photos of us sitting in the grotto. He took individual portraits of each of us, and then various small groups of two or three sitting in the grotto. Last he took several photos of us all together. We'd use these shots for RIO's publicity as well as in Gary's article in *Ecosphere*.

The photos Gary took showed a jolly group, happy and filled with the glow of achievement and camaraderie. I knew his article would be a success, and it would make a great promotional tool for the opening of our newest business venture. It was a win/win for *Ecosphere* and RIO.

Davy Jones was covering for Stewie in the dive shop, but since it was a quiet time of day, he came out to stand in the shade behind the shop to check out the festivities. While he was out of the sun's glare, he removed his dark glasses and placed them on his head.

Even from a distance, I could see sadness in his bright blue eyes. I smiled at him, feeling guilty because I still hadn't told him I was planning to shut down the submarine attraction that was his responsibility within the next few weeks.

When Gary finished taking the pictures he needed, we all peeled off our tails and carefully extracted our monofins. Benjamin and Stewie had created a special drying zone adjacent to the secure employee locker area where we could store our monofins and tails. But before we dispersed, Benjamin had one last announcement.

"According to the tradition here at RIO, we have a congratulations party for all graduating classes. Today's party will be in the lobby atrium, and it's open to the public. See you all there."

I smiled happily. Benjamin was even better at his new VP of business development role than I'd hoped. He thought of everything, and he was so nice that everybody wanted to pitch in to help. If we all worked together, I was sure we could soon make RIO self-sustaining.

Chapter 15
After the Party

By tradition, RIO graduation parties were short, and this one was even shorter than usual. Gary joined us, took a few photos of the buffet table, wandered around making sure he had a recognizable image of everyone in attendance, and took a final picture of Liam and me dancing, my head resting dreamily on his shoulder. The glare of Gary's flash shattered my peaceful state, and I jumped a mile.

Liam wisely stifled his smile at my startled response. Then he smoothed the hair back from my forehead and kissed me. "Any chance you're ready to set a date for our wedding yet?" he whispered.

"Any chance you're ready to tell me about your secret life yet?" I whispered back.

He sighed. "It's not that I don't want to tell you, but you're safer if you don't know anything."

I glared at him. "If it's so dangerous that I can't even know what it is, then in my opinion, it's way too dangerous for my future husband to be involved in."

He thought a moment. "Okay. I never thought of it like that, but you're right. I'll tell you tonight. Can we take one of RIO's rental boats out for a spin?"

"Uh, I guess so. But you know we can always take *Tranquility* if you don't want to use *Enviroman*." His reluctance to use *Tranquility* was puzzling. We'd been together several years now, and we almost always used my boat, even after he'd bought *Enviroman*.

He nuzzled my ear and then whispered. "I know we could take *Tranquility*. And so would anyone who might want to listen in."

I reared back in shock. Liam smiled, stepped back, and twirled me around, under his arm and back again.

We didn't usually do fancy dance steps. Liam could handle them, but I'm not a good dancer. More often than not I stumble and step on his toes. But this time, I was so surprised by his words I followed him without even thinking about it.

Who did he think might want to listen to our conversation? And if they'd be listening tonight, did that mean they listened all the time?

The song ended, and we looked around. The other members of the mermaid class had departed without saying goodbye. The only people left were the catering staff and the maintenance team. They were all milling around the edge of the atrium, looking like they couldn't wait for us to leave. It was well after quitting time on a Friday afternoon, so we couldn't blame them.

We said goodnight to them all and apologized for keeping them late. Then we thanked each one individually before we left through RIO's front door.

Liam went to his car. "I need to take care of some stuff at Quokka. I'll be back later."

"Okay. I have work to do anyway." I went back inside and crossed the lobby to the hall that led to the executive area. I sat at my desk and flipped on my MAC, but I wasn't really interested in work. Instead, I spent the next two hours mulling over what Liam might be about to tell me, and why he suspected somebody might be monitoring our conversations even when we were aboard our boats.

Chapter 16
Boating and Secrets

Liam came back to get me a couple of hours later, bearing jerk chicken and all the fixings that he'd picked up downtown. Since RIO's rental boats aren't as comfortable as our personal boats, we ate dinner at the small table in my office instead of aboard the *Tranquility*.

When we'd finished eating, he pulled a hooded sweatshirt off the hook behind my door and tossed it my way. "Let's go," he said.

Ray's Place was hopping tonight. There was a long line waiting for tables, and the crowd was three deep at the bar. Revelers crowded the dance floor and occupied all the picnic tables and hammocks in the recreation area. To ensure that any unknown watchers would miss seeing us depart, Liam and I stayed off the well-lit crushed shell paths and stuck to the shadows by unspoken agreement.

Music and laughter from the bar mingled with the clink of silverware against dishes. The distant sound wafted across the lawn, covering the faint noises I made when I unlocked the chain holding one of our rental Zodiacs in place.

RIO's rental Zodiacs are twenty-six feet long and jet black. They have large powerful engines, but Liam stopped me before I could push the engine's electric start button. "Shh. Let's wait until we get out of sight to start the motor," he whispered.

We sat on the center bench and together, we rowed out to RIO's Training Spot One. I'd always thought Training Spot One was very close to RIO's marina, but I'd never had to row all the way to it before. It obviously wasn't as close as I thought because it took us quite a while to get there under our own steam, although it was less than a five minute trip in the *Tranquility*.

Instead of tying up to the mooring, Liam just pulled in the oars and let the boat float free. He turned and straddled the bench so he could face me. "I never want to hurt you, you know that, right?" he said softly.

I blinked back sudden tears. Was he going to tell me he was still married to Amelia despite the legitimate looking divorce papers he'd shown me when he returned from his year in Australia? Or had he met someone else? Was he sick, and traveling for experimental treatments? Every horrible thought that might explain his frequent absences and secret trips went through my mind.

"Tell me," I said. "I need to know. I can handle whatever it is."

"I know you can." He paused a moment. "You remember I'm the guy who wrote Oh! Possum, and the object of the game is to follow clues to find out where in the world the possum is or has been. And then if he's already gone from somewhere, you have to figure out when he was there. And he moved around all the time."

I nodded wordlessly. I'm not a gamer, but I'd been with Liam long enough that I knew the rudiments of the hit video game he'd authored.

He continued. "And remember how when we were all looking for the drug dealers a while ago Oliver said it must be a coincidence that if you could unlock certain levels, the possum was always someplace where a big drug bust had occurred shortly after his arrival? And remember I told him never to mention it again?"

I was annoyed. I thought he was just putting off what I wanted —no, what I **needed**—to hear. "I don't want to talk about the game. I want to know what's going on in your life. Especially when you're away and out of touch."

He nodded. "I know. And I'm telling you. But it's complicated, so bear with me." He took my hand. "After Oh! Possum had been out for a while, a group that told me they were from an international law enforcement agency approached me. They thought the game would be a great way to communicate with agents around the world, alerting them to locations where they suspected bad guys were manufacturing or distributing drugs."

"They asked me if I could create a special version of the game with hidden levels that only their agents could get to. So if anyone saw them playing the game or borrowed their device, it would look just like the commercial version of the game, as long as you didn't enter a certain complicated sequence of keystrokes that unlocks the hidden levels."

He shifted on the bench. "And I was flattered and arrogant enough that I believed them, and I didn't bother checking them out to see if they were telling the truth. I did what they asked and created the custom version they wanted. And just like they promised, they distributed it all over the world."

He turned away, a bitter look on his face. "It was only later I learned they weren't an elite international police force. They were actually the bad guys. And now they were using my creation to hide what they were doing. I'd made it easy for them to distribute their vile products and evade the real police."

"I didn't know what to do to stop them. When I confronted them about their lie, they said they'd kill me and Amelia if I told anyone what they were doing or how they were doing it. But I couldn't let them continue using me and my work to hurt innocent people. I had to stop them. So I decided to get out from under their control by selling my company."

"That's when I met your father. Newton was heading up a group that was interested in buying Oh! Possum. I liked Newton right away when we met, and I was worried that the drug consortium would put the new owners under the same threats they'd used against me. I didn't want that to happen to him."

He drew in a huge breath. "So I told him what was going on and advised him not to buy the company. It was a huge risk on my part. We both know your father's reputation for honesty and integrity. I could only hope he'd believe me and keep my secret and not turn me in to the police. I was putting myself in his hands, and I was scared to death."

"After I told him, Newton was quiet for what felt like an age and a half. Then he told me that he already knew about my involvement with the drug cartel. He confessed that he actually did work for an international law enforcement agency, and that the agency was interested in buying my company to gain access to the insider info. They had thought I was part of the cartel, and they'd been planning to take me down along with rest of the whole nasty crew."

"Newton found a way to get me out from under the cartel's thumb. He sent me here to the Cayman Islands, where I was supposed to lay low for a while. But a few times, he asked me to interact with the bad guys again to help him get information. You remember you saw me one time in my other persona—Jameson?"

I nodded. "And that was the time they figured out you weren't really on their side and almost killed you."

"Correct. Meanwhile, well before that happened, I gave Newton's organization the code to unlock the hidden levels. Once they knew where the drug factories and distribution centers were, they raided them and shut them down. Eventually, the cartel figured out their scheme wasn't working any longer, so they stopped using Oh! Possum to communicate. Those levels Oliver unlocked when Lily had drugged him were never supposed to be accessible, and Newton and I were shocked that he was able to connect the drug busts to the possum's locations in the game. We both realized it was time for a new method of tracking the bad guys. And honestly, for a time, because he'd cracked the code so easily, we suspected Oliver had gone over to the dark side."

That was a chilling thought. "But he hasn't done that, right? He really is my sweet brother?"

Liam nodded. "It seems so."

"But to continue..." he said with a grim smile. "Sometimes the good guys still call on me to undertake a mission against the bad guys. That's what happened that year I was gone in Australia when I told you I was getting a divorce from Amelia." He paused. "Don't panic. I really did get the divorce. But I spent most of the time I was away undercover."

"And you remember the time I told you I was going to Switzerland, but I was really on Seb Lukin's yacht just outside Cayman Harbor." He paused. "And there were a few other times. But Newton and I agreed not to tell you what was going on because we wanted to keep you safe."

"But Maddy knows," I said, remembering how she'd always trusted Liam and hired him as RIO's CFO without even a single interview or checking any references.

He shrugged. "She might know about it if Newton told her. But I honestly don't think he would have. He wants to keep her safe, the same way he wants to keep you safe. I think she just trusted me because you and Newton do."

My head was spinning. "So, are you still involved in this international crime fighting organization?"

He bit his lip before answering. "Yes. It's one of the reasons I set up my environmental cleanup company the way I did. It gives me a good cover story when I'm gone for long periods of time at short notice. Sometimes the good guys ask me to go on a mission. Up until now, I've always said yes. I'd like to continue working with them if you're comfortable with it."

Now I was biting my lip. I'd seen how dangerous this undercover work could be. I'd nearly lost Liam a few times, and I hated it when he disappeared and didn't communicate with me. It reactivated all my abandonment issues from when Newton had left me as a little girl. It left me lonely and scared. All alone, worried sick about him.

Liam could follow my train of thought. "Don't ever tell him I told you, but Newton didn't abandon you when you were little because he didn't love you or couldn't care for you. Not even because of that story he told you about not wanting to confuse you when you saw Maddy and Ray together."

"The only reason Newton abandoned you back then was

because he didn't want anyone to realize how much you mean to him and empower them to use his love for you against him. You know all the bad guys would have to do is threaten to hurt you and Newton would give himself up in a heartbeat. So he stayed away from you all those years so they couldn't see how much he loves you."

My head spun at this new way of looking at my father's actions. I'd never understood how such a kind, loving man as Newton could have walked away from his own child. And then stayed away for all those years, without so much as a text message. "Did Maddy know why he left?"

Liam shook his head slowly. "I don't think so. Newton wanted her to be safe too…"

"I have another question," I said at last. "If we get married, isn't this dangerous for both of us? If they know we're married, won't they use me to get to you?"

He nodded. "They very well might try."

"Give me a minute to digest this," I said. It's a lot to take in." Even though I'd occasionally suspected something like this, I always told myself it was too crazy to be real. Yet here it was.

Liam waited patiently for a few minutes before breaking into my thought process. "You know we always said we wanted a life filled with adventure…"

I nodded. "Yes, but I always thought we'd have those adventures together. I guess that's not what you meant. It feels like you want to have your adventures all by yourself while I stay home and worry."

He shrugged. "Your entire life is an adventure, but the adventures I'm talking about are too dangerous for you. I could never let my wife go up against this group. They are very bad people. Ruthless, in fact. They'd have no qualms about killing you if they even suspected you were working undercover."

"Let me?" I said quietly. "You could never let me?"

He shrugged again, obviously missing the point. "While I'm around, I do everything I can to take care of you and show you how much I love you. Just because I'm away doesn't mean I don't love you, even if you don't know where I am. You should know that."

"I'm the first to admit I have a very easy life, and it's even easier when you're around. But I need to be an equal partner in our lives, not the one sitting at home waiting for permission to live my life or wondering when or if you'll ever return. Would you consider giving up working with…"

He interrupted me. "No. Not ever gonna happen."

I needed to think this through. The life Liam envisioned for us was totally different than the one I'd imagined. It wasn't even close to the way I wanted to live my life, and I was pretty sure Liam understood that. We sat in silence for quite a while, letting the black Zodiac drift at will, practically invisible in the shadowy night out on the deep dark sea.

Chapter 17
Bump

A SOFT BUMP against one of the Zodiac's inflatable pontoons interrupted our quiet contemplation.

"What do you think that was? Shark bump maybe?" whispered Liam.

I shook my head. "Don't think so. Too gentle." I leaned over the side and gasped. Then I reached out to grab the limp, pale hand of the body drifting alongside our boat. "Yikes! We have another body. Hand me a line and a marker buoy. I'll secure the body and mark the location while you text Dane. Then we need to get back to shore ASAP."

Liam scrambled toward the dry box in the boat's stern and pulled out a length of line. "Let me know when you're ready," he said. "I'll get us back to shore as quickly as we can go." He pulled out his phone and holding it below the Zodiac's pontoons to shield the light, he started texting.

I used the line to corral the body, being as careful as I could under the circumstances not to do anything that might destroy evidence. When I had the body in a secure loop, I wrapped the other end of the line around one of the Zodiac's cleats.

I dropped the marker buoy's anchor but then I wanted to dive down to make sure it was secure. The anchor, designed for deployment on a sand bottom, was just a heavy bag of sand rather than the more traditional metal trident or bar.

I grabbed the underwater flashlight out of the dry box, took a deep breath, and rolled off the boat's pontoon. When I reached the bottom, I gave the anchor a tug to make sure it was firmly in place. There usually isn't enough current in our little cove to cause much of a problem. The anchor seemed secure, so I headed back to the surface.

I climbed back up the ladder and sat shivering on the bench. I used the compass from the survival kit in the dry box and took a heading on the mermaid grotto so I could find my way back to this spot in case the marker drifted. Then I turned my attention back to the actual body. While I was contemplating the best way to get the patient into the boat, Liam put his phone back into the pocket of his cargo shorts..

"Dane's on his way to RIO," he said.

"Good. Be right back." I sat on the Zodiac's pontoon and slipped into the water again. Close up, I realized that the body was another young woman. All I could see of her appearance was moonlight glinting off her long matted blonde hair. I swam in front of her and pulled her to the front of my body and wrapped one arm around her torso. Then I used my other arm to maneuver to the stern of the boat where there was a small platform and a short ladder.

"Help me get her aboard," I said softly.

Liam scooted to the stern and crouched down to pull her up. As soon as she'd cleared the water, I climbed the ladder and went to the engine. "Sorry, Liam. I'll be as quiet as I can, but I want to get her to shore quickly."

I put the engine in low and steered toward RIO. As we drew near, I veered off away from the part of the marina where we typically kept the rental boats and went past the dive shop and the new mermaid lagoon. At this point the buildings and other structures hid us from the crowd at Ray's Place, so I felt safe heading for shore.

I heard the sound of a text whizzing off into the ether. Liam must have texted Dane about where to find us.

I grabbed the flashlight again to help guide us toward the ironshore without accidentally ramming into it. After flipping it on, I kept the beam pointed down and close to the water to avoid spreading light that someone might notice.

It was very dark over here, away from the security lights and the tiki torches that surrounded Ray's Place and the recreation area. I hoped Dane and his team would be able to find us, but I needn't have worried. I'd barely got us up next to the ironshore when I heard Roland's booming voice cursing the lack of light and bellowing about a stubbed toe. Morey's subdued laugh broke off quickly when Dane hissed. "Quiet, you two. There must be a reason she wanted to meet us way over here, and I told you Liam asked us to be quiet. I don't think those requests had much to do with avoiding the bar crowd."

I heard a splash and aimed the light toward the shore, but I was too late to keep Morey from stepping off the edge of the ironshore and plunging into water that was over his head.

When he bobbed up, he cursed and began to wail. "My phone. My watch. My radio. My suit."

Dane hissed, "Be quiet, at least until we find out what all the secrecy is about."

I looked at Liam. "Sorry about all the noise."

He shrugged and tossed the bow line to Roland who waited on shore. "It's alright. You know what you need to know to make your decision, and we don't have to say anything else right now. The only thing I need from you is a yes."

His smile was breathtaking, although short-lived.

"I need time to think it over…" I said slowly. "I just need a little more time be sure I know what I'm getting into."

He looked surprised, but he didn't say anything because Dane and his team were standing on the shore waiting for us.

"What do you have for me?" asked Dane, putting a quick end to our discussion.

I took a deep breath. "Looks like another drowned woman. I

don't think she's been in long. We found her pretty close to where we found the other one."

"Did you find anything else? Any ID?" Roland asked.

I shook my head. "I didn't have time to check her, and it's too dark to do an underwater search right now. We'll be on it at first light. I took a heading, and I left a marker on the location where we found her. We shouldn't have any trouble identifying the spot to start the search later."

Dane broke in. "Why are we whispering? And why no lights?

I glanced at my watch. Ray's Place should have closed a few minutes ago, and Liam and I were no longer discussing the bad guys or our futures. There should be no one around and there was nothing more to hide. "No reason. Why don't you set up some floodlights so you can see?"

I climbed from the Zodiac onto the ironshore. Liam followed close behind, then we both leaned over and each took an arm to pull Morey up onto dry land.

Roland radioed for an EMT team, and Morey went to see about getting some floodlights delivered. I called Doc to see if she was still around. I hoped she could help us identify any signs of foul play on the body.

"You just caught me," she said. "I've been waiting for Stewie to close the dive shop, then we were going home for a quiet dinner. What's up?'

"Can you put that dinner off for a little while longer? I promise I'll make it up to you." Then I told her what we'd found.

"Be right there," she said before disconnecting the call.

A few minutes later I saw the beam of a flashlight bobbing along the ground, lighting the way for Doc. As soon as she reached us, she switched off her flash and slipped it into the pocket of her white lab coat. She knelt next to the body on the ground and immediately checked for vitals. "She's dead," Doc said, "but I imagine you already knew that."

"Nice to have confirmation from an expert though," said Dane. "Anything else you can tell us?"

"Not without more light..." she started to say when Morey

flipped on one of the portable floodlights he'd carried over from his police van. She smiled grimly. "Never mind."

She leaned back on her heels and took in every detail of the woman's body. "No signs of foul play. No bruising or marks. Can't have been in the water long because the fish haven't done any damage. I'd have to check her lungs and stomach to be sure, but it seems obvious she drowned." She looked up at me. "Where did you find her?

I bit my lip. "Near Training Spot One. Not too far from where we found the other woman."

Dane looked at me sharply. "Is there much current out there?"

I thought for a minute. "A little more than usual, but you know with the winds we've been having lately, we're dealing with lots of unexpected and shifting currents."

Dane looked away. "Given what you remember about the current, can you make a guess as to where she went in?"

I shook my head. "These aren't the usual currents, so there's no way of predicting for sure, but given that both bodies were found near the same place, I'd guess they originally went in near the same spot. The trick will be to find that place."

He nodded. "I thought that would be the case."

"Do you have any ideas about where it is?" Liam asked.

"No," Dane said. "But I'm hoping Fin can help me figure that out."

Chapter 18
Search

EARLY IN THE MORNING, Liam had an international conference call with some advertising prospects for Quokka Media, so Stewie and I were going to do the search of RIO's cove together. We met near the mermaid grotto at 5:30 AM. Stewie carried two stainless steel mugs of hot black coffee, and he handed me one as I walked up to him.

"Bless you," I said. "You can't imagine how much I need this."

"Nobody's imagination is that good," he said with a laugh.

From where we were standing, we could just about see the marker buoy I'd dropped last night, so we marked out imaginary quadrants using the buoy as the center point. We were planning to use the mermaid grotto and the edge of the deep wall as our nearshore boundaries. We extended those imaginary lines about another hundred yards out beyond the marker buoy for the other half of the total square area we'd be searching.

Stewie had wheeled over a cartload of tanks and parked it near the grotto. I finished my coffee just as Dane, Roland, and Morey walked across RIO's dewy back lawn. I pointed out the search area Stewie and I had decided on and said, "We can expand that if you need us to, but if you do, we'll want to call in some other divers. It's already a huge expanse for just the two of us to do in a day."

Dane thought a moment. "Nope. If it's too far from the spot

where you found her, we'll have a hard time tying it to this case. And if you don't find anything today, we'll probably lose whatever it is to the ocean anyway. I trust you and Stewie to do a good job."

Out of the corner of my eye I saw Stewie's face take on a glow of pride. Not very long ago nobody would have trusted him with anything more difficult than fetching coffee, so this was a big change. I was proud of him and the way he'd turned his life around.

"Will you be here all day?" I asked Dane as I stepped into my dive suit.

He shook his head. "I doubt it. We'll drop in several times during the day, and of course, please call me if you find anything and we'll be here within a few minutes. But it doesn't make sense for us to stand here all day watching your bubbles."

I laughed. "Agreed. If there's nothing else you need to tell me, then Stewie and I should get started."

Stewie was already wearing his dive suit, and he'd set up both our regulators on fresh tanks. I thanked him as I lifted my BCD and tank assembly over my head, slipping my arms into the armholes in the buoyancy control vest as I did. It slid down my body, ending up perfectly centered on my shoulders and back. After fastening the cummerbund and tightening the shoulder straps, I donned my mask, put my regulator in my mouth, and stepped off the ironshore.

The water was about ten feet deep, and I didn't quite touch bottom before I bobbed back to the surface and gave Stewie the okay sign. He flashed the sign back, and then entered the water a few feet away from me.

We kicked out to the marker buoy and split up, each of us taking half the area. We worked in squares, counting our kicks for each side of the square, and making each square slightly smaller than the previous one. We were working from the outer perimeter of the search area inward.

It was hard work. We both stopped a few times to change our tank or grab a drink and a bite to eat, being sure to mark the position where we stopped our search before we swam to shore. Noah had set up a cooler with water, pitchers of lemonade, sandwiches, and cookies for us so that whenever we took a break, we could grab a drink, eat a quick snack, and get right back to the search with minimal time lost.

The second time I needed to change my tank, Dane was sitting on the edge of the iron shore when I surfaced. He looked at me with hope in his eyes, but the hopeful light dimmed when I shook my head. I hadn't found anything at all, and my catch bag was still empty.

I needed to spend some time off-gassing the nitrogen I'd absorbed over the morning's dives, so I pulled myself up on the ironshore and sat beside Dane. "Any news?"

He shook his head. "No ID on the body. No signs of foul play. No bumps or bruises, so it doesn't look like she fell out of a boat. Just like the other woman you found. It seems like they're just swimming out until they drown, then they float on the current until someone—make that you—finds them. It doesn't make sense. One victim I could see. Maybe two. But three is getting crazy. We have no clues, and no insight into what's going on. We don't even know who most of these women are. We don't know anything about them—not even where they went into the water."

I thought about what Dane had said and had an idea. "What if I go out there and try to backtrack through the current? Maybe I can figure out where they went in. And to be honest, I should have thought of this earlier, but if they dropped anything that might provide a clue to their identities, it probably happened closer to where they went in than to where we pulled them out. So it might help us figure this case out if we could see where this particular rip current started. And I'll need to do that right away before this crazy wind dies down and the currents go back to normal."

Dane stared out to sea. "I don't know. I think it's too dangerous. If there's a rogue current that's pulling these women to their deaths, I don't want you anywhere near it."

He patted my hand, and a lump formed in my throat. I knew Dane thought of me as a daughter, and it warmed my heart, especially after he'd told me about what had happened to Sydney, his biological daughter.

Before I responded, I rubbed his back to let him know I understood. "It'll be fine. I'll be underwater near the bottom, where the current is often different than it is near the surface. No matter what, I'd bet I'm a better swimmer than any of these women were. I'll ask Stewie to follow me in one of the Zodiacs, so he'll be right there to pick me up when I surface. I'll deploy a dive flag to make it easier for him to follow me than it would be if he tried to track me just by my bubbles. He'll always be nearby if I run into trouble. And I'll take a scuba scooter with me, so worst case, I'll be able to use its power to go crosswise out of the current before it has a chance to wash me out to sea. And even if I do get caught in the current, I just have to surface and Stewie will be right there to pick me up. This new plan will make it easier to do the search and increase the odds of finding something. What do you think?"

He snorted. "I think you're crazy. But your plan may be exactly what we need. Let's start in on it as soon as you and Stewie are ready to go again."

I slipped back into the water and banged three times on my tank with the scuba scissors I keep in my BCD pocket, trying to get Stewie's attention. Over the years we'd been doing searches together, we'd worked out a series of sound signals. This one meant to surface. His head popped out of the water a few minutes later and he spun in a circle looking for me.

He caught sight of me bobbing near the shore, and I waved him in. He put his right hand to his head in the alternate okay sign and began the surface swim toward us.

When he reached the ironshore, I gave him a hand getting out of the water. He shrugged out of his tank and BCD and laid them down on the grass before he sat beside me. "What's up?" he asked.

He listened while I explained my plan. "Sounds good. But why don't you let me do the swimming and you follow in the boat?'

"No," I said. "I'm closer to the size and weight of the drowned women, so if that affected their trajectories at all, it's better if I'm the one following the current."

Stewie looked at me like I was crazy, but before he could say anything, Dane spoke up. "I agree with Fin. She's closer to the body size of the victims we've found so far and that may give her an advantage in finding how they got to the cove here."

Stewie and I both knew that the premise didn't make any sense because I'd be traveling against the current, following it to its origin instead of letting it sweep me along. But even so, Dane's words settled the issue.

Before we started the search, Stewie and I needed to fuel up with some food, and we needed a little more time to off-gas anyway. We called Noah at Ray's Place and asked for a couple of cheeseburgers and a huge stack of fries.

"Can you bring everything to the mermaid grotto without anyone noticing, please?" I asked. "We're trying to stay out of sight."

Stalwart Noah didn't ask any questions. "Will do," he said. "I'll send Austin. He can be practically invisible when he wants to be."

Chapter 19
The New Methodology

Austin delivered the food we'd requested a few minutes later, and Stewie and I devoured it as though we hadn't eaten in a week. Dane nibbled on a single fry and shook his head in amazement at the food Stewie and I packed away. He wouldn't have been at all surprised at our intake if he'd been diving with us all day.

After we ate, we packed up all the trash and put it in the delivery basket Austin had used to bring the food over, and Stewie carried it back to Ray's Place. I stayed on the steps of the mermaid grotto while Dane sat on the edge of the ironshore. I wanted to wait at least another forty-five minutes before I went back in the water, just to be on the safe side, and I didn't want to be visible to the crowd at Ray's Place while I waited.

Some days nobody recognized me at all, and other days my appearance set off a flurry of autograph requests. I didn't want to be stuck signing autographs or to have zealous fans follow our boat out when we started the search, so everyone agreed it was best if I stayed in seclusion.

Stewie left to load up one of the Zodiacs with multiple tanks, a diver down flag on a reel, and extra rescue gear, just in case we ran into any trouble. Since he's always puttering around the boats and the dive shop, we were pretty sure nobody would pay any attention to him while he gathered the required gear. Plus he's changed so much since his successful stint at rehab that outsiders usually don't recognize him from the old documentaries. Since then, he lost a lot of weight along with that bleary look to his face.

Dane cleared his throat as soon as Stewie was out of hearing distance. "I was wondering…" He stopped. "If you have time…" Another pause. "Would you be willing…" The words were stuck in his throat.

I'd already sensed that Dane wanted to restart his diving lessons now that he and my mother were back on solid footing, but he seemed to be having trouble asking me—probably because he'd quit so abruptly a few years ago when Maddy and Newton got back together temporarily. For weeks now he'd start to make the request, then he'd hem and haw, but never quite manage to ask the question.

I decided to put him out of his misery. "Oh for heaven's sake, Dane. Yes, I'll do it. When do you want to start the diving lessons?"

He jumped. "How did you know that's what I was going to ask?"

"You're not that subtle. I can read you like a book." Then I decided to mess around with him a little bit more. "That's not a very good trait for a person who does interrogations for a living."

He looked affronted for a second before he realized I was teasing him and laughed. "Lucky for me the bad guys don't know me as well as you do."

Before we'd finalized the start date for Dane's scuba training, Stewie rejoined us on the ironshore. "The wind on the other side of the dive shop is brutal, and it's blowing sand and dirt everywhere. It felt like someone was sandpapering my face over there. I'm glad we're on this side of the shop so at least the building can break the wind a little bit. No wonder we're dealing with rip currents all over the island."

The freak winds were unpleasant, but there was nothing we could do about them so we waited on the ironshore until we'd off-gassed enough that we were back close to normal. When we were ready to go, Stewie fastened the chin strap on his hat and pulled the flaps down to protect his ears and the skin on his face. Then he left to get the Zodiac he'd already loaded.

As soon as he pulled up to the ironshore where I was waiting, I donned my scuba gear and stepped off the edge into the boat. Stewie piloted us out to the spot where we'd left off the earlier search.

I did a backward roll off the boat's pontoon. When I surfaced to give Stewie the okay sign and gather the gear I'd be carrying, the current on the surface nearly swept me away because it was so strong. Luckily, I was able to grab a weighted line Stewie had dropped overboard for me to hang onto. He handed me the motorized dive scooter, and I clipped its tow line to a strap that went around my waist and had loops to go around each thigh.

Attaching the scooter to the waist cinch would significantly reduce the burden on my arms and transfer it to my hips while the scooter was in use. It was awkward making the connections in the water while battling the current, and I knew that on the next dive I'd attach the scooter while I was still in the boat, have Stewie hand it down to me after I'd made my entry. That way, all I'd have to do while in the water would be to tighten up the line connecting the scooter to my waist strap.

Once I had the scooter set up, Stewie handed me the diver down flag on the reel of line I'd unspool as I descended, which would allow the flag to float on the surface to mark my location.

Now that I had all my equipment squared away, I gave him the okay sign and submerged, letting the flag's line unspool behind me as I went.

I'd only descended about ten feet when the vicious current completely slacked off. It was such a relief not to be fighting that killer current that I sighed into my regulator.

The current at depth was going in totally the opposite direction from the surface current, which was lucky. The surface rip current was roaring into RIO's cove, but the underwater current was heading in exactly the direction I wanted to search. I said a quick thank you to the universe that I wouldn't have to fight that monster rip current to get back to shore. When I was ready, I'd simply planned to surface and ride back in the boat with Stewie.

On the bottom, I looked around to get my bearings, and realized Stewie had put me almost exactly on the spot where I'd finished my last dive. I kicked along a few feet above the sandy bottom, moving back and forth so I could cover a wide swath of the ocean bed.

I'd covered a patch of the search area about thirty feet long and about 25 feet wide when I saw something bright pink caught on a nearby branch of staghorn coral. I swam over to investigate.

The item was a woman's canvas sunhat with a wide brim. The dangling chin strap had tangled in the horns of the coral, and now it was waving in the current like a beacon. I pulled my small underwater camera out of the pocket of my BCD and took several photographs of the item in situ from every angle and then I photographed the entire surrounding area.

Once I'd put my camera back in my BCD pocket, I began carefully unwinding the hat's snarled strap so I could retrieve it without damaging the delicate coral. Once it was free, I placed it in a plastic evidence bag and put it in the catch bag attached to a D-ring on my BCD. Then I tied a fluorescent pink plastic ribbon marker on the spot where I'd found the hat in case I needed to return for some reason.

I looked up at the surface, and I could see the Zodiac hovering right above me. Stewie was obviously doing a good job following my bubbles, and he'd positioned the boat between the spot where the bubbles broke the surface and where the diver down flag bobbed nearby. I wasn't anticipating any problems, but I was glad I had Stewie positioned on the surface just in case. He was a good man to have watching my back.

The rip current was so strong that it created a visible distortion in the water, making it easy for me to follow the path back to its origin without having to fight against its power. Once I'd secured the bag with the hat inside, I looked up to make sure I was continuing to move directly under the rip current and started searching again. About forty-five minutes later, my tank was at 800 PSI. I'd found nothing else since the hat, and I wanted to surface with enough air in my tank to be safe in case I had trouble connecting with the Zodiac in the strong surface current. I would need plenty of air if I had to fight to reach the boat.

I began my ascent, rising extra slowly to facilitate off-gassing the nitrogen in my body just in case the current caught me, which might force me to finish my ascent hastily.

Chapter 20
A Struggle

THE POWERFUL RIP current on the surface had been moving steadily in the opposite direction from the mild current near the bottom, which had made it easy for me to follow it. It's very common for currents to switch directions at various depths in the ocean—one reason divers always check the current on the surface and then again when they reach depth.

It's good diving practice to start a dive swimming into the current so you'll get a little extra help on the return leg of the dive, rather than fighting against strong currents when you're tired. That wasn't what I'd done on this dive, but with good reason.

As I ascended to about twenty-five feet and entered the rip area, the mild bottom current gave way. The surface rip current slammed into me with great force, pushing me away from Stewie and the Zodiac.

Not only was the rip current moving fast along the ocean's surface, but it had also developed a powerful downdraft. It kept pushing me down toward the bottom, and I was having trouble rising through the current at all.

I pushed the button to inflate my BCD, hoping the added buoyancy would help me reach the surface. But once again, the rip's powerful downdraft pushed me toward the bottom despite my increased buoyancy.

I quickly switched on my scooter and aimed it up toward the surface and directly into the current. I had to push the scooter to full power to make any headway at all. It took everything I had—and that the scooter had—to make any progress, but every time I'd gain a few feet another surge of current would push me back down again. I could not reach the surface because the downdraft kept pushing me deeper.

I was kicking as hard as I could, and the scooter was whining as I tried to get more power out of it. I turned my head up to see where the boat was, and the current's fury tore my regulator out of my mouth.

I took my hand off the scooter's throttle to recover my regulator, and the current pushed the heavy machine back—hard, and directly into my stomach. I gasped from the impact, letting all the air out of my lungs as I did. Now I was in real trouble.

I transferred the reel for the dive flag from my right hand to my left. I looked up and saw the Zodiac getting further away by the second as the rip current pushed me along at high speed, deep under water. Desperately, I swept my arm around behind me to recover my regulator.

As soon as I stopped pushing hard to move forward, the current grabbed me and spun me around, so the regulator was always behind me and just out of my reach. I quickly switched to the octopus regulator attached to the front of my BCD and took a slow, deep calming breath.

Once I'd recovered from the brief moment of panic, I let the air out of my BCD and dropped down below the rip current to regroup and try to recover my primary regulator. A quick glance at my pressure gauge showed 450 PSI. Not much left of that comfortable margin of safety I'd started my ascent with.

As soon as I was on the bottom and free of the current, I did the arm sweep again and recovered my primary regulator. I clipped the dive flag reel to my BCD and grabbed the scooter again.

I looked up and saw that the current had pushed me even

further away from the boat. In fact, I was further away now than I'd been when I started trying to reach it.

The scooter's battery gauge clicked over into the red. It was almost out of power.

I swam crosswise to the rip current, peering up anxiously so I could determine when I was outside its coverage area. I swam for quite a way, but I never found the current's edge. It must have widened or switched direction. And still, whenever I tried to ascend, it pushed me down deeper and deeper until I was just a few feet above the bottom.

The current was so vast that I couldn't swim crosswise outside its range, and its downdraft was so strong that I couldn't get through it to the surface. I kept struggling to make any headway toward the open air, but invariably, the current forced me down again.

I pushed the scooter's throttle and got nothing. The battery was totally dead. I unclipped it from my BCD and let it fall to the bottom. It was a $15,000 piece of equipment, but it wasn't worth my life. I pushed the button to refill my BCD with air. I needed the buoyancy to make it through the downdraft.

I looked at my pressure gauge again. 300 PSI.

Not good.

In fact, very not good.

I'd have to swim as hard as I could toward the surface, and just hope I made it. I could tell immediately when I rose high enough to be inside the current's grip because it began pushing me back down the way I'd come. I was struggling for every inch of rise through the water.

If I'd started back earlier, I could have let the current push me all the way to the cove, which would have been fine, except I no longer had enough air to make it all the way back.

I couldn't swim against the mighty current. I couldn't get out of it. I couldn't fight my way through the downdraft. I was exhausted.

The only thing I could do was swim as hard as I could for the surface and hope Stewie could somehow fish me out.

I was at the bottom of the current, still about twenty-five feet under the surface, when I saw a weighted line drop from the boat. Luckily, it quickly sank to my level and within reach of my arm. I grabbed it, holding on as tightly as I could. I gave it a couple of yanks to let Stewie know I had a hold on it.

Relieved, I took a breath from my regulator and got nothing. My tank was now completely empty.

Stewie must have been watching for my response, because almost as soon as the line twitched, he angled the boat across the width of the current instead of moving directly against it as he had been. He pushed the boat slowly enough that I could hang on, but fast enough that we made real progress. Eventually, we escaped the grasp of the rip current.

My inflated BCD popped me to the surface, and as soon as my head broke the water, I gasped in a deep breath. He started hauling me toward the boat using the line I clutched. I tried to help Stewie haul me to safety by swimming toward the boat, but my strength was nearly gone.

When I finally put my shaking hand on the ladder, Stewie took the dive flag from me and helped me climb aboard. I slid my tank into an empty spot on the rack and took off my mask. Then I pulled my camera out of the BCD's pocket and dropped it in the catch bag. Dane would want the photos and the hat right away.

Exhausted, I collapsed to the gunwale. Stewie was staring at me, concern etched across his face.

I had to try hard to control my breathing before speaking. "It's pretty hairy down there. I'm glad you were here following me. The swimmers caught in that rip didn't have a prayer unless they knew to swim across the current rather than against it. Even then, they'd have had to fight pretty hard. And it would be a long swim—it's the widest rip current I've ever seen." I gulped. "And there's a down current. The thing is a killer."

Stewie folded his arms, and his lips were tight. "You're not going down there again. I barely got you out of there this time, and you had the scooter and the boat to help you fight the current. It's too dangerous. I won't allow it."

Stewie obviously expected a fight from me, and I knew he was ready to dig in his heels. I saw surprise on his face when I said. "You're right. I'm stubborn, but I'm not stupid. I'm done here. Let's go home."

He didn't waste any time. He quickly turned the Zodiac back toward RIO and gave the boat maximum throttle. Between the engine thrust and the rip current pushing us in that direction anyway, we were back at RIO within a few minutes.

Stewie pulled up near the ladder at the shore dive entry point and held the boat steady while I rolled out and swam the few strokes to the wall, my arms and legs shaking with exhaustion. I climbed the ladder and turned to give him the okay sign.

He signaled back, then turned the Zodiac away to return it to the area where we stored our rental boats. I trudged around to the back of the dive shop where Dane and his team were anxiously awaiting my return.

Chapter 21
Important Realizations

My legs were still shaking violently as I took those few steps toward Dane and his team. Underwater, I hadn't realized how hard I was fighting to keep the current from sweeping me away, but I'd used up every ounce of energy I had. I was thankful Stewie had been there to tow me to safety, and that he was skilled enough to manage it without putting me in even more danger than the rip current alone had presented.

I knew that I might eventually have been able to swim around the current, especially deep underwater where the current's direction was very slowly pushing me away from danger anyway. If I'd had more air in my tank, I would have ultimately been fine no matter what.

But I didn't have more air in my tank. I'd been reckless and overconfident.

The entire dive had been difficult. It was scary, and I was never scared underwater.

My heart bled for the poor women that wicked current had caught and pushed beyond their ability to fight back. They must have been terrified.

I couldn't imagine why they went swimming in the angry ocean anyway. There were signs posted along the beaches warning people to stay out of the water. The newspapers and TV stations had been broadcasting information about the unusual rip currents and the best way to break free of its grip if you were caught up in one. Why hadn't they paid attention?

I knew that at least three—and possibly four—women so far had lost their lives fighting an impossible battle. I was comfortable in the water, a strong swimmer, and superbly trained, yet even I'd had trouble making it to safety against the malevolent current. And I'd had help.

I respect the ocean. I admit sometimes I do foolhardy things in the water, but never without first weighing my abilities against the risk and reward for my actions, however crazy those actions might look to others.

And I always know that it doesn't really matter. When the ocean wants you, it will win.

Hands down. No contest.

You will lose.

And those poor women had lost everything.

My feet were leaden as I crossed the grounds to join Dane, Roland, and Morey, who were anxiously watching my approach.

"What happened?" Morey said. "You look exhausted."

He stood up and took my arm to lead me to the bench where the other members of the team were sitting. As soon as I sat down, he poured a glass of water from the nearby cooler and put it in my quivering hands. The look of concern on his face was so intense it was frightening. My reflection in his sunglasses told the tale. I looked truly awful.

I drank most of the water before speaking. "Those poor women must have been scared to death. The current was horrible. I barely made it myself. Thank God for Stewie." I took another sip of water and choked a little bit.

Dane took my hand. "No more searching for clues. We can't take a chance on losing you, and if it's that dangerous..."

I leaned over and refilled my cup from the nearby cooler. "It is definitely that dangerous. You have to close the beaches. Anyone caught in one of those monster rips is doomed." I started shivering, remembering my fear when I couldn't reach the surface or swim out of the current.

Morey draped a dry towel over my shoulders. I was grateful for its warmth. "Thanks," I said.

Then an idea occurred to me. "There's something odd going on here. Why are all the drowning victims women? Even most men don't swim as well as I do, and if I could barely make it out alive, very few people of any gender would have been able to make it. Yet so far at least, every drowning victim is a woman." I turned to Dane. "Something—or someone—must be luring women into the water."

I saw the dawning realization grow in Dane's eyes.

He knew I was right. "That makes it murder," he said. "Or at the very least, manslaughter."

"Exactly," I said. "And by the way, I found this snagged on some coral just beneath the current. I don't know if it will help. I marked the spot where I found it, and I have pictures."

I handed my catch bag to Roland. He removed the camera and popped out the mini-disk before handing the camera back to me. Morey took the card and loaded it into his computer while Roland snapped on some latex gloves.

He pulled the plastic bag containing the sunhat out of my catch bag and opened it. He withdrew the hat. "Maybe we got lucky," he said. "This brand of hats usually has a waterproof pocket inside. Maybe there's something there we can use to identify its owner."

He flipped the hat over, and I heard the ripping sound of Velcro as he opened the pocket. He carefully reached inside and drew out a small wad of cash, a credit card—and the real prize, an ID.

"One victim at least will be identified," he said, holding the card in front of Dane's face so he could see the picture and name on it. "She look familiar to you?"

I stared over Dane's shoulder at the ID, and my heart sank. The woman in the picture was the same one Liam and I had pulled out of the water yesterday.

"Suzanne Wilkins," I read. "At least now we know her name."

Roland nodded and slipped everything into evidence bags. While he was creating his chain of custody notes, I shut my eyes and tried not to cry. I hated not knowing who the victims were, but I hated it just as much when I uncovered their identities. Knowing their names made them real. Real people with real parents, friends, lovers, kids, pets. Lives that mattered to them. All gone in a flash.

I was still feeling grief when Liam rushed up with a bag of my favorite chocolate chip cookies from the café. "Stewie called me and said you need me. Are you okay?" he said, putting the bag on the picnic table. He pulled me to my feet and clasped me in a major bear hug.

When he finally stepped back, he looked deep into my eyes. "I've never seen you look so wiped out. You need to replenish your energy." He reached around me to grab a cookie from the bag and handed it to me. "Sit. Eat."

He sat on the bench next to Dane and pulled me down on his other side, throwing an arm over my shoulders and drawing me close. I huddled against him, trying to get warm and forget my lingering terror. I felt like crying, but I blinked my eyes rapidly to hold back the tears. I wouldn't give in.

It wasn't like me to ever show any weakness whatsoever. I often berated myself harshly for my perceived—and real—failures, but I kept it all inside. The horrifying experience with the rip current had left me shaken to my core, and I needed to rethink my own ideas about who I truly was. I remembered Maddy telling me often not to count on luck to pull me out of tight spots, and I realized that she was right.

But on the other hand, I hadn't felt like crying until Liam arrived, and I wondered what had truly set off the deep despair I felt.

Meanwhile, Dane signaled to his team. "Let's go back to the station. We need to find out all there is to know about Suzanne Wilkins."

Roland and Morey gathered their things and walked slowly toward the parking lot.

After a few steps, Dane turned back. "I'm sorry, Fin. I shouldn't have let you try something so dangerous." He sighed. "Take good care of her, Liam."

Chapter 22
Planning

L‍IAM WAITED until they were out of earshot before he said, "Where do you want to stay tonight? Newton's, the *Tranquility*, or home?"

The last few days had left me shaken. For the first time in my life, I didn't want to be in, on, or under the ocean. I only wanted to be someplace where I felt safe enough to stop trembling, even if it took all night.

And I needed to be alone. I didn't want to be with Liam or anyone else. I just needed time to sit by myself and figure out who I was, way down deep.

"Home, please," I said.

"Right you are," he said. "Wait here. I'll get your stuff." Then he stopped. "Will you be okay for a few minutes by yourself, or should I get Doc or Genevra to sit with you?"

"I'll be fine," I said.

I watched him walk away and disappear from view when he took the corner around the front of the dive shop. A few seconds later, I caught sight of him walking along the dock toward my boat. Then he was on his way back, carrying my canvas tote bag. He crossed behind the dive shop on his way to RIO's back door. A minute or so later, he was beside me again, with both my computer bag and my canvas tote bag slung over his shoulder.

"Ready?" he asked.

I nodded and got to my feet. Liam held my hand as we walked across the lawn toward the parking lot. I was starting to get my energy back, although I didn't feel ready to get back into the water just yet.

Liam drove his EV to my house on Rum Point and pulled into my driveway. He slung an arm across my shoulders and used his other hand to carry my belongings as we walked to the front door, where he handed me my tote bag so I could fish out my keys.

Since I never knew when or if even I'd be at home, the air conditioning was off inside, making it hot and stuffy in the house. Liam dropped my bags inside the door and walked around opening the windows and the sliding door in the back to air the place out. I stood in the entryway watching him, too beat to move, and still shivering with residual nerves.

Once he'd opened up the windows, Liam went into my bathroom and started the shower. "Go on in. You're freezing, and the hot water will help warm you up. I'll see what I can find to eat, and I'll let you know when dinner's ready."

We both knew the search for anything edible in my house would be futile, but we also knew Liam had a freezer stocked with food and a garden full of fresh vegetables in his backyard. I watched him exit through the slider before I went in to take my shower.

The water on the island never really gets hot, but it was always soft and warm. I was happy to get the salt off after a long day in the ocean. After washing my hair with an expensive shampoo Newton had given me and enjoying its subtle fragrance, I added conditioner and then washed the salt off my body. When I finally stopped shivering, I rinsed the conditioner out of my hair, letting the water run until it was silky smooth.

Liam had put a couple of towels on the towel warmer outside my shower, and I was delighted to wrap myself in a fluffy hot towel to dry off. I slipped into a warm terrycloth robe. Then still barefoot, I padded out to the patio.

Liam was sitting in a chair next to my grill, sipping a lemonade and watching Chico and Henrietta, our free-range chickens, pecking in the dirt. The smell from the grill was heavenly. A pot of hot cocoa and an open bag of marshmallows waited for me on the table next to a RIO-branded stainless steel mug.

I sat in the chair next to Liam's and poured some of the warm, creamy chocolate drink into the mug. There wasn't much call for hot cocoa in the Caymans, and I wondered why he had it on hand or how he'd obtained it so quickly if not.

But it was just what I needed. After adding a couple of marshmallows to the mug, I sat back, took a sip, and sighed. "Thank you."

Liam was always so good to me. When he was around, he treated me like a princess. I only wished he was around more. Or that I knew where he was and what he was doing when he was away. I need to know he's safe, the same way he needs to know I'm safe. I was annoyed that he didn't seem to get that.

As if he'd read my mind, he smiled at me and stood up to flip whatever he was cooking on the grill. "I might have lost you today," he said, not looking at me. "That would have killed me. Please take better care of yourself. Show some caution. If you don't care about yourself, then do it for me. Please." His voice wavered on the last word, nearly breaking my heart.

"I will," I said. "It was reckless of me to keep pushing on when the current got so strong. I realize that now. I'll try to think things through better in the future. You won't have to worry."

He lowered the cover on the grill and returned to his seat. "The other day, when we were out in the Zodiac, you said you needed time to think about what I told you before you could commit to getting married. Have you had time to think things through?"

I nodded. "I did. I told you before that the only thing standing between us was the truth about where you go when you disappear, but that turned out not to be the whole story. I'm not sure I can live with not knowing where you are, when you'll leave again, or when you'll come home." I bit my lip. "Or even if you will be coming home at all. I need to know that wherever you are, you're safe. Do you understand that?"

He nodded. "I do understand. But it's important to me to keep doing what I do."

"Then I need a little more time to figure out if I can live with your decision." I sipped my cocoa. "It won't take me long to decide what to do. I love you. That's not the issue. Like I said, I just need you to give me the time I need to be sure I can live with your conditions."

He grimaced when my phone rang, interrupting our serious discussion. Caller ID said it was Oliver. I put the call on speaker. "Hey, Bro. What's up?"

My brother spoke in a rush. "I heard what happened to you today. Please be more careful. Genevra and I are on our way over with pizza. We have something important we want to talk to you about. We'll be there in five minutes." He disconnected without saying goodbye, a bad habit he'd probably learned from Newton.

"I'd better go put some clothes on," I said.

"And I'll slip some extra shrimp on the barbie for them," Liam said, laughing at his use of the old Australian Tourism Commission catchphrase.

Chapter 23
An Announcement

DRESSED in an old pair of terry shorts that reached my knees and a long sleeved tee, I slid my feet into a pair of ugly shearling lined sandals that looked like a discarded pair of Fred Flintstone's shoes. I'd just come back out onto the patio when I heard the doors on Oliver's car slam shut. He and Genevra were laughing as they came through the gate to my backyard. They were holding hands, and their faces were glowing. Oliver was balancing three large pizza boxes in his free hand.

Since there was potential food involved, Chico and Henrietta ran over to greet the newcomers. Chico, the big rooster, stopped in front of Oliver, barring his entry.

We'd made a big fuss over Chico a while back when he'd saved my life from a bad guy intent on doing me harm, so now he took his responsibility to keep newcomers out of the premises very seriously until either the newcomer gave him food or I told him it was okay to let them in. Either option was fine with the rooster.

I was laughing at Chico so hard I could barely speak. "Chico, that's Oliver and Genevra. You know them. It's okay to let them in."

Chico gave me a hard look telling me that he'd be the one to decide who was allowed to enter the premises, and he stared a beady-eyed glare at Oliver and Genevra to ensure they knew he was still in charge. Satisfied that we all knew our places, he stepped back so they could pass.

Oliver laughed and put the pizza boxes on the table. "Only you would have a guardian rooster," he said. "Is he ever going to get used to us? He doesn't try to keep you out, does he, Liam?"

Genevra rolled her eyes at Oliver's words, and we all laughed.

"Nope," Liam said. "But I'm here all the time. Or maybe it's because I feed him. You should try that. Meanwhile, what can I get you two to drink?"

He and Oliver went inside to fix drinks, and Genevra sat down at the table next to me. "I heard about your adventure today. You need to be more careful. It sounded awful."

"Yup," I said. "It was the scariest thing that ever happened to me in the water. But I'm still here. I'm very lucky."

Genevra knocked on the teakwood table. "Don't get cocky."

We both laughed, but I knew she was serious. So was I.

Oliver came outside carrying an IPA in a bottle and a glass of lemonade for Genevra. Liam had a stack of plates and napkins in one hand and a lemonade for me in the other. He placed the icy glass carefully in front of me. "Unless you want more hot chocolate?" he asked. "I can make another pot."

I shook my head. "No thanks. This is good. Hey, what kind of pizza did you guys bring? Liam has been cooking marinated shrimp, and I think he made a salad. It's still in the kitchen staying cool. We'll have quite a feast tonight."

We spent the next hour or so devouring our food and laughing at silly stories. It was exactly the kind of evening I needed. When we'd finished our dessert—a coconut cream pie Liam had brought over earlier—Oliver said, "We need to talk to you guys." He looked serious.

"Sure. What's up?" I said. "Okay if I get a refill before you tell us?"

Oliver smiled at me. "We're practically bursting with excitement and we can't wait any longer to tell you our news."

"Go ahead then," I said. "I can wait."

Oliver and Genevra joined hands. "We're getting married," she said. "As soon as we can make the arrangements. Fin, I want you to be in my wedding party. And Liam, would you walk me down the aisle? I don't have any relatives except my younger sister."

Oliver looked at Liam. "And I'd be honored if you'd agree to be my best man too. So you'll have two jobs at the wedding."

Liam and I were surprised, but we tried not to act like it. We weren't surprised they'd decided to get married. It was obvious they were perfect for each other, but we were surprised it seemed to be happening so quickly.

"That's great news," I said to Genevra. "I'd love to be in the wedding party."

"Good. Thank you." she said. "Now we just have to keep you safe—at least until after the wedding."

Liam shook Oliver's hand. "Congratulations. You're getting a real prize in Genevra." She'd been Liam's assistant at Quokka Media for a few years before she came to RIO. They knew each other well, and they were close friends.

Liam raised his glass in a toast to the happy couple. Then Oliver toasted his beautiful bride-to-be. Genevra toasted to my health and safety. There was much laughter and good humored teasing. It was a wonderful evening.

At last, Oliver looked at Liam and me. "I was so excited about our news I almost forgot to ask what's new with you guys? So what's up?"

"We do have some news," Liam said. "It's about a change in our relationship…"

I kicked Liam gently under the table. I didn't want him to stomp on Genevra and Oliver's happiness by sharing our own more distressing news at this point. And really, we hadn't settled anything. We'd been engaged for a long time, but so far we hadn't ever gotten around to actually committing to marriage. So nothing there had changed. Yet.

Liam raised his glass. "Compared to your news, ours is no big deal. We've decided to launch a new title at Quokka Media. Totally dedicated to living in the Caymans. We'll be kicking off the project next week."

My mouth dropped open. This was the first I'd heard of this idea.

But Oliver and Genevra thought it was great.

"What's the title? Have you finalized it yet?" Genevra asked.

I thought I could see a little bit of envy in her eyes. Although I was nominally the editor of *Ecosphere*, in reality, Genevra did all the work. And thank the universe for that.

Impulsively, I said, "That's where you come in. We're hoping you can take this on as editor-in-chief of the new title. If you can fit it in with your responsibilities at RIO—and at *Ecosphere*."

For a moment, Genevra's face glowed. Then the glow faded as she realized what she'd be taking on. "With everything else on my plate, I don't think I could do it alone," she said. "I'm sorry."

Liam jumped in smoothly. "No need to go it alone. Gary will be there to help at *Ecosphere*, and you can hire an assistant editor. In fact, maybe you and Fin can share an assistant so you can give up your work on *Ecosphere*."

Now I was the one who wasn't happy about the idea. I knew what a jewel Genevra was, and selfishly, I didn't want to give up any of her time or attention. And superstar performers like her don't come along every day. But I would never do anything to hold her back, so I swallowed my concerns and smiled brightly. "Congratulations. What a great opportunity for you," I said.

Genevra smiled. "Thanks. You sure you're okay with it?" At my nod, she continued. "Because if you're really sure, I have someone I'd like to recommend as my replacement. I think you'll find her more than satisfactory. She's smart, well-educated, and a hard worker."

"So, a lot like you?" I said with a laugh.

Genevra grinned. "More alike than you know. I'm thinking of my sister, Bari."

Although Genevra had occasionally mentioned a sister, she didn't talk about her very much. I'd assumed they weren't close at all. In fact, I was pretty sure this was the first time Genevra had ever told me her sister's name.

"Bari? What a lovely name. Is it short for something else?" I asked.

Genevra shook her head. "Nope. Just Bari. Bari Blackthorne."

Liam broke in. "Is Bari looking for work?"

She shrugged. "I don't know for sure, but she just finished a Master of Fine Arts in creative writing program, so I assume she is. I'll call her and see if she's interested in this opportunity."

Oliver looked curious, so I gathered this was all new information to him too. "Where does Bari live?" he asked.

"Arizona," Genevra said. "But she's tired of the desert and would like to live someplace near the ocean."

Liam smiled at that. "We certainly have plenty of ocean here. Would she consent to an interview over the internet? I'd like to get moving on this quickly."

I stood up to get more lemonade. "I don't need to interview her. The fact that she's Genevra's sister is all I need to know. Genevra, if you'll let her know she'll be hearing from us right away, I'll have HR call her to make her an offer."

Genevra and I 'high fived' each other, although I still felt uneasy about losing her assistance at *Ecosphere*. I tamped down the twinge of discomfort and assured myself all would be fine.

Probably.

Chapter 24
Davy Jones

THE NEXT MORNING, I was at work bright and early, as usual. I was determined to put yesterday's scare behind me, and to approach life as fearlessly as I always had before.

But that didn't mean I was looking forward to my first task of the day. I had to tell Davy Jones that the submarine ride business he led was not living up to expectations, and was in fact, costing us money. Davy had not stepped up as a leader the way I'd hoped he would, and it was time to shut down the business. We couldn't afford to support a losing proposition.

I picked up a pot of coffee and a half dozen warm blueberry muffins on the way to my office. I was a firm believer that food always helps bad news go down a little easier. I sat down at my desk and poured coffee into my stainless steel RIO-branded mug and took a sip. Davy was due here any minute, and I needed the caffeine hit to be able to face my unhappy task.

I'd finished two cups of coffee before Davy showed up, forty minutes late for our meeting. His rumpled shirt, bleary eyes, and uncombed hair told me quite clearly that he'd just gotten out of bed.

He poured a cup of coffee for himself before he sat down in one of the visitor's chairs in front of my desk. "Sorry I'm late, Boss," he said. "The alarm didn't go off."

If I didn't know I was just about to shut down his business unit, I'd have pointed out that it seemed like his alarm never went off. He started work late most days. But since I was going to terminate his employment along with the business, I didn't see any need to pile criticism on top of pain.

"You're here now," I said. "Help yourself to a muffin, and then we'll get started." I moved over to the small table in the corner of my office and chose a seat near the wall.

"Don't mind if I do," he said, putting two muffins on a small plate and topping off his coffee. He sat down across from me and began peeling the paper off his first muffin.

I waited until he'd swallowed a few bites before I started. "We've talked several times about how the submarine business is not performing the way we expected. I understand that outside events may have frightened some potential customers away."

I was referring to the recent personal submarine implosion that had occurred on a trip to the Titanic. "But as far as I've seen, you haven't done anything to draw in new customers or to help them understand the differences between our commercially built sub and the jerry-rigged one that imploded."

He held up a hand in protest. "People are scared right now. They don't want to hear it."

"Really? How do you know that? Did you run a focus group? Post an online survey?"

"Nope," he said. "I just know. People aren't interested now, but they'll come around someday." He crossed his arms stubbornly, daring me to question his assertions.

"I see. And what have you done to help facilitate this change in attitude? How have you spent the advertising budget I gave you? I haven't seen ads in tourist or trade magazines. No billboards or signposts around town. There's not even an easel display in the lobby. So what have you spent that money on? Because I've noticed you're a little over budget." Actually, he was a lot over budget, so I was keenly interested in his answer.

He shrugged. "I take the concierges and divemasters around town out for a meal or a few drinks. I talk up our sub and ask them to refer their customers."

"Have you seen any business come from that approach?" I asked. "Because from where I'm sitting, it doesn't seem to be working."

He took a huge bite of his muffin. "Nothing yet. These things take time."

"Which is not at all what you said when I offered to let you run the business unit. As I recall, at the time you thought we'd be turning away business within a few weeks."

He shrugged. "I was wrong."

I looked at him with sympathy, because I knew what I was about to say would hurt him. "I explained when you came on board that each new business at RIO needs to start turning a profit almost right away. We can't justify a unit that isn't bring in enough revenue to support its own needs, never mind missing its planned contribution targets to the research budget."

Abruptly, he sat up straight. "What are you saying?"

"I'm sorry to have to tell you this, Davy, but we have to shut down the submarine ride business unit. We'll be closing it within sixty days."

"I see. So then what? I'll be working in the dive shop full time?"

"No," I said. "I'm sorry but I'll be letting you go at the end of the sixty days. Take the time between now and then to work on shutting down the submarine unit, and you can spend as much time as you think is right looking for your next opportunity."

"You can't do this to me," he said. "After all I did for you."

I nodded. "I agree you did help me get my friends back when Seb Lukin kidnapped them. But that doesn't give you a free ride at RIO's expense for the rest of your life. Everybody here needs to pull at least their own weight. I'm sorry but I can't justify keeping you on."

Davy glared at me for a minute, his eyes hard and cold. Then he threw the remains of his second muffin on the floor, dumped the ones still on the tray on top of it, and then ground them to bits under one of his flip-flops. "We'll see about that." He slammed the door behind him when he stomped out of my office, leaving a trail of squashed blueberries and crumbs behind him.

I waited a minute, then went in search of some wet paper towels to clean up the mess, wondering if I'd done either of us a favor by letting Davy stay on for the promised sixty days.

Chapter 25
First Commercial Mermaid Class Graduates

A FEW MINUTES LATER, Benjamin popped into my office with another handful of wet paper towels. He knelt beside me. "I was passing by and saw the mess. What happened?"

I sighed. "I told Davy we're shutting down the submarine ride business unit and letting him go. He didn't take it well."

"I was afraid of that," he said. "You should have let me tell him. He thinks you owe him." He gathered all the dirty paper towels into a bunch and stood up.

"I wish I could have, but it was only right he should hear the bad news from me. I hired him, and he reported to me for most of the time he worked here. I knew he'd be upset, but I didn't expect this kind of childish response."

Benjamin paused a moment, his hands full of blueberry stained paper towels. "We should let him go right now. He obviously feels like you owe him more than a job, even though you were the only person that would hire him when he finished his jail time. We can pay him through the sixty days you promised him if you want to, but let's get him off the premises today. Who knows what kind of mischief he'll get into, and neither of us has the time to watch him twenty-four seven. If you like, this time I can be the one to tell him."

Benjamin was now the VP of business development, so the submarine business unit actually fell under his span of control—and he'd volunteered. But it was my responsibility. I would never shirk an unpleasant duty like letting someone go.

"No thanks," I said absently while sending Stanley Simmons, a member of RIO's maintenance team, a text asking him to come by to empty my now overflowing trash bin.

Benjamin dumped his wad of dirty paper towels on top of the pile already in my trash bin and put it out in the hall. "Okay. But right now, I need your help."

"Sure. What's up?"

"Today's the day our first mermaid class graduates, and I'd appreciate it if you could come by and say a few words. Then later if you could join us at the graduation party…"

"Sure. What time do you want me?"

"The class should end around noon, so that's when the party will start. We'll be serving lunch at the mermaid grotto. We'd all be thrilled to have you join us for that, of course, but if you could come by for about ten minutes to say hello any time before the class ends, I know the students would be thrilled."

I laughed. "How could anyone resist a deal like that? If it works for you, I'll come by around 11:30, do the meet and greet, and then stick around for lunch. How's that sound?"

Benjamin grinned at me. "And you'll stay for some photo ops too, won't you?" he said in a wheedling tone.

I laughed. "You'd better be serving a terrific lunch then, Mr. Brooks. If so, I'll be there."

Benjamin laughed too and left to finish teaching his class, and I sat at my desk working on extending the topic calendar for my *Ecosphere* column. I like to keep a plan that goes out at least six months ahead of publication so everybody involved with the zine has time to prepare.

One way that I work out my calendar is to review news articles, research papers, and the competition, although I scrupulously avoid looking at *Your World*, where I used to have a column. My ex-husband, Alec Stone, runs it now, and I had no wish to see what kind of hash he was making out of the once-revered title.

That is, until I did a search for ocean news and found a recent link that included *Your World* and my name.

This could not be good.

My finger hovered over the link. Whatever was behind the link was sure to ruin my day, and I didn't want to face a class full of eager mermaids with a sour disposition. I forwarded the link to Newton to let him take whatever legal action he thought best.

As soon as I forwarded it to my father, I couldn't help myself. I clicked, and almost fell off my chair. It was a public letter of apology for all the times over the years *Your World* had erroneously attributed my work to Alec Stone. It included every image, every article, and a corrected attribution for each one. The new publisher, Will Graham, a man I didn't know, had signed the letter and published it prominently in the most recent issue.

I wondered what had happened to Alec's job, but then again, I didn't care. Whatever had happened, I could only hope he'd gotten what he deserved. I spent a moment appreciating the way the universe had eventually made things right. I was still savoring the feeling of vindication when the alert on my calendar beeped, letting me know it was time to head down to the mermaid class.

The final skill needed to pass the mermaid course was to go into open water wearing mermaid gear and perform the required mermaid skillset, so I headed toward the grotto instead of the pool. I could hear high pitched laughter and squeals as I approached. It sounded like the class was having a great time.

Benjamin saw me coming, so he blew his whistle to get everyone's attention. The mermaids were in the shallow cove, treading water with big joyous smiles on their faces. They all turned and faced him just as I reached the grotto to stand beside him.

Benjamin introduced me, and the class applauded enthusiastically. Some of them weren't fully adept at treading water in their mermaid tails, and two of them sank underwater when they lifted their hands out of the water to clap.

Within seconds, they popped to the surface again, laughing and sputtering. Benjamin waved everyone over to the seats built into the grotto, and the class perched on the rock platforms, playfully swishing their tails in the sparkling droplets spewing from the fountain.

Benjamin left the top seat of the grotto open for me. When everyone was in position, he took photographs of each mermaid and of the group as a whole. Then he told them it was time for questions and turned off the fountain to make it easier for them to hear my answers.

Before I started taking their questions, I asked each of them to tell me their name, and as they did, I congratulated them on passing the mermaid course. Next I asked them what they planned to do with their new credential. Some of them said they wanted to get a job in a water park or on a cruise ship. A few said they'd taken the class just for fun, because they already knew how to scuba or freedive and they wanted one more credential.

Emma, a young girl who looked barely old enough to take the course, said she'd taken it purely to get over her life-long fear of the ocean.

"Wonderful. Did it work?" I asked her.

Her glowing face and enthusiastic nods gave me my answer, even without her shouted, "Yes."

"That's great," I said. "You should be very proud of yourself for facing your fears."

After everyone had their chance to speak, I told the newly certified mermaids that they'd always be special to us here at RIO because they were graduates of our first mermaid class.

"Now I want to give you a few words of hard earned advice. Always respect the ocean. It's an alien environment, and you're a stranger there. You need to recognize and be aware of its power. Don't dive or swim alone, and always make sure someone knows where you are and when you'll be back. Never go beyond the limits of your training and experience, and always listen to that little voice inside when it says, 'Don't do it.'"

The class laughed uneasily, and Benjamin gave me a funny look. Obviously, I was still processing my ordeal from the other day. I'd never before told any class so clearly that the ocean is a big scary place. I needed to change the subject before the entire class went screaming back to dry land.

I looked at the dive watch on my left wrist. "Now it's time for you to ask me whatever questions you want," I said. "I think we still have a few minutes before lunch gets here."

There was a moment of shy silence before the questions started coming from all directions. Most of them were about what it was like to work at RIO and live in the Cayman Islands. I answered each one, realizing as I did that I was indeed one of the luckiest people in the world to do what I do and live where I live.

Noah and Austin Gibb approached wheeling carts laden with the food for the party. While they were setting up the buffet and the sound system and getting the nearby grill going, I said, "I think we have time for one more question before lunch is ready. Anybody?"

Emma, the young one who'd been afraid of the ocean, said "I have a question. Are you and Liam Lawton ever going to get married?"

I could feel my cheeks flaming as they all stared at me avidly, looking for an answer. Benjamin was giving me the side-eye, and I realized that he still had an interest in my answer to this question.

I didn't say anything, just held up my left hand where for once I wore the large, ornate, and crazy expensive ring Liam had given me a few years ago. The ring sparkled in the sunlight, sending rainbows through the water droplets from the fountain and across the tiny wavelets in the sheltered cove. It was gorgeous, but I rarely wore it. Partly that was because of its size, but mostly it was because of the always precarious status of my relationship with Liam.

Chapter 26
A Mermaid Struggles

STEWIE WANDERED over from the dive shop, the tantalizing aromas from the grill telling him the party was just about to begin. Doc and Maddy came out the back door, followed a few minutes later by Genevra and Joely. Liam and Rafe strolled across the lawn from the parking lot, making several hearts—including mine—skip a few beats. Tate Crusoe came out of the locker room and joined them for the last few steps to the party area. As they approached, Austin turned up the music, and the party atmosphere was complete.

The class wiggled out of their mermaid tails and, after carefully removing the monofin from the tip, folded their prized tails. One by one, they joined the buffet line. At first they were shy, especially with some of the more famous members of the team like Rafe Cummings. But he and Tate mingled with the students, and Tate had brought a dozen photographs for Rafe to sign for the class. Rafe personalized each photo for the recipient, and he was so nice and down to earth that he soon broke the ice even with the shyest of the mermaids.

The food was plentiful. Simple cookout food but very welcome, especially for the group who'd already spent most of their day in the water. After sandwiches, burgers, and salads, we finished up with ice cream sandwiches made in house with RIO's famous chocolate chip cookies. When we'd finished eating, the RIO team drifted away one by one. When it was just Benjamin and me left, he helped everyone pile their belongings onto a small cart and he rolled it to their cars so they wouldn't have to carry it all. I waved goodbye as they left and then went inside to my office.

A few hours later I leaned back in my chair and stretched. I wanted a break, and a short quiet dive in our cove sounded like exactly what I needed. I headed to the dive shop to pick up my gear from the employee storage area. After slipping into my shorty dive skin, I poked my head into the dive shop's open Dutch door to let Stewie know where I was going and when I'd be back.

He nodded. "Stay away from the area where the rip current is. I don't want to have to fish you out again."

I laughed, but Stewie didn't, so I knew how worried he was.

"I'll be careful," I said. "I'll stick to the other side of the cove."

"Good. But I'll keep an eye out for you anyway." He calmly kept on checking in rental tanks, but he peered over his reading glasses like he thought I might argue with him.

He was sort of right to be worried. I had a habit of diving alone and not letting anyone know where I was going. I considered telling him that I was a big girl and a world renowned diver, so I didn't need a babysitter to dive a few yards away from shore. Then I remembered that if he hadn't been "babysitting" me the other day, I might not be here now.

"Thank you," I said meekly. "I appreciate it."

I thought Stewie was going to fall off his stool with surprise, but he didn't say anything else. I went outside to grab a tank and set up my BCD and regulator on it. I clipped my fins to a D-ring on my BCD vest and hung my mask around my neck. Then I walked over to the tiny sand beach near Ray's Place, where the water was calm and shallow. I donned my gear and waded in.

The water was clear and warm, and there was no current to speak of. There was also very little to see. I swam under the dock, which is usually a hotbed of sea life, but today it too was deserted.

I tried to be content with the feeling of freedom and peace that always comes over me in the water, but it wasn't working today. I found myself finning over toward the other side of the cove.

I swam slowly across RIO's cove, past the shore dive area—which we had closed today because of the unpredictable currents running nearby. The surge picked up slightly as I neared the far edge of the cove, passing by the narrow opening between the artificial reef we'd built and the natural coral that marked the end of the mermaid grotto and hid the deep wall just a few feet beyond it.

I let the gentle surge push me along. The tide was coming in, so it was pushing me along parallel to the ironshore. I neither saw nor felt any evidence of a rip current. Since the wind had died down to near normal, I began to think that maybe the danger had passed.

The current here naturally ran in and at a slight angle to the shore. I was just floating along with the current, not trying to swim at all, when suddenly I felt a small spurt of turbulence. It wasn't a rip current or anything that felt natural. It was almost like the turbulence you'd feel if a boat passed overhead when you're down deep.

But I was in a 'no boating' area, so that couldn't be it.

I rolled onto my back and looked up. Something was splashing near the surface. It looked like the death throes of a very large fish, its tail slapping out of the water every few seconds.

It took me another moment to realize that the tail was one of the mermaid tails we sold in the dive shop, and its wearer was obviously in trouble.

In shock, I realized she'd met up with the last of the rip current I'd struggled with. Even in the few seconds I'd been watching, the current had pushed the hapless mermaid down deeper and dragged her further out to sea. I could see her small hands trying frantically to get out of the mermaid tail.

She didn't realize that the monofin was probably her only hope of escape from the killer current. Or at least, it had been until I arrived on the scene.

I swam toward her, staying below the rip current until I was directly beneath her. Her struggles were growing weaker, and I knew it was only a matter of a few seconds before she succumbed to the ocean's might. She didn't seem to realize I was there.

I rose slowly through the water, careful not to let myself enter the rip current with its deadly downdraft and powerful push. I reached up.

My fingers touched the ends of her tail, but I didn't want to dislodge either the tail or the monofin inside, which might be the only thing that would save her if my attempt failed. I reached up a little further and tried to tap her leg so she'd know I was there. The powerful current grabbed my arm.

I snatched it back before it overwhelmed me too. It was still dragging the mermaid out to sea. I followed below her, although I had to work hard at keeping up with her, given the speed at which she was moving.

I quickly realized if I didn't get her down below the current in the next few seconds, we might both be lost. I looked around. There was nothing I could use to help save her, so I did the only thing I could.

I gathered my strength and lunged for her, hoping to be able to grab her high enough on her legs that it wouldn't dislodge her tail and the precious monofin. My arms encircled her mid-thigh, and I immediately swam toward the bottom, still holding her in my arms.

She had no idea what had hold of her, and she had been panicking anyway, so she thrashed and wiggled, trying to escape my grasp. I held on with all my strength and kept swimming crosswise away from the rip current and down toward the slower, less lethal bottom current to escape the rip and its deadly downdraft.

As soon as I felt us come free of the grip of the killer current, I turned to the mermaid. It was young Emma, the student who'd been so afraid of the ocean. I was pretty sure this episode was going to be the stuff of her nightmares for years to come.

I let go of her thighs and grabbed her hand, then I tugged her toward me. I handed her a small spare air tank I'd taken from the pocket of my BCD. She took it and inhaled deeply. Once she'd taken a few breaths, I started dolphin kicking toward shore, holding her hand, and pulling her along with me. After a few strokes, she started kicking in unison with me.

Her kicks were weak, but at least she was trying. My kicks were strong enough to propel us both, so we were making good progress. But I was worried that the spare air wouldn't last her long enough for us to reach shore.

No sooner did I complete that thought when I saw the panic rise in her eyes again when she tried to inhale and nothing came out. I quickly took my primary regulator out of my mouth and shoved it into hers. In case she panicked even more, I stayed as far away from her as my hose allowed. I plugged my octopus into my own mouth and resumed swimming.

I was elated when we passed the newly built artificial reef and exhausted by the time the ironshore came into view. But I knew that now we were home free. I led Emma over to the ladder that led to the top of the mermaid grotto's wall. The ladder's top rung was wide enough to be a seat, and she quickly turned around to remove her tail and monofin while I hovered on the surface. She let both items drop to the bottom, then she turned and scampered up to dry land.

I ducked down to retrieve her belongings, although I figured she'd probably never use them again.

Then I took a deep breath and paused with my arms on the ladder, waiting for my heartbeat to return to normal. I shut my eyes, willing away the images of all the horrible things that could have happened to Emma. Or me.

Worse yet, to both of us.

I tried controlling my breathing, but no matter how slowly and deeply I tried to breathe, within a few seconds I was panting and gasping again. I leaned my head against the cool damp metal of the ladder rails.

"Do you need a hand?" Emma's soft voice came from nearby.

I lied. "No thanks. I'm fine."

She probably knew that I was lying, but she pretended not to notice my discomposure. "Thank you," she said. "I was in a total panic, but once I knew you had me, I was sure I'd be safe. You saved my life."

I tried to smile, but even I could tell my smile was wobbly. "What happened anyway?" I asked. "What were you doing out there alone? Didn't we train you to know and respect the limits of your experience? You were way outside the parameters of your training."

She shrugged. "I know that now, but at the time, I thought I could handle anything. I've learned my lesson. I'm lucky you were around to save me, because I couldn't break free from that current on my own, and I was too scared to take a minute to think about the best thing to do. But it'll be okay. I won't swim beyond my abilities and training ever again."

I smiled at her and hoped that she truly meant what she said. Then I climbed out of the cove to join her in the grotto. I'd saved her. She was unharmed, and that's what mattered.

Chapter 27
Bari Arrives

I WALKED out of the locker room after my shower and strolled under the arbor to the main RIO building. I'd spent a long time thinking under the semi-hot water, and I'd had an epiphany.

It had been foolish for me to try to rescue Emma. I knew how bad the rip current was. It had nearly killed me not that long ago. The smart thing would have been to call for help. Get Stewie to jump in a boat and go after her.

But I'd seen her flailing underwater, and I knew that even a few seconds of delay might have been a few seconds too many. Instead of sitting in Ray's Place devouring a toasted cheese and tomato sandwich with a heap of golden french fries like she'd been when I left her, she'd have been on her way to the morgue. I would never have been able to live with that outcome.

My epiphany was this.

I've been blessed with incredible water skills and the ability to evaluate the odds of various situational outcomes at lightning speed. I'd known, deep in my soul, that I could save Emma. And even if I hadn't known that truth in my heart, nothing, not even that scared little voice in my head, could have stopped me from trying. If that tiny, insecure, and terrified voice had had its way and

I didn't try to save her, I wouldn't have been able to live with myself. Instead, I'd put aside my panic and done what needed doing, just as I usually do in emergencies.

I recognized that a big part of my purpose in life is to save other people's lives. Sometimes I do that by teaching them to swim or dive safely. And sometimes I do it by rescuing them when they get into trouble.

When something beyond their ability to manage happens to someone, and they're in danger, I never hold back. I never waste time dithering over what's the right thing to do, because I know the right thing will always be to use my gifts to help others.

And if I did that, with my whole heart and soul, everything would work out exactly as it should. My incredible luck—which is as much about skills as it is about random chances—would hold up.

At least my luck would hold up until someday maybe it wouldn't. But when and if my luck gave out, I would be okay with that. In the meantime, I had to do my best to train people to respect and love the ocean and themselves. I had a solemn duty to do whatever was in my power to keep the ocean clean and healthy, and to teach people to have the proper respect for its mighty waters. That way, everyone I helped could enjoy the incredible underwater realm, and I'd have the satisfaction of knowing I'd done everything possible to keep safe the people I know—or would meet in the future.

I could hear Ray in the back of my mind saying, "Good job, Fin. You've recognized that the universe gave you those skills so you could use them to fulfill your life's purpose. I'm very proud of you."

Hearing Ray's voice in my head made me smile, as it always did, and I felt my breathing return to normal and my shoulders drop back to their usual position rather than tensely brushing up against my earlobes.

I walked down the hall, but turned toward the lobby rather than my office when I came to the end. I wanted to pick up a few cookies to munch on while I worked. As I crossed the stunning glass-walled atrium, I noticed a petite blonde woman walking toward the reception area. I could only see her back, but I felt sure this must be Bari Blackthorne, Genevra's sister.

"Bari," I called out, loudly enough to get her attention but not so loud as to make a spectacle of myself if my hunch turned out to be wrong.

The woman turned around to see who had called her name, and I stopped, stunned by her resemblance to my friend. Bari's hair was blonde and her eyes were blue, but the unmistakable elegant bone structure of their faces was exactly the same.

She was as petite as Genevra, who barely hit the five foot mark. Genevra was very fit and deceptively strong. She worked out daily, ran for miles every week, practiced martial arts, and swam and dove almost as well as I did. She was a powerhouse packed into a tiny package, and from all outward appearances, Bari had sprung from exactly the same mold.

Bari walked my way with a big smile on her face. "You're Fin Fleming," she said. "I'm so happy to meet you. I'm a big fan."

I could feel myself blushing, but I tried to laugh it off. "Did your sister tell you to say that?"

She chuckled. "Yes, she did. She said it would make you blush, and she was right, as usual."

I nodded. "In my experience, Genevra is usually right. If you decide to join us, you'll have big shoes to fill."

Bari looked down at her tiny feet. "I might have some growing to do…"

We both laughed.

It seemed that Bari also had her older sister's sense of humor. Right away, I knew I was going to love working with Bari, just as I'd loved working and hanging out with Genevra.

I waved down the hall toward the administrative offices. "Let me show you the way to HR, then after you talk to them I'll take you on a tour of our facilities. Have you checked into a hotel already? I can drop you off later and then we can have dinner if you're free."

"No hotel needed. I'm staying at Genevra's for a few days until I find a place of my own, but I'd love to have dinner. Thank you."

I opened the door to HR and poked my head in. "I have Bari Blackthorne here. Remember, she's taking the position of assistant to Genevra and me. Please give her the usual orientation—just the good parts, please—and then let me know when you're done. I'll take her on a tour of the facilities when you're finished."

"Will do," said the head of human resources. "Welcome, Bari. I know you already spoke to Liam, and of course you know Genevra, but I assume you'll have at least a few questions. We can start with those." She pulled out a stack of pamphlets and forms, so I left, shutting the door behind me to give them some privacy.

About an hour later, the HR leader and Bari were at my door. "We're finished. Are you free to talk to Bari now?"

I came out from behind my desk. "I am. Are you ready for that tour, Bari?"

I took her around the office area, showing her each of the executive offices, and the small cubbyhole next to my office that would be hers. I brought her through the institute's aquarium, explaining the schedule of shows and giving her the history behind each exhibit.

We went into the gift store, and I watched while Bari looked at the variety of inventory we kept. Although the merchandise assortment tilted heavily toward t-shirts, hats, posters, photographs, and branded mugs, we had everything from cheap postcards to expensive handmade jewelry and artistic figurines and wall hangings.

While Bari explored the store, the manager and I watched her to see if we could identify something extra she really seemed to like. The manager knew I'd want an assortment of hats, tees, and bric-a-brac along with at least one really nice item that had caught Bari's eye. After we left, the manager would gather the welcome packet and leave it in my office for me to give to Bari when we'd finished our tour.

After we left the gift shop, I took her down the long hall that led to our pool, where we taught most of our dive classes. I explained the pool's unique construction, and the reasons for the large shallow area and the almost equally large and unusually deep area.

Then we checked out the fully equipped gym next door, and after that we doubled back so I could show her the locker room. HR had already assigned a locker to her. We could tell because someone from maintenance had put her name on the door using a sharpie and a piece of painter's tape.

Then it was time to see the research labs, which I always like to save for last. The research labs are a series of interconnected rooms in the center of the building. There's only one entrance and no windows, because maintaining consistent light and temperature levels is crucial to our research.

We started by working our way around the main lab, moving clockwise as I told her about the inhabitants of each tank and what we were hoping to learn by studying them. Unlike many VIPs who take the tour and merely feign interest in our research, Bari seemed fascinated by each project. This was good, because part of her new role would be managing research grants and funding requests from the scientists on RIO's staff. Personally, I would have been horrified at the prospect of spending so much time with numbers and spreadsheets, but Bari seemed excited to dig in.

At last we came to the small alcove which houses my favorite exhibit. Rosie, the Atlantic pygmy octopus lives in this tank. I'd had Rosie for a long time—far longer than the expected life span of most octopuses, but Rosie is still going strong.

As soon as we approached her tank, Rosie peeked out of her shell home and jetted to the surface. She extended one tiny delicate tentacle, indicating that she wanted to hold hands. I'd washed my hands before we approached the tank, just in case, because more often than not, Rosie wanted to touch me.

As soon as I put my hand in the tank, she wrapped her tiny tentacle around one of my fingers and held on tight. She blinked her inscrutable eyes at me, and I wondered what she was trying to tell me.

After a few minutes, I used my free hand to take the small deck of cards off the shelf under Rosie's tank and explained to Bari how Rosie could identify the object depicted on the card and deliver it from a random pile of similar objects stacked haphazardly in a corner of the tank.

Bari exclaimed in wonder when every time I held up a card, Rosie unerringly delivered the correct object. Each time she completed her task, I dropped a small bit of clam into the water. Rosie's tentacle whipped out to secure the morsel, and then she delivered it to her beak by passing it along the length of her tentacles. Her quick flash of a deeper pink color conveyed her thanks.

Then I showed off Rosie's latest trick, which was opening a locked plexiglass box with a reconfigurable maze inside. The prize for successfully navigating the maze was a whole clam, and Rosie claimed her reward in record time.

I glanced over at Bari.

Her eyes were wide and filled with awe. "She's so smart."

"Yes, she is," I said proudly. "Would you like to touch her?"

Bari scrubbed her hands and then dipped a finger into Rosie's tank. Rosie eyed it suspiciously for several seconds before shooting one of her tentacles over for a tentative touch. Just as quickly, she withdrew the tentacle and jetted away.

When Bari didn't move, Rosie came back over and touched her again. Within a few minutes, she'd wrapped tentacles around each of Bari's fingers. They stayed that way for quite some time.

"How long until she lets me go?" Bari finally asked.

"Until she gets bored, or you ask her to let go. Like this." I showed Bari how to gently remove the tentacles from her hand so she wouldn't hurt Rosie.

When I'd freed her from the tiny tentacles, we washed our hands again before leaving the lab. At the door, Bari turned back to the tank where Rosie was watching us.

"Bye, Rosie," she said. "See you soon."

I shut the door behind us and then paused.

"I'm half starved. Are you ready for dinner yet, Bari?" I said.

"I could eat," she said, and I heard another hint of Genevra's wry humor in her answer.

"If you're anything like your sister, I know that deceptively mild response means you're starving. Am I right?"

She grinned. "Spot on."

"Ray's Place okay with you?"

She nodded. "I've been dying to eat there for months. Gen is always raving about the food and how much fun the place is. I'm ready if you are."

We walked down the hall to the back door and then along the paths to Ray's Place. Bari's head swiveled as she took in every detail. Candy shouted, "Look. It's Fin Fleming," when we walked in, and Bari laughed with delight.

When Noah had seated us, she said, "Ray's Place is even more spectacular than I expected. I mean, I've seen it in Genevra's social media feeds, but seeing it life-size, in real time, is mind-blowing."

I laughed. "If you like the vibe, wait until you taste the food. Noah is a great host and restaurant manager, but he's an even more amazing chef."

I ordered my usual lemonade and Bari ordered iced tea with sugar. We both selected the night's special. Under Theresa's tutelage, Noah Gibb had indeed turned into a top-tier gourmet chef, and the food he served was worthy of acclaim. It was certainly a far cry from the pre-made sandwiches from the convenience store that was my usual dinner when I ate alone at home or on the *Tranquility*.

By unspoken mutual agreement, we concentrated on the food rather than conversation. I didn't want to put Bari through the typical 'getting to know you' interview questions while she was trying to get a feel for me and RIO. And truth be told, I really didn't care what her answers were. Two of the people I trusted most in the world had already vetted her. If Liam and Genevra both thought she was right for the job, I wanted to hire her.

So when we pushed away the plates that had held our dessert—a fresh baked almond coconut pie with chocolate sauce—I said, "So, is there anything you need to know or that you're not certain about? Do you have any more questions I can answer?"

She nodded. "Just one. When can I start?"

"Whenever you want," I said.

We agreed that Bari would take a few days to settle up her affairs in Arizona, pack and ship her belongings, and then maybe take a couple of days of vacation before her start day. We settled on the first day of the coming month, a little over two weeks away. It seemed like a long time to wait to add her to the staff at RIO.

Chapter 28
Shark Feeding

THE NEXT DAY Rafe and I had scheduled our dive in the shark tank at the Turtle Centre. The Centre usually didn't hand-feed the sharks, so the experience would be almost as new to them as it was to us. Gary had expressed some trepidation about joining us in the tank, especially since while we'd be hand-feeding the sharks.

To accommodate his concerns, the Centre's manager, Rafe, and I all agreed that it would be better if Gary filmed us from outside the tank, and Rafe and I would take turns filming each other from inside. Rafe and I were actually both relieved that Gary had made it so easy for us to keep him out of the shark tank. It was obvious to me that Rafe didn't trust him as a dive buddy any more than I did. I hoped it wasn't quite as obvious to Gary.

Hand feeding the extremely well-fed sharks in the tank probably wasn't dangerous, but you never know with wild creatures. And despite the fact that they spent their lives in a giant tank with plenty of food to eat, these sharks were wild creatures.

We all knew that no matter what, Gary would never be as comfortable swimming with the sharks as Rafe and I were. Our unspoken concern was that the wily sharks might somehow sense his fear and decide to haze him a little bit.

Not necessarily to hurt him. Just to scare him.

For fun.

Or what passes for a shark's idea of fun.

Very early that morning, Rafe and I hauled our tanks and gear to the top of the tank, which required climbing up several flights of stairs in the already hot sun. In addition to our usual gear, we had heavy chain mail dive skins that Gary, as publisher of *Ecosphere*, had procured for us to wear during the dive. The suits would cover our entire bodies, and they also included boots, hoods, and gloves to keep us safe if a shark got overexcited and decided to take a test bite. If a shark decided to rip off an arm or a leg, the chain mail probably couldn't stop that, but they would prevent injuries from bumps and the occasional test nip.

These metal suits were heavy. Very heavy. We were both perspiring by the time we finished lugging everything up to the platform at the top of the predator tank.

The metal platform stuck out over the open water of the tank to allow the shark's usual feeders to toss food to the tank's inhabitants. The tank itself was made from a heavy plastic amalgam that was scratch resistant, strong enough to hold back the water, and optically engineered to eliminate distortion.

We rested on the platform for a few minutes while we discussed where Gary should take his positions during the dive, and we decided on specific images we wanted him to try to get. We definitely wanted shots of sharks taking food directly from our hands, preferably with our faces visible to viewers, and multiple shots of sharks approaching us from behind.

It was always interesting to see the size of these predators, so we wanted several pics that showed the sharks alongside us. Lots of teeth. Bump shots. Video taken from above while Gary stood on the platform where we were now, and film taken from the ramp that wound up along the outside of the tank where Gary would be for most of our dive. In addition, the Centre's director was hoping for some publicity stills taken from inside the clear walk-through tunnel, where patrons could stay dry while viewing the underwater goings-on when the Centre was open. We promised to provide them as a thank you for allowing us this unprecedented access.

It was a long list, but we weren't asking Gary for anything too difficult. As a group, we decided it would be best for Gary to start on the lower part of the ramp, shooting up at us as Rafe and I fed the sharks from the platform.

Then we'd enter the water, descend to the bottom of the tank, and hand-feed the sharks at various levels and landmark spots within the giant aquarium, moving toward the top of the tank as the dive progressed. With luck, Gary would be able to occasionally get close ups of our hands encased in the chain mail gloves while the sharks tore at the food in our grasp. Finally, before we exited the tank, we wanted Gary to position himself on the upper platform and shoot down into the water, catching us interacting with the sharks from above.

Just as the sun began to rise, we were ready to begin. Rafe and I began helping each other into our chain mail dive suits. They were heavy and awkward, especially the gloves and boots, so luckily Gary was there to help.

When we were ready, we gave Gary a few minutes to get in position down below. I wished I'd thought to bring Liam or Stewie to help us gear up so Rafe and I wouldn't have had to wait in the hot sun while Gary trotted down the ramp to set up his own gear. We were sweating buckets in the heavy chain mail, but eventually, Gary's ready text came through our phones.

Rafe and I picked up our baskets of shark food and we each dropped a small piece of fish into the water. Almost instantly, the water began to churn as the sharks and the rest of the tank's lesser denizens chased after the food. We dropped in a few more pieces to be sure they were well fed, but once the sharks had eaten them, they began patrolling the area under and around the feeding platform. We knew they'd keep this up until they were convinced there was no more food in the offing, so we waited a few minutes for them to calm down.

When the sharks had resumed their normal patrols, Rafe and I sat down on the platform and eased our way into the water. Within a few seconds, the sharks were all around us. The slight turbulence our entries created attracted them, along with the lingering smell of fish on our hands and the enticing scent wafting from the containers of food we held.

We were more heavily weighted than usual by the chain mail, so we began sinking almost immediately. We maneuvered around each other so we were back to back, and we descended at the same pace. We scanned the area around us side-to-side as we went. My job was to look above every few seconds while Rafe's was to check below. This positioning and assigned surveillance areas gave us the ability to see the sharks from all angles as we increased our depth.

When we neared the bottom of the tank, I saw Gary filming us, his camera pressed up tight to the glass to prevent or at least minimize distortion. I smiled around my regulator and waved, then Rafe and I carefully danced around so he was facing Gary for his own turn to wave.

When Rafe completed his wave, we each took some larger pieces of fish from our buckets and fed the sharks, who tore the food from our hands. The trick was to hold on to the food long enough for the shark to get close enough to make the images amazing, but not so close they might bite your hand while trying to take the food. Even with the steel chainmail gloves, a shark bite could exert enormous pressure and leave a horrendous bruise or even break a bone.

Staying steady in the direct gaze of a feeding-frenzy crazed pack of sharks required nerves of steel. I consciously kept my breathing slow and regular, and I could tell Rafe was doing the same. The stiffness in his body told me it was taking some effort for him to keep his nerves in check. Or maybe I was just feeling the rigidity of the chain mail.

I had a healthy respect for sharks, and I'd been diving with various shark species many times before. I'd been in a cage when I'd taken that famous shot of Maddy facing down the great white, while she'd been alone in the open water, face-to-face with a known man-eater. She hadn't flinched or even blinked, just gazed at the shark with open trust until he'd turned away.

Today's close up experience made me respect Maddy's courage even more. My heart swelled with pride in her.

I tapped Rafe's leg with my fin, the signal we'd agreed on to start our journey to the surface. Our ascent plan called for us to pause periodically near one of the artificial reef's outcroppings to give Gary a landmark he could use to position himself as we rose. The first stop in our plan required us to ascend about ten feet and move slightly to the left so the backdrop of the pictures Gary shot would be different.

But the aquarium was round, and we were in the center of the tank, so saying "the left" had little meaning. As I felt Rafe's body peel away from my back, I realized we should have used cardinal directions like east or west, or even hand signals. I reached over to clasp his hand at the same time he reached for mine.

We dove so well together that we'd simultaneously recognized the problem and spontaneously come up with the same solution. Rafe swung around to regain our back-to-back stance and extended his right forefinger so I'd know which way he intended to move. I reached my arm around toward my back, trying to ensure my okay signal would be visible to him, but before I'd raised it more than a few inches, a large shark charged in, bumping me out of the way.

I whirled around just in time to see him chomp down on Rafe's arm, midway between his elbow and wrist. Rafe yelped in surprise, and his regulator dropped out of his mouth.

Without thinking, I pounded my fist down as hard as I could on the shark's snout, hoping that would be enough to convince him to let go of Rafe's arm.

The shark turned my way and glared at me with those cold, dead shark's eyes before he turned and swam away. I quickly grabbed Rafe's now free-floating regulator and stuck it in his mouth. After I hit the purge button to blow out the water so he wouldn't choke, I gave him the okay sign.

His bitten hand was hanging limply by his side, and his other hand was still holding the basket of fish, so he didn't signal back. I didn't see any blood seeping from the bitten area, so I figured he'd be okay for at least the next few minutes. Probably long enough for me to get him out of the tank.

Except I didn't like the way the sharks were acting. They were swimming circles around us, moving in close and then darting away. I'd seen the shark show many times here at the center, and I knew this wasn't their normal feeding behavior. Our presence had obviously upset them in some unexpected way.

I reached around my back so my hand was in front of Rafe's face. I made the thumbs up sign that means to ascend. I pumped my arm a few times, hoping Rafe would realize I meant to skip the remainder of our planned feeding stops and go right to the surface. He bumped my leg with his fin, the only way he could signal me for now. I put a quick hit of air into his BCD by reaching around him and pushing the button on the inflator hose. Then I did the same for my own BCD.

We began swimming slowly and gently toward the surface, still back-to-back. It sounds easy enough, but the chain mail is so heavy that it took a lot more effort than it normally would have, despite the added air in our vests. Although my nerves were twanging—and I'm pretty sure Rafe's were too—we both stayed calm and swam steadily up at the usual rate of ninety feet per minute. At that pace, it took about a minute and a half to reach the top of the tank.

Gary was on the platform when my head broke out of the water. I pulled my regulator out of my mouth and commanded to Gary. "Help him." I swung us around so Rafe was nearest the ladder, then I reinserted my regulator and ducked under where I could keep an eye on the sharks.

A few seconds later a metallic clang told me that Rafe was safely on the platform and it was my turn to climb the ladder. It only took me one kick to reach it. I held onto the top rung and used my other hand to pass my fins up so I could climb out unencumbered. Rafe took my fins in his good hand, and I scampered up the ladder and out onto the platform. I quickly shrugged out of my BCD and put it down on the platform before peeling back my steel hood and gloves.

Rafe had already removed one of his chain mail gloves. He was having difficulty using the injured arm, so I helped him remove his BCD and lower it to the platform, then I tugged off his other glove, his steel hood, and his booties. A large dark bruise marred the skin of his right arm and hand, all the way from the tips of his fingers to well above his elbow.

While I was helping Rafe, Gary was still filming the sharks circling below us. He was on his knees, leaning over the platform's edge with the lens of his video camera in the water. From this angle he couldn't really frame out his shots, so I guessed he was just winging it hoping to get some usable footage. He turned around to see how Rafe and I were doing, and he accidentally knocked the basket of fish into the water. The contents spilled out, and the sharks went into a wild frenzy.

Gary leaned forward putting his camera in the water again, but this time, he overbalanced and fell in headfirst, free-falling through the water. In his panic, he dropped his camera and began thrashing around, attracting the sharks just as much as the food had. Their unwelcome attention caused him to struggle even harder, and they moved in closer, bumping against him as they passed.

It was a vicious circle. The closer the sharks came, the more he floundered. The more he flailed, the more excited the sharks became. If someone didn't pull him out quickly, there would be a tragedy here today.

I pulled on my fins and then picked up my BCD, shrugging it down over my shoulders and fastening the cummerbund even while I stepped off the platform. Putting my regulator in my mouth as I moved, I swam after Gary and grabbed him by his shirt collar. I was swimming toward the surface as fast as I could. Meanwhile, the sharks kept circling, and Gary kept struggling, making it even harder for us to reach the safety of the surface.

I took my primary regulator out of my mouth and stuck it in Gary's, pushing the purge valve as soon as his lips clamped around the mouthpiece. I hoped that knowing he had a secure air supply would calm him down, but it didn't. Swimming with him was like trying to hold onto an overexcited eel. Even so, we made steady progress.

When my head broke the water's surface, I spun around and put Gary's hands on the ladder's side rails. Out of the corner of my eye, I saw Rafe reach forward with his good arm to try to help Gary onto the platform, but he kept up his panicky struggling, making it nearly impossible for Rafe to get him out of the water.

But if anyone could do it, I knew it would be Rafe Cummings. The best thing I could do now was to get out of his way and make sure he didn't have to rescue me too.

While I waited for Gary to get out of the way, I sank about a foot underwater to be able to keep an eye on the sharks, who kept coming closer each time they passed. The biggest shark of the group bumped me, then swam away. The rest of the sharks followed his lead.

They bumped me from the right. From the left. From the front, and from behind. This was not good. I knew I had to get out of the water right away, even though Gary was still blocking the ladder.

I didn't have the time to swim the few feet to the other ladder, and anyway, I didn't relish the idea of standing on the lower rungs with my back to the frenzied beasts while I made my way up the ladder. Instead, I gave a mighty kick and grabbed onto the platform with my arms as I rose a little way out of the water. I used my arms to lever myself onto the platform, completely discarding the idea of going up either ladder. It was too dangerous to wait, and I didn't have even a nanosecond to spare.

Pulling myself up wasn't easy. I weighed a lot more than usual because of the heavy chain mail I still wore. I silently thanked my friend Christophe Poisson, the world famous freediver. He'd taught me to lift heavy weights, because to be a good free diver, you need both mental and physical strength. And I thanked my stepfather Ray, who'd taught me to think and act quickly in an emergency.

My upper body was draped across the platform, and I crawled forward to get the rest of me to safety. Seeing I was in trouble, Rafe gave me one of his hands and pulled. Just as I hauled my upper thighs over the edge of the platform, the angriest shark jumped up out of the water behind me, snapping his jaws at my feet and legs. I quickly drew them further onto the platform.

The big shark took a bite of my fin, shook his head, and nearly pulled the fin right off my foot. I snapped my leg completely out of the water onto the platform. Then I hastily scooted back away from the edge and gratefully counted my limbs. Luckily, they were all still there.

I drew in a shuddering breath. Gary had curled into a ball on the platform, quivering and quaking with fear. He made small mewling noises, and his arms covered his eyes as though he expected to see a gruesome scene.

Rafe put down the video camera he'd been using to film the rescue and the shark frenzy even while he helped pull me across the platform to safety. "You okay?" he asked. "I got some amazing footage. You were brilliant."

"I bet. Maybe next time forget the filming and just yank me out sooner, okay?"

Rafe looked surprised, then contrite. "I'm sorry. I wasn't thinking like this was real life. In my day job the first rule is to always get the shot." Rafe was the hottest action movie star on the planet, famous for doing most of his own stunts. He was well known for always getting the shot.

I nodded. "I totally get it. But remember, in your movies the sharks are usually mechanical."

He paled. "I...I'm sorry. I wasn't thinking. It was inexcusable."

I smiled at him. "It was. But it was also brilliant. Let's get out of here so we can have Doc look at your arm. And my leg. Once she gives us the once over, we'll view the footage. We've got a Pulitzer with our names on it, for sure."

Rafe gave a crooked smile. "Ya think? If we do, it's all you."

Gary finally sat up. "Are you two okay? When those sharks were all around me I thought I was a goner. I never expected to get out alive."

I shrugged. "As long as you're breathing, you can't ever give up. Always just keep going, no matter how hopeless it seems."

He looked at his feet. "I'm sorry. I didn't expect them to act like that. I shouldn't have…"

Rafe and I looked at each other, puzzled. This sounded ominous.

"Shouldn't have what?" I asked, my voice cold with suspicion.

Gary looked at his feet. "Last night I soaked the chainmail dive suits in a tub of fish guts. I thought it would make for more dramatic footage. The sharks got a little bit crazier than I expected. I didn't realize they'd react like that."

"A little bit crazier? Rafe might have lost his arm, and I nearly lost my leg and my life trying to save your worthless hide when you fell in deep water roiling with a bunch of sharks high on fish fumes. What were you thinking?"

He shrugged. "I wanted to show you I could handle the photography for the new column. I thought this would prove I was good enough. At least as good as Cummings here."

I tried to hold back my anger, but it was too powerful. He could have killed us all. At the very least, he should have asked us if it was okay with us for him to do what he'd done or told us about it and let us make our own decision about whether or not we thought it was safe to dive.

"You're fired," I said. "Clean out your desk at Quokka headquarters and be gone before I get to the office."

He licked his lips. "I don't work for you. You can't fire me."

"Wanna bet?" I said.

Chapter 29
Liam

As soon as Rafe and I got back to RIO, I walked him down to the infirmary. I was limping along, carrying both our dive bags because I'd volunteered to clean our gear while Doc checked him out. He was biting his lip, and his face was ghostly white. I knew he was in great pain, but action heroes never complain. Rafe would never utter a word of complaint even if he was on his deathbed.

Which he was not. Or at least, I was pretty sure he was not.

Doc was sitting at her desk, studying a new DAN report on decompression illness symptoms. DAN, the Divers Alert Network, is the top source for information about diving-related illnesses and accident prevention, and I knew Doc read all their reports cover-to-cover.

She glanced up, and as soon as she saw the look of pain on Rafe's face, she dropped her report and rushed to him. "What happened?" she asked me.

"Shark bite. Luckily he was wearing chain mail, but the shark was a big guy. Put a lot of pressure on his arm."

Doc pursed her lips. "I see. What were you two doing to provoke the shark?"

"Feeding them," I said, looking down at my feet.

She glared. "You know better than that. I thought your policy was never to feed the wildlife."

"That is my policy, but this shark isn't exactly wildlife. We were in the big tank at the Turtle Centre." I knew what she was going to say.

"Confinement in a tank or a cage doesn't make wildlife any the less wild. You two could have been badly hurt." While we'd been talking, Doc had been checking out Rafe's arm, looking for punctures and broken bones. "But I've seen people feed those sharks many times, and they've never attacked anybody. You must have done something to provoke them."

"Yep," I said. "Someone soaked our chain mail in fish guts."

She gasped. "Who would hate you that much?"

"Gary Graydon did the soaking, but I don't think he was trying to kill us. He was just looking for a dramatic photo."

Her voice was sharp. "He should have known better. I hope you gave him a good talking to."

"I did more than that," I said. "I fired him."

"Good. Now get out of here and let me work on poor Rafe. I'll let you know when—or if—he's free to go."

As I turned to leave, she noticed my limp. "Not so fast. Get back here and let me check you out too."

"I'll come back," I said. "First I have to let Liam know I fired his best friend."

I picked up our gear bags and hobbled out of the infirmary to call Liam from my office, but he was sitting at the corner table when I arrived. He stood up and faced me, anger in every line of his body.

"You tried to fire Gary? I know I give you a lot of leeway at Quokka Media, but you're not authorized to fire the publisher. What were you thinking?"

"I was thinking I wasn't going to work with a guy that nearly got Rafe and me killed with his stupid stunt. I foolishly thought you'd rather have a living fiancée than one who'd been shredded by sharks. I assumed you would agree with my decision. Or am I wrong?"

Liam's assumption that whatever had gone down between Gary and me had been my fault enraged me. I was livid that he hadn't asked me for my side of the story before jumping down my throat. And I was beyond furious that Gary had immediately called Liam and complained about my actions before I'd had a chance to talk to him.

Liam sucked in a breath at my angry response. He inhaled slowly and steadily, then sat down at the table in the corner of my office. "I apologize for jumping on you. What happened? And where's Rafe?"

"He's in the infirmary and lucky to still have all his limbs. Or I hope he'll still have them once Doc finishes assessing the injuries he sustained."

"How did he get injured?" Liam asked mildly. "I thought you two had planned to dive in the shark tank at the Turtle Centre today. I've seen that show, and it's pretty tame. Did you guys do something to provoke them? That's so not like you. Must have been Rafe then."

I stood up in utter fury. "It was NOT Rafe. He's the victim here, and he nearly lost his arm, if not his life. And I nearly lost the lower half of my body trying to out-jump an irate shark. All because your idiot friend wanted a chance to take a one-of-a-kind picture. And the joke's on him. Nobody outside the dark web would ever have published gruesome films of two celebrities being eaten alive by sharks."

Liam dropped back onto his seat. He swallowed. He bit his lip, swallowed again. "I…I don't understand. What went on today?"

"Your so-called friend decided to spice up the pictures he planned to take today. He soaked our chainmail diveskins in fish guts yesterday, so the scent would inflame the sharks. He never told us. Just sent us off to dive after turning a bunch of normally docile sharks into man-eaters. Then he stayed safely on the ramp, shooting video of us while we tried to get out of the tank without getting eaten alive."

"One big shark chomped down on Rafe's arm. We're just lucky he didn't decide to tear it off. I think Rafe'll just have a bad bruise, but Doc is still examining him. And I nearly lost my leg. A huge shark jumped up onto the platform and tried to tear it off." I showed him the ripening bruise that ran from my knee to my ankle.

"In fact, it was so close that he ripped the fin right off my foot. He spit it out and it floated to the surface. I have it here. Look." I pulled the mangled fin out of my bag. Most of the blade was missing, and the tooth marks and ragged edges went all the way to the toe pocket.

Liam turned white and gulped. "I didn't realize what went on. I could have lost you."

"Yeah, you could have. And that's why I fired your buddy. I thought you and I were a team. You should have at least asked me what happened before jumping down my throat. Now go away and give me some time to calm down."

Liam stood and reached out his hand to me. "Gary and I go all the way back to our days at uni. We've been best buddies for years. I don't want to fire him. Let me think about this a little more."

"Consider this. *Your World* has a new editor-in-chief. Name's Will Graham. I don't know him, but he took the initiative to apologize for all the times the 'zine stole my work by attributing it to Alec. Maybe you should try to poach him. Or better yet, buy the whole enterprise. The market's too small to support two titles that are so similar, and you know they both end up struggling. But either way, I won't be working with Gary anymore. If you don't want to call Graham—no problem. Because I will. Not to suggest you buy the magazine. I'll be asking for a job. Either Gary goes or I go."

"I just need a little time to think things through..." Liam said.

Liam hates confrontations with people he cares about. I could tell he was hoping I'd give in and change my mind once I'd calmed down.

But I wouldn't. I don't calm down easily when somebody does something that could get me killed.

I turned my back and limped out of the office to return to the infirmary.

Part Three
Bari

Chapter 30
Bari

SHE WASN'T STARTING her new job for a few days, so Bari was making the most of her free time on Grand Cayman. She'd been exploring the island, seeing the sights, and enjoying the food at all the amazing restaurants near her sister's condo. It had been a blissful respite.

Today her plan was to visit world famous Seven Mile Beach. She'd been on the island several days already, and she hadn't been to the renowned beach even once. It was early in the morning of what promised to be another gorgeous day.

She started getting ready for her adventure. The beach was practically right across the street from Genevra's condo, so she didn't need to bring much with her. If she decided later that she needed something else, it would be easy enough to run back and get it.

She slipped into a tiny pink crochet bikini with delicate string ties on her hips and behind her neck. She'd bought it yesterday on a shopping excursion to Caymana Bay. The swimsuit was something she'd never have worn at home, but somehow, it felt just right here on this cosmopolitan island where people from all over the world came to enjoy themselves.

But still, she slipped a white t-shirt on over her bikini. She could always remove it once she was at the beach, and she'd feel more comfortable walking around if she had something on that provided a little more coverage than just the bikini. She pulled a striped beach towel out of Genevra's linen closet, then picked up a folding beach chair from her sister's storage locker in the building's basement.

She put a broad brimmed sunhat on her head but pushed it back so the strap was around her neck while the hat hung down her back. It was dim in the basement, and the broad brim had blocked the meager overhead lights, making it hard for her to see where she was going. She carefully made her way out of the gloomy basement and stood by the door for a minute, blinking in the glare of the hot sun before setting out.

When she arrived at the beach, she saw signs everywhere warning swimmers to beware of rip currents. She wasn't quite sure what a rip current was, but she felt certain that if it was something really bad, either Genevra or Fin would have mentioned it to her.

So she promptly put the warnings out of her mind. She wanted to relax, veg out, and enjoy her time in the sun.

Right now, her life was almost too perfect. If she didn't know better she'd have been convinced she was dreaming. She felt like she should pinch herself to make sure she was really awake.

Be happy. No worries.

That was her new motto.

She set up her chair under a handy palm tree and spread her towel on the sand nearby. She'd covered her body in SPF lotion earlier, so she didn't waste any time. She lay down on her stomach in the sand and gave a deep, contented sigh.

The hot sun and the soothing sound of the nearby waves was better than any sleep aid or hypnotist. Within a few minutes, Bari started to drift off to sleep.

So she was really annoyed when a shadow fell across her back, blocking the sun.

"Excuse me," said a quiet male voice. "Do you mind if I sit down?"

She growled. "It's a public beach. Just don't talk to me. I'm trying to relax." She didn't look up or turn her head.

There was silence for a few minutes, and she'd almost drifted off when he shattered her relaxed state again.

"You're Bari Blackthorne, aren't you?"

She flipped over quickly. "Who are you?"

"I'm a friend of Genevra's. I've heard your sister talk about you. She's pretty excited that you'll be living here on the island.

Bari had heard her sister mention several male co-workers, and Genevra liked them all. She could tell by the logo on the t-shirt he wore that his man worked at RIO, and therefore, he was probably someone Genevra liked. She couldn't ignore him if he was a friend of her sister's as well as a future co-worker. She sat up.

"I'm very pleased to meet you. Sorry if I was rude before. I don't like to talk to strange men."

He nodded. "Very prudent. But I'm not that strange."

He grinned at her, and she started laughing.

His sense of humor appealed to her, and he was very easy on the eyes. Very.

His light brown hair was streaked blonde by the sun in several places, and a few locks curled down over his forehead. His eyes were a deep blue, set off by the matching t-shirt with the RIO logo on the chest, and the sleek stretchy brown shorts that fit closely on his lean frame. The sun glinted off his perfect cheekbones and long dark eyelashes. Two clear silicone dive masks dangled by their straps from his left hand.

He smiled at her, and she couldn't help but smile back. He seemed so nice.

He buried his feet in the sand and stared at the horizon. "It's so hot here. Want to go for a swim?"

"Aren't we supposed to stay out of the water? The signs say there's a rip current, whatever that is."

He shrugged. "They're nothing to worry about. See, even the little kids are going in." He pointed down the beach where two young children waded in the shallow surf, both holding one of their father's hands.

It looked idyllic, not life threatening, and nobody on the beach seemed concerned.

"Okay," she said. "I've been dying to swim in the ocean here. Is it really as warm and clear as they say?"

He nodded. "It is. And you can soon see for yourself." He held the two scuba masks in one hand, but he put out his other hand to help pull her to her feet. She took it and rose gracefully. His eyes swept up and down, and she could tell he thought she was beautiful.

But even if he was a friend of Genevra's, something in his scrutiny made her uneasy.

He held onto her hand as they walked across the beach to the water. She dug her toes in the soft white sand as the waves washed over them, and giggled when she felt the water pull the sand right out from under her.

"Feel that?" he said. "That's the rip current. I told you there was nothing to worry about. Let's go in. I brought that extra scuba mask so you can see the stingrays and other fish on the bottom." He paused a moment. "Last one in buys the first round of drinks at dinner."

She was a little surprised that he seemed to take it for granted that they'd be having dinner together, but she didn't want to be stuck buying drinks if she decided to accept his invitation. She hadn't actually started her new job yet, and money would be tight until she received her first paycheck. She'd had a lot of moving expenses, and although RIO would reimburse most of them, it wouldn't be until she actually started working there.

So she shrugged and took the mask he held out with one hand. Then she grinned and splashed water in his face. While he was rubbing his eyes, she ran into the water and dove under a chest deep wave. When she surfaced, she put on the mask and after ducking her face into the water, she checked out the area below.

All she saw was sand and a few bits of broken coral. Maybe she wasn't out far enough yet to see the promised stingrays.

She swam out a few more strokes and turned to see where he was. He was still in the same spot he'd been in before, just a few inches from shore.

"You coming?" Her voice was slightly taunting, implying he was too chicken to follow her.

"Yes, but I prefer to go in slow and easy." He took a half step toward her. "But you go ahead and swim out a little further. If you get out far enough, you can see stingrays and parrot fish in the sand below you. Don't worry. It doesn't get very deep, and I'll keep an eye on you until I get there."

His smile was sweet.

She stared at him for a minute, but then the lure of seeing stingrays in the wild proved too much for her. She turned back to the open ocean and swam out a few more strokes. She was just about to look back to see where he was when she caught a flash of black and grey from below.

A stingray.

She smiled with delight and floated on her stomach, watching the graceful creature glide and swoop, totally unaware of its own beauty. He swerved off to her left, and she kicked along in his wake. He was fast, and she had to kick hard to keep up with him.

After a few minutes, keeping up with him got easier. It felt like she was flying. This must be the feeling Genevra always talked about—the feeling of weightless joy she said she felt while in the ocean.

Bari wondered where her new friend was. He was missing out on the sight of the stingray. She flipped upright in the water, and it was only then she realized how deep it was. The water here was so clear that it was deceptive. Everything on the bottom looked like you could just reach down and touch it, but it was about twenty feet down.

She looked to shore and sucked in a breath. She'd had no idea she was out this far. She certainly hadn't been swimming hard. It looked like a mile or more back to the beach, and nobody seemed to be paying any attention to her. She didn't see the man from RIO—or anyone else—nearby in the water.

Even while she stared at the distant beach, she noticed that the ocean was pulling her further away from safety at an alarming rate. How could that be?

With a sinking feeling, she realized the harmless erosion of the sand under her feet when she stood at the edge of the ocean had not been the dangerous rip current the warning signs had been referring to. This—this current moving at the speed of a freight train, pulling her out so far and so fast that she knew in her heart she'd never make it back to shore—this was the deadly rip current.

With that realization, she knew she was doomed.

She felt a tear trickle down her cheek, and she let her body go limp in the water. She'd been foolish not to pay attention to where she was going in the open water, but to be fair, she'd never been in an ocean before.

She'd had no idea how big an ocean actually was.

Or how dangerous.

Then she remembered the man on the beach. He was from RIO. He must know the ocean well. He was probably calling together a rescue team right now.

She scanned the shore again but didn't see anyone who seemed to be looking for her. Of course, at this point she was so far away that the people on the shore looked like gnats. There was no way she could tell who was there or what they were doing.

She inhaled. She'd gotten herself into this mess. It was up to her to save herself.

She started swimming toward shore, kicking her feet and scooping water with her arms for all she was worth. When she'd winded herself, she looked up to see how much progress she'd made.

Yikes.

She was even further away than before.

She floated on her back for a minute, gathering her strength. When she looked back toward shore, she was again further away. She couldn't take even a moment to rest or she'd end up in the middle of nowhere.

She looked around. She was already in the middle of nowhere. She didn't know what to do or how to escape the wicked current. All she could do was swim.

At least until she couldn't swim any more.

Part Four
Fin

Chapter 31
Rescue

It was mid-morning, and I'd already done my first dive of the day. When I returned to my office, I repeatedly reviewed the footage of the shark attack that Gary, Rafe, and I had taken yesterday, and although it scared me to see the sharks acting so aggressively toward Rafe and me, I knew it was excellent footage.

Even so, I was still angry about the underhanded way the situation had come about, and I didn't think I'd ever get over that.

But the footage Rafe and I had obtained was riveting. The question was how to find the best use of this extraordinary film. I'd been pondering that very question for a while now. Whenever I saw the video, I got angry at Gary all over again. He'd endangered my life to further his own career, and he hadn't even given me a heads up. Or apologized afterwards.

Last night, we were at his house when Liam implied that I should have been just as angry at Rafe as I was at Gary. I thought about that long and hard. In my mind, the difference between the actions of the two men was simple.

Gary, an experienced nature photographer, had set us up in a dangerous situation without so much as a hint that we should expect the sharks to be much more aggressive than usual. We'd gone in unprepared, and when the situation got out of hand, instead of helping in any way, Gary had simply kept on filming while we were in mortal danger. And then when he found himself in trouble, he'd panicked and expected me to rescue him.

On the other hand, Rafe was a Hollywood star. As an actor, he knew getting the best shots on film quickly was always the first priority. He was a good diver, but I was better and more experienced, and I'd been his mentor as far as diving and underwater filmmaking were concerned. And when he saw me struggling, he'd immediately given me the help I needed, even though he'd kept on filming while doing so.

Rafe hadn't played any part in over-exciting the sharks. He was as much Gary's victim as I was. There'd been no malice in his continuing to film while I exited the water. He was simply doing what they paid him to do in his real job, secure in the assumption that with a minimum of help from him, I could safely deal with the danger. He was right about that, and because of that belief, he was right to continue trying to get the shot. And he had pulled me to safety when he saw I was in trouble, even while he continued filming.

To me, there was no contest. The whole debacle was Gary's fault, and he deserved firing for recklessly endangering us. I was so angry at Liam for arguing to keep him on at *Ecosphere* that I couldn't even speak coherently on the topic. We'd argued deep into the night before I went back to my own house to sleep.

The next morning, I got up super early and crept into Liam's kitchen through the open rear sliding door. I wrote a note telling him how I felt and breaking our engagement on a paper towel. Then I left the diamond engagement ring he'd given me and the note on his kitchen counter, right next to the coffee maker that I knew would be his first stop when he got up. Then I left for work well before sunrise so I wouldn't have to talk to him about it anymore. Cowardly, I know.

Now I was sitting at my desk worrying about whether I'd done the right thing when my cellphone rang. Caller ID said it was Dane Scott.

"What's up?" I said when I answered.

"I think we may have an ID on the body you and Liam found when you were kayaking. I had a call this morning from a hotel. Guest had the room for a month. She was supposed to leave the other day but she never checked out. Housekeeping finally ignored the "Do Not Disturb" tag on the door and went in. The room hadn't been touched since the last time they serviced it. Clothes, toiletries, shoes, and jewelry all still there. I'm on my way over. Do you want to join me?"

"Sure do. Where are you headed?" I needed to get out of the office, and this was the perfect way to do it.

Dane named a guest house that wasn't too far away and right on the water.

"I'll come in the *Tranquility*, prepared to search if you decide we need to. I'll meet you there." I said.

He laughed. "I'm standing on the dock next to the *Tranquility*. Can I catch a ride with you?"

We clicked off and I stuck my feet into the flip-flops under my desk. I grabbed my boat's keys and limped out the back door. My leg was killing me, and I knew I should have had Doc take a look at it right after the event in the tank. It wasn't something I should keep putting off, but Stewie was already loading full tanks into the racks on the *Tranquility*, and Dane needed me. I'd be fine.

"Are you coming too?" I asked, hoping the answer would be yes.

He shook his head. "Nope. Sorry. There's nobody on duty who can cover the dive shop."

I frowned. "Davy's not in today?"

Stewie frowned. "Haven't seen him for a few days. I thought you'd already let him go and just forgot to mention it."

I exhaled a sigh. "Put in a requisition for a new hire, will you please? We need at least one person on staff to back you up."

He gave me a mock salute and then trotted back into the dive shop.

Dane and I boarded the *Tranquility*. I checked out my gear to make sure Stewie had loaded enough tanks and everything else I might need while Dane went below and started a pot of coffee.

By the time I finished checking my gear, Dane had returned with a stainless steel RIO-branded mug of hot coffee for me. I took a couple of quick swallows, then put the lid back on top to keep the coffee from spilling while we were en route.

"Ready?" I asked Dane.

At his nod, I climbed the ladder to the flying bridge and started the engines. Dane undid the line holding us to the dock and coiled it neatly. As soon as we were free, I backed out of the slip and took off.

I headed straight out to sea for quite a long way because I wanted to avoid bucking the rip current that I knew was raging between me and our destination. I thought if I could get out far enough, I wouldn't have to fight against the current, and it would be a smoother ride for Dane, who was not a great sailor.

Up ahead, I could see the area where the rip current petered out. I could tell it was the spot because there was a small area of turbulence where I knew there was nothing nearby to cause any sort of disturbance. I made a wide, shallow turn to go around the seething water.

Just as I'd completed the turn, I saw something out of the corner of my eye.

No. No. It couldn't be.

"Dane, will you please bring me my binocs?" I called down.

He climbed the ladder and walked unsteadily to the captain's chair where I sat. "Here you go."

"Thanks." I put the strap around my neck and lifted the binoculars to my face, focused them, and shuddered. "Oh my God. There's a body over there." I pointed.

He took the binoculars and focused them. "You sure? It couldn't be just driftwood or…"

Then we both saw the person straighten up and look around. I could see the despair in the droop of her head when she realized she was still so far away from shore.

So not a body. But definitely another potential victim of the rip currents though. I vowed not to let the current take this one, whoever she was.

I picked up my microphone and keyed it to project my voice. "This is the *Tranquility*. We're not far behind you. Do you need help? Wave your arm if you do."

I'd barely finished speaking when the person's arm shot straight up and waved vigorously back and forth.

"Stay calm," I said into the mic. "We'll come to you." I positioned the *Tranquility* behind the person and set the engine speed to low—just enough power to keep us steady against the current. With each passing second, the current pushed the person closer to the boat.

I watched through the binoculars, keeping one hand on the wheel to hold the boat steady. Within a few minutes, we were close enough that I could tell the person in the water was a woman. Another second or two, and she turned to see where we were.

"That's Bari Blackthorne, Genevra's sister," I told Dane. "I'm sure of it."

He shrugged. "Doesn't matter who she is. We're gonna save her one way or another. What do you need from me?"

"How's your pitching arm?" I asked. "I want to get close enough to toss out a life ring. Then at least we'll have her and we can reel her in once we get her out of the current."

"I can toss a ring," he said. "You tell me when."

"OK. Get ready," I said. "I'll let you know."

Dane scurried down the ladder and pulled the life ring off the side of the transom. He made sure the line was securely tied around the ring, then he clambered up on the *Tranquility*'s bow, leaning against the wheelhouse while he waited for my signal.

Bari was treading water, her eyes trained intently on the *Tranquility* as the rip current brought her further from shore but closer to us. I could see she was losing strength by the second. She already looked more exhausted than she had when I first caught sight of her just a few minutes ago.

"Now," I shouted to Dane.

He tossed the ring. It landed about three feet in front of Bari.

She reached out to touch it.

Help was so close.

She missed.

Her body sank under the water. A second later, she bobbed up again, but she was barely holding her head above water.

"Reel it in. Throw it again," I shouted. "Hurry. We don't have much time. She's fading fast."

Dane pulled the line in, coiling it around his arm.

"Now," I shouted.

Again the toss was short, and the ring shot away from Bari before she could grab it.

I put the boat in neutral and ran down the ladder. I skinnied along the gunwales to the bow and grabbed the ring from Dane. "You go up and drive the boat. Put it in low and keep her to the same heading." I bent over to put on my fins.

"But I don't know how..." he started to say, but then whatever he'd been about to say was irrelevant.

I was in the water, swimming as hard as I could across the current to reach Bari with the life ring. I bit my lip, ignoring the pain in my leg. I cursed Gary and his stupid scheme all over again.

I swam until I was directly in line with her, but then I stopped trying to beat the current by swimming to beat it. All I had to do now was hold my ground and the current would bring her right to me. "Hang on, Bari. I've got this," I shouted.

We were so close I could see the wild panic in her eyes.

And the despair.

The current was merciless. I was swimming against it as hard as I could, especially given the intense pain in my shark-bitten leg. I was trying not to let it push me away from her, but the fierce current was relentless. Despite my efforts, I was losing ground.

By now, Bari wasn't swimming at all. Her arms and most of her head were below the surface. Her eyes were glazing over.

She was drowning right in front of me.

I was no more than a few feet away and yet I couldn't save her.

Yes, I could. I would. I was determined.

I waited until we were both in a trough in the waves, then I gave a mighty kick to lift myself out of the water. Bari was just out of arms reach. I tossed the ring, and it landed around her head.

"Grab the ring, Bari. Hold on," I shouted.

She was too far gone to hear me.

I wanted to pull on the life ring's line, hoping that would bring her near enough that I could lift her head above the water's surface, but I was afraid if I pulled too hard it would slide right over the top of her head and I'd lose her for good.

I thought as fast as I could, but there was no other way. If I didn't get a hold on her in the next few seconds, she was lost anyway. One way or another, I had to try.

I pulled gently on the line. I saw the ring move and bump against the back of her head. Her eyes were closed.

"C'mon, Bari. Try." I gave another tug, and she moved a little closer.

Her eyes fluttered.

"Grab the ring, Bari. C'mon. I've got you." I shouted.

One hand came out of the water and brushed against the surface.

I gave another little tug. She was still just out of my reach, but if I didn't act now it would be too late for her.

I lunged forward, throwing myself on top of the ring. My momentum knocked Bari below the surface, and she was so tired she was just letting herself sink.

I reached through the center hole of the ring and grabbed her floating hair. I lifted her up by a handful of her hair and positioned the life ring over her head. It probably hurt, but I hoped she'd thank me later. I ducked under and pulled one of her arms up through the center opening and draped it over the ring.

Now that we were together and her head was out of the water, I didn't have to fight against the current. I took a deep breath and then swam across the raging current, pushing the ring as I went. I could tell when we emerged from the rip current because we shot forward with a lurch that almost made me lose my grip on Bari.

But I didn't.

We were safely out of the worst danger.

Now I just had to get Bari on the boat so we could take her to the medical help she needed. I hoped my leg would hold out long enough for me to get her there.

I looked around for the *Tranquility*, and saw her straight ahead, about fifty yards away and just outside of the treacherous current. I began the swim toward safety, towing Bari with me.

When I was close to the boat, I shouted to Dane. "Shut her down. We need to get aboard and I don't want to take a chance on losing Bari while the engines are running. Then come down to the dive platform and help me get her aboard."

Dane did the 'hand on top of his head' okay sign and shut the engine down. Then he practically flew down the ladder to the stern.

I swam for the boat, pushing Bari ahead of me. She wasn't moving, so all I could do was try to keep her head above water as I swam. After a minute, Dane helped by pulling on the line so we made even faster progress toward safety.

Once we'd reached the dive platform, I stood on the bottom rung of the ladder, with Bari and the life ring wedged between me and the dive platform. I lifted her as high as I could, and Dane put his arms under hers and pulled her the rest of the way aboard.

I climbed up, ready to start resuscitation efforts, but Dane was already working on her. While he'd waited for us to cross the final stretch of open water, he'd pulled the emergency oxygen out of the boat's first aid kit. By the time I stood next to him, shivering and exhausted, he had the cannula inserted in her nose. While I watched, he turned her on her left side to help her clear her lungs.

I scurried up the ladder to the flying bridge and started the engines, turned *Tranquility* back toward RIO, and called ahead to let Doc know we were on our way.

It was only as I pulled the *Tranquility* into her slip at RIO that the full enormity of what had happened sank in. I'd gone back into that hellish current, after swearing I would never do that again. I thought I'd done it to save Bari because I knew her, but I realized I'd have done exactly the same thing no matter who was in the water.

I'm good in emergencies, and when I can, I save people. But I hadn't just jumped into that awful current willy-nilly without thinking about what I was going to do and whether I had a good chance of pulling off the rescue safely. I thought it through, but I thought fast. I'd had a plan.

It's what I did the other day when I jumped into the tank to save Gary, even though I knew the tank was full of frenzied sharks. I knew I could save him, and I knew he'd probably die or at least sustain serious injuries if I didn't rescue him. I'd balanced the risk to me against saving his life, and his life outweighed the risk to me.

It's also what I'd done a few years ago when a silky shark was attacking a team member. We were diving without tanks, and back then, I knew there was no way I could save him. If I'd tried to intervene, we'd have both died that day. He wasn't a nice man, but still, my inability to save him sometimes ate at me late at night when I couldn't sleep.

It's who I am. Yet the realization that I would always act to save someone when I could didn't stop me from shaking uncontrollably when I remembered being in that awful rip current again.

I relived the terrifying moments from the other day when the down draft had kept me from reaching the surface when I was doing the search. When I realized I couldn't even swim out of it crosswise. I remembered the fear when I'd rescued Emma. And when I realized how awful it must have been for the women who had needlessly lost their lives to that unbeatable current.

By this time, we were back at RIO, and I pulled into my slip. Doc's team was already wheeling Bari away while Dane was still tying off the line.

My hands were frozen on the wheel. I don't know how long I stood there before Dane came up and draped a sweatshirt over my shoulders. "C'mon," he said. "She's going to be fine, and right now, I think you need Doc as much as Bari does." He took my hand and led me to the ladder. He helped me down, and then walked me all the way to the infirmary where he turned me over to Doc.

Chapter 32
Recovery

Bari was already asleep when Dane and I entered the infirmary, so Doc was able to give me her full attention. Dane left as soon as she started her exam. I figured he'd gone to get Maddy and Newton.

Doc examined my leg and gave me a painkiller. The shark bite the other day had left me with a massive bruise and a lot of deep pain, even though the skin was intact.

"I'm surprised you could swim against that current with your leg in such bad shape," she said.

I shrugged my shoulders. I did what needed doing.

Doc gave me a sour look and asked me to change into clean, dry scrubs and while I was doing that, she made me a cup of coffee from the pod-type machine in the nearby waiting room. She called the café and asked them to send up a sandwich and a plate of my favorite cookies, and then she blew dry my hair, which was still soaking wet from the rescue.

By the time I finished my sandwich, my eyes were barely open, so I didn't protest when she told me to lie down. She covered me with a soft, warm blanket. That was the last thing I remember until the next morning.

The smell of hot coffee woke me shortly after dawn. Liam was there, holding a stainless steel mug and a warm banana nut muffin. I smiled at him and reached out for the mug.

He waited until I'd taken a couple of sips before he spoke. "I'm sorry. I didn't know the whole story, and I should have asked you for your side of things before doing anything. Rafe read me the riot act last night, and he was right to. Gary's stupid idea endangered you both, and what's worse, he didn't even tell you what he was doing so you could make your own decision about the risk."

I took another sip of coffee. "And…?"

He flushed. "And I think he's learned his lesson. He's agreed to leave things as they were and never to interfere in your work again. If—and this is the big condition—if you agree."

I just looked at him, too tired for this discussion. I'd had several really difficult days in a row, and my first inclination was to tell Gary to forget about ever working with me again. And to tell Liam I'd truly meant we were over when I'd left his engagement ring behind.

But the sensible part of my brain—the part that speaks in Ray's voice— said, "Wait. Think it through."

I handed Liam the empty mug. "I'll let you know what I decide." Then I snuggled back into the hospital bed and immediately went back to sleep.

The next time I woke up, Bari, Genevra, Doc, and Dane were all sitting beside my bed, watching me sleep. I jumped when I opened my eyes and saw them. "You guys, that is so creepy. What are you doing?"

"We need to talk," said Dane. "Is she ready?"

I nodded slightly, and Doc said, "Yes, I believe so. But you don't need me for this, so I'll leave you to it."

I sat up and swung my legs over the side of the bed. "What time is it?"

Genevra handed me a coffee. "It's already tomorrow, so don't even worry about the time. Bari needs to talk to us."

"You're okay?" I asked Bari.

She nodded. "Thanks to you."

I stifled a yawn. "That's good. So what do we need to talk about."

She looked uneasy, and she cast her eyes toward Dane. "Is it illegal to swim with the signs posted on the beach? The ones about the rip current."

"Not illegal. Just stupid." He smiled to soften the words. "Can you tell us what you were thinking?"

She bit her lip. "Someone lured me into swimming, tricked me into going out too far, and then left me to fend for myself in that current. If you hadn't come by, I'd have drowned for sure. I think that's exactly what that man wanted to have happen."

"I believe you," I said. "Did he tell you his name?"

"No, but I remember what he looked like. He had brown hair and he was wearing brown shorts and a blue t-shirt with the RIO logo on it. That must mean he works here, right?"

"Not necessarily," I said. "We sell those items in the gift shop and the dive shop. And they sell them in several stores around town too."

Dane broke in. "Anything else you remember? Height, eye color, build? Tattoos or other identifying marks? A name?"

She shook her head. "No, sorry. It's all pretty much a blur."

"Would you recognize him if you saw a picture?" Dane asked.

She shook her head. "I'm not sure. I think the trauma of nearly drowning wiped the details of our conversation right out of my head. I'm sorry."

"Don't be," I said. "It doesn't matter. The important thing is you're safe, and maybe in a few days you'll remember more. But even if you don't, no worries. We'll find him soon enough."

Neither Dane nor I wanted to tell her exactly how lucky she'd been. Not every woman caught by that current had been as lucky.

Chapter 33
The Face of a Charity

BARI HAD BEEN DISCHARGED from the infirmary, so she and Genevra went off to get lunch while Dane and I sat in the infirmary's comfortable waiting room and talked about the diabolical murder scheme.

Dane started. "Just so you know, we have an ID on the unidentified woman you found while you and Liam were kayaking. Name was Stella St. Francis. A would-be actress from LA. Her roommate back home got worried when she didn't return on schedule. Said she was here hoping to meet Rafe Cummings and thinking maybe she'd get him to cast her in one of his movies."

My heart filled with sorrow. "Broken dreams. So sad."

Dane looked pensive. "Yep. It's a pity. She was a lovely young woman. And you know, even if we figure out who has been luring these people out into the danger zone, I'm not sure we could ever prove it was an intentional murder."

He rubbed his chin. "There's no evidence he ever touched them. Nobody saw or heard him tell the victims it would be okay to swim in the current. Heck, if it wasn't for you saving Bari, we wouldn't even know for sure there was someone involved in luring people into swimming into the current."

"That's true. Maybe we should put some decoys on the beach. See if anyone approaches them. I could do it."

Dane scowled at me. "You could, but you won't. I won't let you. You've done enough, and I'm not sending you out into that deadly current again. Besides, your mother would kill me if I let you do it."

I laughed. "She sure would."

I looked at the dive watch on my wrist. "I'm still not entirely certain about what day it is, but I think you have a charity event to attend tonight, don't you?"

"Yikes. I do. Thanks for the reminder. Will I see you there? Are you up to going?"

"Of course I'll be there. Free food and puppies? Just try to keep me away."

The shelter organization had recently named Dane the "face" of the island's shelter for lost and abandoned dogs. He'd made a few PSA ads imploring people not to leave their pets behind when they leave the island. His handsome face had even been on a few posters hanging around town. There was a fundraiser tonight, and Dane was the keynote speaker.

He departed to get ready for the event, and I left the infirmary. I stopped by my office where I had a blue linen short suit hanging behind the door for emergency dress-up needs. I took the clothes and then strolled to the locker room, where I showered and dressed for the event this evening. Luckily, it wasn't a formal event, or getting ready would have been a much longer process.

I was still annoyed at Liam, but I sent him a text telling him I'd meet him at the fundraiser. Then I walked out to the parking lot, where I bumped into Rafe and Tate. They were both headed to the benefit, so we decided to drive over together.

The goal of the charity event was to raise money for the pet shelter and to find homes for some of the pets who lived there. Unlike many Caribbean islands, the Caymans don't have a big feral pet problem. Occasionally we have a cat or a dog left behind when their owners lose track of them and have a flight to catch. Most of those animals soon find a good home, and they're kept in a very nice shelter until they do. In fact, we have more free-range chickens than we do abandoned cats or dogs.

And we even have more iguanas. We have lots of iguanas.

We arrived late, just as Dane finished his presentation, and people crowded around him, asking questions, congratulating him, or handing him envelopes containing their donations. Dane was smiling, so I assumed his presentation had gone well.

Now came the best part of the evening, as far as I was concerned. Volunteers led the leashed pets out so they could mingle with the crowd. I love dogs, but I'd never had one as a pet. Ray and Maddy had explained dogs don't do well on research vessels, and as a kid I'd spent at least six months of the year on RIO's research vessel *Omega*.

Even as an adult, my life was too chaotic to expect a pet to adjust. At least Chico and Henrietta could take care of themselves, and I thought regretfully that they might be the only pets I'd ever have. My lifestyle was just too hectic for me to add a dog to the mix.

Rafe and I were standing together near the podium where Dane had been speaking. The cutest dog I'd ever seen pulled her handler over to us and sat at our feet, smiling up at us while her tail wagged at the speed of light.

She was tiny—just a few inches tall, although she had a long dachshund body. Her curly fur was a beautiful reddish blonde color. As though we'd rehearsed it, Rafe and I sat down and reached for her at the same time.

Her handler said, "This is Penny. She's a young, wire-haired dachshund. Not quite two. Her owners were heartbroken to leave her behind."

"I can see why," I said, burying my face in her fur. "I can't imagine ever letting this little sweetheart go."

Penny gave me a tiny lick, then she gave Rafe one too.

Her handler said, "Her original owners declined to come back for her or to pay to have her flown to them. She's available for adoption."

"I love her," I said kissing her little button nose.

"We'll take her," said Rafe.

I looked at him sadly. "Neither one of us leads a lifestyle conducive to dog ownership. I'm away a lot on photo shoots, and you're away a lot on movie sets."

"But we love her, and she loves us," he said. "She's meant to be ours. We'll make it work. She can stay with you when I'm away filming, and with me when you're off shooting your documentaries. In between, we'll share her. And if we're ever stuck with conflicting schedules, we have loads of friends who can watch her for a few days."

He looked at her handler. "We'll take her," he repeated firmly.

Penny rolled over on her back, showing me her soft belly covered with downy, almost-white fur. I gave her a tentative rub, and then I nodded. "Yes. We'll take her."

There was a fair amount of paperwork involved in the adoption, plus at least a half hour convincing Penny's handler that we really could take care of her despite our lifestyles. I wrote a very sizable check to the shelter, and Rafe matched it with a check of his own.

Eventually, I motioned to Dane to join us. "Would you please tell Penny's handler that Rafe and I will be excellent puppy parents. You know we'll take good care of her."

Dane looked startled. "You and Rafe?" he asked. "Not you and Liam?"

"Yes. Rafe and I want her, and we've agreed to share her. C'mon, Dane, you know us. You can be sure we'll love her and take care of her and never let anything bad happen to her. Please tell them to let us adopt her."

I could see him pondering—but only for a millisecond—before he turned to the handler. "I can't think of anyone in the world who would make better pet owners. Please let them have this dog. If they ever need a dog sitter, she can always stay with me." He looked at the tag attached to her collar. "Please let them adopt Penny."

The handler smiled. "Okay. I'm convinced. Since Dane vouched for you, she's yours."

Chapter 34
Puppy Love

Rafe and I were ecstatic about adopting Penny. The shelter team told us they'd need an hour or so to process the paperwork and give her a final medical checkup, so we borrowed Tate's car and rushed out to the pet supply store in Camana Bay to buy two of everything we'd need for her to be comfortable and safe, regardless of which of us she stayed with.

We bought her two collars, two leashes, two beds, two bags of food, two car seats, and two of every treat and toy they had in her size, which was very, very tiny. By the time we finished, we were practically staggering under the weight of our purchases. We dumped the whole pile of bags in the trunk of Tate's car and sped off to pick up our new pet. We couldn't wait to make Penny ours.

Dane was still at the shelter, helping some of the event attendees pick out the perfect pet from the few that were still unadopted. Tate was at a corner table waiting for us, leaning back on his chair with his long legs stretched out into the aisle.

My heart plummeted when I saw all the people leaving with their newly adopted pets. I was terrified that someone might have given Penny away to someone else by mistake.

I already loved her. I couldn't lose her.

We rushed up to Dane. "Where's Penny?"

He smiled. "I believe that's her heading your way right now."

Rafe and I both whirled around. Maddy was walking toward us with Penny on a leash. The shelter had given the pup a bath, and she had a jaunty pink bow on the top of her head. Although it was curly and a little bit wild, they'd brushed her thick wiry fur until it gleamed. As soon as Penny caught sight of us, she strained forward on her leash.

Maddy laughed as she walked Penny over. "She already knows who she belongs to."

Rafe and I fell to our knees and scooped the little dog up for hugs and kisses. She rolled right over for us to rub her belly. The poor little thing seemed starved for affection.

The shelter administrator came out of her office. "She may need to go outside. It's been a while, and this has been a big day for her."

Maddy was standing next to Dane, holding his hand. "Fin, we have something we want to talk to you about, so if you could come back in once Penny has done her thing I'd appreciate it," she said.

"It's okay," said Rafe. "You can talk now. Tate and I can take her out and bring her back when she's ready."

"Thank you." Maddy smiled at him. "We won't be more than a few minutes."

"No problem," he said. "This little beauty can keep me entertained for hours." He winked at me as he said it, and I knew he wasn't only referring to our new dog. He took the leash from Maddy's hand, and walked out of the shelter looking like he was walking on air.

"She's very cute," Maddy said. "And well behaved." Her eyes followed Rafe as he showed Penny how to navigate the revolving door. "You've chosen well."

I had the feeling Maddy wasn't only talking about my new pet.

Dane raised their clasped hands and kissed the back of Maddy's hand. "We have something we wanted to tell you, but we'd like you to keep it a secret for a while."

"Sure. What's up?" I asked. His solemn air was making me nervous.

Maddy's face broke out in a huge grin. "Dane and I are

engaged. We're going to get married as soon as we can. But we want to keep it a secret until after Oliver and Genevra's wedding. We don't want to steal their thunder."

I reached out to hug her. "That's wonderful news. I'm so happy for you both." I turned to Dane and kissed his cheek. "Congratulations. It's been a long time coming, but you hung in there."

"Your mother is well worth the wait," he said with a happy smile.

I thought about whether I should tell them that Liam and I had broken off our always iffy engagement, but then I thought better of it. I didn't want to tell them and spoil their joy, and they'd figure it out soon enough anyway.

Now that I thought about it, I was glad we weren't engaged anymore. He'd been extremely angry that I'd fired Gary without consulting him. And I'd been beyond furious that he hadn't immediately backed me up. Even without the issue of his other career, I couldn't see a way forward for us.

I sighed. After all this time, we were really over. We no longer seemed to be able to talk through our differences. When things in our world were going well, we got along beautifully. But any little hiccup sent us right to the brink, every time. That couldn't be good.

While I'd been ruminating about my relationship, Maddy and Dane had been chattering about their own wedding plans. "And of course, you'll be my maid of honor," Maddy said.

I brought my attention back with difficulty. "Thank you. I'm honored."

"Now I have a question for you," Dane said. "Newton and I have become very good friends. Do you think he'd be willing to take on best man duties?"

I pasted a smile on my face. "Probably. But you'd have to ask him yourself," I said.

I knew Newton would agree to sever his own arm if Maddy asked him to, and I knew being in their wedding party would be a request on just about the same level of sacrifice. But I also knew he'd do it if he thought it would make her happy.

Newton loved her that much. I could only hope she came to her senses and talked Dane out of asking Newton to be in the wedding party before Dane got around to asking him.

"I've got to run," I said. "Rafe and Penny are waiting for me. But I'm so happy for you both. Let me know when it's time for the big reveal."

"You'll be the first to know," Maddy said.

We'd agreed that Penny would spend her first few nights at Rafe's house, because I was still exhausted from rescuing Emma, Bari, Gary, Rafe, and myself. It had been a tough few days. Tate drove me home, and Rafe and I split up our purchases so I had everything I'd need to keep Penny safe and comfortable when she was at my place. Then they headed to Rafe's home in Hell.

When I unlocked my front door, carrying bags of dog toys, blankets, treats, and food, Liam was sitting on my couch with his feet up on the coffee table, reading a book.

"What's all this then?" he asked when I started unpacking the dog paraphernalia. "Are we pet sitting?"

"Not exactly. Rafe and I adopted a dog. She's a wire-haired miniature dachshund puppy, with red-blonde curly fur, and she's adorable. Her name's Penny. We're going to share her."

He put down his magazine. "You and Rafe? You two adopted a dog together? It didn't occur to you to check with me?"

I shook my head. "No, sorry. It didn't actually. We were at the fundraiser for the shelter, and when they let the dogs out, she came running right over to us like she knew she was ours. Neither one of us can care for a dog full-time, but we figured we could synchronize our schedules so one of us would always be around to care for her. Dane promised to take her if we were ever in a bind. Or worst case, Newton could take her for a day or so."

"You still should have checked with me first." He snapped his magazine open to the page he'd been reading.

"Then you probably should have been at the fundraiser. We could have discussed it." I was still angry with Liam about the way he'd handled the situation with Gary, and it was spilling over into this conversation.

He looked over the top of his magazine. "It's okay. You can have a puppy if you want one."

"I didn't ask for your permission," I said.

I walked through the house to my home office and shut the door. I was too upset to work, so I mostly paced from one end of the small room to the other.

About an hour later, Liam knocked on the door. "I made dinner. Do you have time to eat?"

"Not hungry," I said.

I heard a deep sigh and then there was a long silence. The sounds of Chico and Henrietta clucking were all that broke the stillness until the clang of a gate closing told me Liam had gone through the back fence to his own house.

Chapter 35
Morning

The next morning, we were both pretending there was nothing wrong between us. As usual, Liam woke me up with a cup of hot coffee and a warm muffin. I dressed quickly and ate the muffin in his car on the way to RIO.

We had a senior leadership staff meeting scheduled for the first thing this morning, so we couldn't be late. After helping ourselves to more coffee from the conference room sideboard, we sat in our usual side-by-side chairs.

Although Rafe wasn't technically part of the staff, he was on the board of directors so he attended the meetings whenever he was in town. To my delight, he'd brought Penny with him this morning.

She raced across the conference room as soon as she saw me, barking her delight. I picked her up and she licked my face. I melted all over again. Surely now Liam would see how amazing she was.

Obviously, I'd had to adopt her. Nobody in their right mind could let such a little sweetheart go, and I wondered how her original owners could have been so cold-hearted that they left her behind.

Rafe pulled up a chair beside mine, and we spent most of the meeting giving Penny belly rubs. Liam watched us without saying anything. When the meeting adjourned, he finally relented and scratched under her chin.

"She is cute," he said grudgingly.

"She needs a walk," Rafe said. "Let's touch base later." He put her down and headed toward the exit to RIO's back lawn.

Liam and I walked down the hall to my office without speaking. I expected him to bring up the engagement ring I'd left on his kitchen counter the other night, but that wasn't what he had in mind.

Liam closed the door behind us. "I still wish you'd discussed this with me before you made the commitment to adopt Penny. You know if you wanted a dog, we could have adopted one together."

"Maybe we could have," I said, "but as usual, you weren't there. You're never there. And I wanted this dog. Exactly and only this dog. We're soul mates."

Liam rolled his eyes. "I see. I was under the impression you and I were soulmates."

"So was I," I said. "At one point."

"What's that supposed to mean?" He sounded angry, and he stood very close, looming over me.

"It means exactly what it sounds like it means." I sat at my desk. "I don't understand what you're so upset about. You love dogs. Or at least you did when you were a kid. Remember Cherry?"

He nodded. "Of course I remember Cherry. She was a great dog. But our situation is totally different than the conditions when I was a kid. Back then I had a stay at home family and we all pitched in to care for Cherry. You and I both travel a lot, and it's hard enough to coordinate just our two schedules, but now we have to factor in Rafe's travel plans too. And you know how he is. He'll be hanging around at our place all the time. It just seems too complicated."

I stared at him for a moment. "Are you upset because I didn't discuss it with you first, or is it because I adopted Penny with Rafe?"

"Yes," he said. "Both."

"Are you jealous of my friendship with Rafe?"

"No." He flushed. "Yes."

"So let me ask you something. If Rafe soaked my dive suit in shark bait and sent me off to dive in a tank full of hungry sharks without telling me, what would you do?"

He gave a small, shamefaced smile. "I'd kill him."

"And if I disappeared for weeks at a time without a word, how would you feel?"

He shuffled his feet. "I'd be upset, and I'd be worried sick."

"If I adopted Penny with Gary, would you be this upset?"

"No, of course not. Gary's my best friend."

I'd always said Theresa was my best friend, but I realized that somehow, over the short time I'd known him, Rafe had become an even better friend than Theresa. But I thought better of saying that to Liam, especially given the mood he was in right now.

"Rafe is my friend," I said, leaving out the 'best' part.

He didn't say anything, so I continued. "Okay. Last question. If I expected you to ask my permission before you did something important to you, what would that say to you about our relationship?"

Now he looked stubborn. He didn't really answer the question, just repeated his complaint. "We should have discussed it before you adopted a dog. I would have given you permission."

I stared at him. "That's the problem right there. You know I don't actually need your permission, right? We're both independent, autonomous people, aren't we? Do you ask me for permission before you make decisions? You don't, even when they affect me."

He turned and left my office without another word. I switched on my Mac and got down to work, wondering if I'd just said goodbye to my heart.

Half an hour later, Liam walked in and slid a plate of chocolate chip cookies in front of me. "I thought about what you said. You're right. You don't need my permission to do anything you want to do, but if we're going to be real partners in our marriage, we should at least discuss things."

I nodded. "You're right too. I'll promise to discuss anything that may affect us both if you'll promise to communicate at least once a day no matter where you are."

He sighed deeply. "I've told you there are times that might put my life at risk."

"Then maybe we should discuss that," I said. "I don't believe I was consulted about that decision."

He laughed like he thought I was kidding, but I wasn't.

I thought it would be best if we let a few days go by so both our tempers could die down, and then we could calmly hash everything out. For now, I'd act like it was life as usual.

"Feel like a dive? I need some serenity in my life," I said.

I smiled to show him that wasn't a dig. I genuinely just needed a dive. Underwater is always where I'm happiest. The ocean just seems to wash away all my troubles, leaving me serene and unruffled when I emerge.

"Love it," he said. "Let's go."

Chapter 36
Dive at Three Sisters

Liam and I strolled out RIO's back door, heading toward the *Tranquility*. I didn't mind that we almost always took my boat. I love the *Tranquility*. We swerved off the path to pick up our gear from the wooden lockers next to the dive shop. We each slung our heavy gear bags over our shoulders and then picked up two fresh tanks each just in case we had enough time for a second dive.

We headed for Three Sisters, a fascinating wall dive along the East End. Because much of the dive is at eighty feet or below, it's beyond the depths allowable for divers with only basic open water certifications. And since it's only accessible by boat and has few novice divers as visitors, the site is in excellent condition.

The reef here starts at between sixty and eighty feet, and the most impressive part of the dive is the three huge coral pinnacles located at the edge of the drop off at about eighty feet. They merge with the steeply sloping wall at around 100 feet, and the area around them is rife with lush coral and abundant sea life.

We swam to the famous swim-through that starts at about sixty-five feet of depth. It's a wide tunnel that drops the diver out on the sheer vertical wall at about 108 feet. Liam went first, and I followed behind. When he emerged, he waited along the wall for me to exit, and then we began exploring the multiple cuts and channels containing plenty of crevices and tiny grottos that make great homes for sea life.

As we explored each cut, we moved slowly, admiring the coral, and looking for cleaning stations, which are very common on this site. At the first one we came across, we saw a line consisting of a dog snapper and a tiger grouper, both waiting patiently for their turn with the gobies working diligently on their current client—a silvery barracuda.

A few feet farther on, we found another cleaning station with no waiting line, so Liam held out his hand and the cleaner shrimp removed a few hangnails. I smiled at him as we watched their careful work.

It was time to head back toward the boat, so we began our leisurely ascent. As we topped the wall we saw a school of blue chromis, a few black durgon, and a pair of brightly colored Spanish hogfish hanging around the reef. We finished our dive with the usual three minute safety stop at fifteen feet. Instead of hanging in one spot under the boat, we stayed over the reef at fifteen feet, swimming in slow circles over the coral, looking for interesting sights.

We lucked out and noticed a trumpet fish hiding in the sea grass and a southern stingray soaring gracefully toward the wall. We also saw several parrotfish, which are a great favorite of Liam's.

When the safety stop was over, he boarded first, and I climbed the ladder as soon as he'd cleared the platform. He took my fins, which he tossed under the bench along the gunwales. Once I was on deck. I walked over to the bench and sat down, fitting my empty tank into one of the racks behind me. Then I unbuckled the BCD vest and went to find something to drink.

I handed Liam a mugful of lemonade and held out a small plastic dish of cut fruit. He selected a piece of mango, which he popped in his mouth before he leaned back to soak up some sun.

I sat on the bench along the other side of the *Tranquility*, sipped from my mug and ate a section of a small tangerine. I drank the whole mug of lemonade. We still hadn't said a word to each other.

Liam sighed and broke the ice. "This site is great. We should come here more often."

I smiled. "We can do that. We could also do a second dive right here right now if you have time."

I could still feel some tension in my shoulders and my throat from our earlier fight, and I recognized that the feeling had been occurring more and more frequently for the last several months. Even though I'd been feeling super stressed for a long time, I hoped another dive would work its magic and complete my transformation back into a calm and focused person.

Liam looked at his dive watch. "Okay. I guess I could squeeze in one more dive. But then I have to get to work."

We waited out our surface interval, munching on fruit. I was chatting idly about Oliver's and Genevra's upcoming wedding while we switched over our gear to fresh tanks. I was excited about the upcoming wedding simply because I loved both Oliver and Genevra.

Genevra's parents were no longer alive, and she didn't have any relatives except her sister Bari. Since she'd known him for so long, Genevra had asked Liam to walk her down the aisle. He'd agreed, and she'd been ecstatic.

But his silence made it clear he wasn't interested in talking about the wedding, so once again we stopped talking completely. The silence was only a little bit uncomfortable, because after all, we were on a boat in the tropics. How bad could anything be?

But it felt bad, and I sensed the mood getting more tense the longer we sat there.

I looked at my dive computer. "Interval's over. You good?"

He checked his own computer. "Yep. Let's go."

I grabbed my fins from under the bench and then shrugged into my BCD. Liam geared up as quickly as I did, and we both went to the dive platform. We agreed on our dive plan while doing our buddy checks, and then we did simultaneous giant stride entries from opposite sides of the platform and immediately began our descent.

This time we skipped the swim through tunnel. It's spectacular, but we didn't want to go as deep on this second dive. We headed toward the middle pinnacle and swam around it, checking out the abundant variety of sea life that made this beautiful spot its home.

I peered into one crevice and found a porcupine fish staring back at me. These puffers are nocturnal creatures who hide out in the coral during the day. I think I startled this one when I appeared in his doorway, because he immediately puffed himself up to at least twice his original size.

I smiled at the sight and moved on so as not to cause him undue distress. A little further on I spotted a Caribbean spiny lobster peeking out from under a tiny overhang, his antennas waving in the mild current. I checked him out as I passed by, but I didn't linger at his front door.

I turned to see where Liam was, and he was facing out into the blue, watching a hammerhead pass by. The shark was moving so quickly that I barely caught a glimpse of him framed between the edges of the coral. Liam hung there for several seconds after the shark passed before turning to follow me.

I continued rising slowly until I crested the drop off at about sixty-five feet. We passed over a cluster of anemones waving gracefully in the current. Nearby, a few feather duster worms withdrew their frothy fronds when they sensed our presence. I stopped, hovering in place and barely breathing, hoping they'd get over their fears. My patience paid off when a few minutes later, they whirled their fronds open again, apparently convinced that there was no danger.

Well, they were right about that. They had nothing to fear from me.

I swam slowly over the top of the reef, admiring all the tiny residents. I saw a butterfly hamlet, a midnight parrotfish, a rock beauty, a Bermuda chub, a couple of black jacks, and a horse-eye jack.

Their serenity and the caress of the ocean water worked its magic, and I was much calmer than I'd been at the start of the dive.

Liam and I still needed to work through our issues, but I felt that at least now I could have a conversation without feeling attacked, or worse yet being the attacker. I inhaled deeply, and then blew out the air through my regulator.

All would be well. It had to be.

Chapter 37
Missing

I PILOTED the *Tranquility* back to RIO's marina. Liam and I didn't talk for the entire trip, but maybe that was because of the roar of the wind and the engines.

Sure. That was the reason.

Liam tied us off on the cleat at the end of my slip, and then we gathered our gear and our empty tanks and started the walk back to land. I missed the peaceful feeling of being underwater, and I could already feel the tension creeping back into my shoulders.

We had just reached the end of the dock when a middle aged woman approached. She seemed highly agitated, wringing her hands and biting her lip. She was sweating and her hair hung wild. Her eyes darted in all directions, and she kept twisting her head around.

"Excuse me," she said. "Are you Fin Fleming?" Her voice was high and stressed. Or maybe she was just overly excited.

If she was excited to see me, it meant she was most probably a fan. Inwardly I groaned, but I pasted a pleasant smile on my face exactly as Ray and Maddy had taught me all those years ago. "Yes, I am. May I help you?"

She nodded. "I hope so. My daughter Jade was supposed to meet me here for lunch two hours ago, but she isn't here and I can't find her. They told me at the restaurant that they saw her earlier with your employee, Austin. Do you know where I can find him? I'm very worried about her, and I'm hoping maybe he'll have some idea of where she went."

I felt a chill go down my spine at her words. We'd had several women taken by a gang of traffickers a while ago. The women had seemingly disappeared without a trace, but luckily, Liam and I were able to recover them safely before anyone hurt them badly. The idea that the bad guys might be targeting RIO again terrified me.

I took in a deep breath to try to regain my equilibrium and looked over the woman's shoulder toward Ray's Place. Austin's brother Noah Gibb was behind the bar. When he caught my eye, he shrugged to let me know he had no idea where either Jade or Austin were, or even if they were together.

Oh, man. This could not be good.

What if she'd gone swimming and the rip current caught her? I didn't want to deal with another drowning victim. That was worse than an abduction, but either one would be terrible.

"I'll take care of your gear while you deal with this," Liam said. He picked up my BCD and gear bag and carried them over to the rinse tank outside the dive shop.

Meanwhile, I drew in a deep breath, trying to hide my own fears at her words. "I'm sorry," I said. "I believe it's Austin's day off today. I don't know where he might be, but if you can hang on for a moment, I'll call him and see if Jade's with him or if he knows where she is. Meanwhile, why don't you wait over there in the shade and have something to drink. Whatever you want. It'll be on the house." I gave Noah the signal we'd worked out for free drinks, and he nodded.

I turned away and pulled my cellphone out of my pocket to hit the speed dial number for Austin. The call went directly to voice mail. I left a short message asking him to call me back and then looked to see where Jade's mother was.

The woman hadn't gone very far. She was sitting right in the middle of the recreation area, very close to the bar, and loudly sobbing. Several patrons in Ray's Place were staring at her. I wanted to talk to her without it becoming a sideshow, so I needed to calm her down and then move someplace more private.

Liam had finished rinsing our gear, so he and I joined her at the table.

I sat beside her. "I'm sorry. Austin didn't answer his phone. He must be tied up."

To my consternation, the woman started to cry even louder. "Please help me. Jade's only fifteen, but she looks a lot older. And she's one of those social media influencers with a ton of followers. People are always trying to get her to go someplace with them or try something she's too young to be doing. I'm so afraid for her. You have to help me find her before something terrible happens." Her voice was rising and falling in a pitiable wail.

Liam's always good at helping people in a panic. He reached out and touched her hand. "Don't worry. I'm sure she's fine. Teenagers lose track of time. They like to push the rules their parents lay down for them, but it's usually not a cause for concern."

"Austin is very responsible. If she's with him, I know he'll take very good care of her. And even if they're not together, you probably don't need to worry. No matter what she's into, Grand Cayman is a very safe place."

His voice was soft and low, very soothing. Jade's mother threw herself into his arms, sobbing against his broad chest. He put his arms around her and patted her back, murmuring words of comfort in a soft soothing voice.

Since Liam is so much better at being nice and showing concern than I am, I left him to it. I walked over to the bar and asked Noah for a glass of water, an iced tea, and a lemonade because I didn't know what she'd prefer. Liam had walked the woman to one of the shadier and more secluded tables near the beach to get her away from the gawkers at the bar, and I brought the drinks back there with me.

I put the tray on the table. "Which would you prefer?" I asked her. She picked up the iced tea and quickly drained the large mug.

By now, even though her tears were still wet on her cheeks, she had gained at least some control. She sat back on the bench. "Thank you," she said. "Now what can you do to find my daughter?"

"Have you tried calling her?" I asked.

She nodded. "Of course. No answer. And that's totally unlike her. She practically lives on that phone. She documents everything she does and everywhere she goes for her followers."

Now she sighed, long and deep. "I don't really understand why, but she makes a fortune through her endorsements. She's already banked enough to pay for her entire college education. She owns an expensive car that she's not old enough to drive yet. She donates tons of clothes, shoes, handbags, jewelry, and designer makeup that she's never even used. And yet, I still don't even really grasp the concept of influencer."

She lifted her head and looked at Liam. "Do you?"

He raised his broad shoulders in a shrug. "I know what it is, but I can't for the life of me figure out why the job exists. Sorry." He smiled kindly. "But I'm glad Jade is successful at it if that's what she wants to do, Mrs…?"

"Call me Cecily. And I'm Jade Abby's mom, of course."

Liam smiled at her. "Nice to meet you, Cecily," he said.

He handed her the icy glass of lemonade, the sides beaded with condensation from the hot sun. "I have an idea."

She sat up straighter, hanging on his every word. "What? I'll do anything to find her and make sure she's safe."

"I know you would," he said. "Do you have a picture, by any chance? We can ask the staff if anybody has seen her."

She opened an app on her phone and shoved it into Liam's face. "See, that's her. Have you seen her?" The girl in the photo was lovely, with bright green eyes and a stunning smile.

"See those amazing green eyes?" Cecily said. "That's why I named her Jade. It just seemed to fit."

"Wow. She's really striking," he said before handing the phone to me for a look. "I'm sure I'd remember her if I'd seen her."

I peered down at the phone, tilting the screen so I could see the image despite the bright sunlight. If the photographer had used a filter when they'd taken that picture, I couldn't tell. The girl in the photo was indeed beautiful.

Her unusual eyes glowed with a brilliant green fire. Her hair and makeup were perfect, and her pose was seductive. She wore the tiniest string bikini I'd ever seen. A single one of my socks would have had more fabric to it than the entire suit she wore. I would never have guessed she was only fifteen years old because to me she looked at least twenty-five. Practically my own age.

I handed the phone back to Cecily and shook my head. "I haven't seen her either and I'm sure I'd remember her if I had. I'm going to call a friend on the police force and ask him to put out a BOLO alert."

Cecily began to sob again. I hit the speed dial button for DS Dane Scott, and stepped aside so I could hear him over Cecily's wails, which were getting increasingly louder. But he didn't answer, so I had to leave a voice mail.

Liam sat beside Cecily and took her hand. "I have another idea that might help too. Fin has a really good friend who's pretty famous. I'm sure if she asked him nicely, he'd agree to call Jade. If she sees this person's name in her caller ID, I bet for sure she'd pick up."

I knew he was referring to Rafe, but I also knew Rafe wouldn't want his personal phone number in the hands of a fifteen year old social media influencer. I also knew Rafe would do it anyway just because he's a nice guy. I smiled hoping Liam would be able to keep Cecily calm while I talked to Rafe.

"Let me track him down," I said. I wondered if I could catch Rafe before he and Tate left for home. The board meeting had ended hours ago, so they might be long gone.

Luckily, they were still here because they'd bumped into Chaunsey, who'd come to RIO to have lunch with Benjamin. The four friends were sitting on two couches in the lobby. Tate and Chaun were picking at the crumbs of their cheeseburgers and potato chips, but Rafe and Benjamin had empty salad bowls in front of them. As always, their dietary discipline impressed me.

But right now, I didn't have time to tease them about it as I usually did. I was on a mission. We needed to find Jade before something awful happened to her.

I rushed over to tell Rafe what I wanted. As I suspected would be the case, he wasn't crazy about the idea of letting his private phone number get into the wild, but he agreed to make the call, just in case Jade really was in some kind of trouble.

When he pulled his phone out, Chaun said, "Put that away. Use my phone. I can fix it so it hides my number and shows your name in caller ID. Your privacy will be perfectly protected, and even if someone somehow manages to crack my encryption, all they'll get will be my number, not yours." He stared down at his lap and sighed. "They most likely won't have any idea who I am, and even if they did, they wouldn't want my number anyway."

Looking relieved, Rafe nodded and put his phone back in his pocket while Chaun's fingers moved like lightning on his own device.

"All set," he said. He handed the phone to Rafe. "Caller ID will show as Rafe Cummings. I blocked the number. They won't even be able to tell where you're calling from. You're as safe as you can possibly be."

"Thanks, Chaun," said Rafe. "You're amazing. After this is over, you'll have to teach me how to do that. It might come in handy again someday."

Chaun looked at him with the patronizing face that tech geniuses use when talking to people who are not tech geniuses. "Sure," he said. "Or just call me anytime and I'll do it for you."

I stifled my smile. Chaun didn't mean to be condescending. Chaun idolized Rafe and they were good friends. I could tell he was excited and happy that at last there was something he could do for his friend.

The five of us went back outside to the table where Cecily and Liam were waiting. As usual, Rafe wore a goofy hat. Its wide brim kept his face in shadow, and the long earflaps covered the sides of his face. He walked hunched over and limped. He always did this when he was in a public place where he didn't want anyone to recognize him, and it amazed me how effectively he could hide his identity this way.

He sat down at the table and removed his hat. Cecily gasped when she recognized Rafe, one of the most well-known—and best looking—of the current crop of Hollywood action stars.

"What's Jade's number?" Rafe asked. He wasn't wasting any time when a young girl might be in danger.

Cecily took the phone from him with shaking hands. Her missing daughter and the sudden appearance of superstar Rafe Cummings had the poor woman overwhelmed. Finally, after several tries, she managed to correctly key in her daughter's number.

Rafe put the call on speaker, but it rang and rang, eventually flipping over to voicemail. He left a message, identifying himself and saying he was really anxious to talk to her. Then he placed the phone on the table, expecting an immediate callback.

Not for the first time I thought about how lovely it must be to be Rafe Cummings. People jumped whenever he asked for anything, and nothing he asked for was ever too much trouble.

Then I remembered how difficult his early life had been, and how demanding it still was in so many ways. Anytime he went anywhere in public, he was in danger from an unexpected mob of fans. He never knew if someone was a real friend or if they were using him to advance their own egos. He worked out hard to stay in action hero shape, and he stayed on a very strict diet. No cheating. Ever.

Fans and paparazzi hounded him pretty much wherever he went. So far, they hadn't figured out that he and I were good friends, or we'd have had a whole herd of them perpetually camped at the bar in Ray's Place, waiting to catch a picture of Rafe. They'd be especially happy if they caught him in an embarrassing moment, so he always had to be on his best behavior in public. In reality, his seemingly enviable life was very restricted.

I realized he deserved every bit of ease he now enjoyed. And yet despite all he'd been through and all the hassles in his current life, he was a genuinely nice guy.

After Rafe finished leaving the message, we sat in silence, waiting for Jade to call us back. We all assumed the phone would ring right away. If she could resist a personal call from Rafe Cummings, she had to be the only fifteen year old in the world who could.

But five minutes passed.

Then ten.

Unasked, Noah brought over a tray of drinks to keep us occupied. He'd included pitchers of lemonade, tea, and ice water, along with an ice bucket, tongs, and several glasses. He'd put a bowl of mixed nuts and a plate of cookies on the tray as well.

Rafe took a single cashew from the bowl. It took him longer to chew and swallow it than I took to eat an entire cookie. Or two.

I blushed, hoping nobody else noticed the difference in our consumption speed. Rafe winked at me when he realized I was well aware of it.

Another five minutes passed with all of us staring at the ground, afraid to say anything for fear we might upset Cecily even more. She was just sitting there on the bench, wringing her hands, and shaking a little bit. Every few minutes, a small moan slipped out. It was obvious she was terrified for her daughter.

I was just about to call Dane again when a shadow fell across the table.

It was Austin. He was coming back from a shore dive, and carrying his prized possession, a Nikon D850 underwater camera in an Ikelite waterproof housing. He'd veered over to join us when he saw us all grouped around the table.

I surmised he'd had a great dive since his face was glowing with joy. He certainly didn't look like a man with anything to hide.

"Hey, Austin," I said. "How was the dive?"

Cecily suddenly stood up and slapped his face. "Where is my daughter?" she said, snarling like a protective tiger mom. "What have you done with my Jade?"

Chapter 38
Dane Arrives

DANE ARRIVED JUST in time to see the slap, and he quickly stepped between Austin and Cecily. "No need for anyone to get physical here. Let's all sit down and we can calmly get to the bottom of this together, okay?"

He took Cecily's hands gently and lowered her back down to her seat.

Dane's arrival and the slap had drawn the attention of several people in the bar, who once again had focused their attention on our little group. Rafe quickly put his hat back on so nobody would recognize him.

Austin's face was beet red from embarrassment, and there was an even deeper red mark where Cecily had slapped him. A small drop of blood trickled toward his chin.

He raised a hand to his cheek. "What was that for? And why are you asking me about Jade in the first place? I barely even know her, and I don't know you at all. I had no idea Jade was your daughter, and she and I only chatted for a few minutes this morning before I went diving. If she's missing now, I don't know anything about it."

Noah had seen Cecily slap Austin, and he left his post behind the bar to see to his younger brother. He lifted Austin's hand from his cheek and examined the ripening bruise. When he saw the mark and the blood, he gasped. In fact, I think we were all stunned at the severity of the marks on Austin's face. That slap had really packed a wallop if it had even broken the skin.

Noah stood shoulder to shoulder with Austin and glared at Cecily. I could feel the tension rising, quickly becoming as thick and heavy as the ocean way down deep. Noah wasn't going to let anyone hurt his younger brother.

"Touch him again and you'll answer to me," he said. His look told Cecily he meant it.

"Let's everybody calm down," Dane said mildly, although he too seemed surprised at the severe mark a simple slap had left. He looked at Cecily's hands, now folded sedately in her lap. She wore a thin silver band on the middle finger of her right hand, but that was all that was visible. Dane stared a minute, then he reached down and turned her hands over.

She had an ornate metal full finger ring that she'd put on upside down, so the ring part, which was the length of her index finger, nestled into her palm rather than enclosing her finger. If she wasn't showing her palm, the ring simply looked like a slim band. But turned the way it was, it could become a serious weapon. There was a drying drop of blood on one of the ring's sharp edges.

Noah surged forward as though he planned to attack Cecily, but Dane put his arm up to stop him. "Austin and I will discuss whether he wants to press charges once we've found the missing woman. Until then, everybody should try to stay calm. We all need to work together…"

And then Cecily's phone pinged.

First we all gasped, then we held our breath. What would the phone reveal?

Cecily's hands were shaking. "It's her," she said. "That's her tone. She just posted something on her social media accounts. She must be okay." Her face lit up with joy and relief as she fumbled with her phone.

The look of joy quickly crumbled, and she bit back a sob. "Oh no," she moaned.

Dane took the phone from her hand and tilted it so we could

both see it. The video was shocking. The same girl in the picture Cecily had shown us was in the scene, but instead of perfectly done makeup and hair, she had a smudge on her face and her long hair was messy and wild, though her extraordinary green eyes still glowed with an intense fire.

She was cowering against a wall of dark ironshore that curved around her and up over her head. The sound of the nearby ocean came through clearly in the background. She wasn't wearing anything but the itsy bitsy bikini she'd had on in the picture her mother had showed us.

In the video, the girl whispered hoarsely. "I've been taken by a very bad man." She looked around furtively, as though she was afraid her captor would return suddenly and catch her using the phone.

My heart stopped. It was happening again. My worst fear was that someone had taken her like the women last year.

Jade's video continued as she described the misery her captor had put her through. She complained about the cold, and a lack of food and water. I was glad to hear that her captor hadn't seriously abused her.

At least, not yet.

But she'd only been missing for a few hours.

With luck, we'd find her before anything worse happened to her.

Then I heard the constant plinks from the phone in Dane's hand. The app was going crazy with all the new likes and comments posted by Jade's followers. There must have been thousands of people watching and commenting on the video.

In the film, Jade started whispering again, her voice hoarse. "I managed to hide my phone when he locked me in here. He doesn't know I have it. I have to find a way to get out before he comes back. I'm all alone, and I'm cold and I'm scared. I need help. Somebody help me, please."

The camera zoomed in on her face. Her lip quivered and her luminous green eyes were huge. She was the perfect image of a woman frightened for her life.

Except I knew enough about photography that I could tell right away by the light that Jade wasn't in a cave, or if she was, she had several bounce lights in there with her. And since she wasn't a very good actress, it was obvious to me she wasn't really frightened at all.

Dane knew it too. "Who do you think is operating the camera?" he asked Cecily.

"How should I know?" she retorted. "Whoever locked her in there, I suppose. You need to find her now, before she gets hurt."

"I have a different question. How did she manage to smuggle her phone in?" I said. "There's no place she could have hidden it from anyone in that bathing suit."

Tate chimed in. "And she's not locked in a cave somewhere. She's filming with a ring light. She's standing under a rocky outcropping for sure, but I can tell by the color and quality of the light that it's wide open to the sun."

Cecily looked cornered for a minute, then she went back on the offense. "You," she spat at Austin. "What have you done with my baby? You were the last one to see her."

He answered quickly, anger in his voice. "Not unless she disappeared in a puff of smoke the instant I walked away. She was sitting right over there in the bar. There were at least twenty or thirty people sitting around drinking or having a late lunch."

"You're in big trouble, and you'd say anything to get out of this. There's no proof that all those people were around," she retorted.

I knew Austin and I knew he wasn't a liar. But before I could say anything in his defense, Noah spoke up. "Let's just go look at the register receipts, shall we? That'll prove how many checks we closed out in the last couple of hours."

Cecily bit her lips. "That won't prove anything. You could have faked them to protect your brother."

"Really?" he said. "How would I have known I'd need to protect him from your stupid accusations even before you made them?"

Dane held up his hands and made a 'calm down' gesture. "Let's worry about all that later. For now, we need to focus on finding

Jade. Austin, what can you tell us about the time you spent with her?"

Austin shrugged his shoulders. "Nothing to tell. We had a soda together in Ray's Place. She was flirting with me, but when she told me she's only fifteen, I left and went diving. I was helping Noah at Ray's Place all morning, and I've either been at the dive shop or underwater for at least the last two hours. Maybe longer."

Dane nodded. "Show me your dive computer, please."

Austin held it out to Dane. I looked over his shoulder. The computer showed a recently completed hour and fifteen minute dive with a maximum depth of eighty feet. He was still early in his required surface interval.

"It looks like Austin is telling the truth. There's no way he could have taken Jade anywhere and still done that dive. So let's start over and see if we can retrace her steps. Noah, we may need those lunch tabs after all."

Liam was still looking hard at Jade's video on the screen of Cecily's phone. "You said Jade is an influencer?" he asked her.

I realized that like me, he thought Jade's disappearance was a hoax. He obviously wanted to make sure Dane knew she had a reason for creating a deception. A gorgeous influencer in a tiny bikini, kidnapped by a bad man and then rescued would be sure to attract a lot of likes.

Cecily didn't catch onto us though. She nodded at his words and began crying again. "My poor baby," she wailed.

"Dane, I think I know where Jade is," Liam said. "She's somewhere near the blowholes, probably in one of the caverns. I recognize the sound in the background."

Dane nodded. "Okay. Let's go see if we can find her."

Chapter 39
Austin

"Austin, you wait here with Fin until Roland and Morey arrive. They'll take care of you from there. Liam, can we use your boat? I don't want to wait for the Coast Guard, and I'd like Fin to stay with Austin."

"Sure thing, mate," said Liam. "Let's go. Tate, do you want to join us? With your eye for lighting and details, maybe you'll recognize the slant of the light or something that can help us find the right spot."

"Sure thing," said Tate. "Whatever I can do to put that poor girl's mother at ease."

I saw Dane and Liam exchange a look, and I could tell neither of them believed anyone had taken Jade. But they would chase down every lead and do whatever they could to return her to her mother.

I watched Liam's *Enviroman* roar off toward the blowholes on Grand Cayman's East End, and then I sat down between Austin and Cecily.

Austin turned to me. "You know I had nothing to do with Jade going missing, don't you?"

I patted his hand. "Don't worry. I know you too well to think that badly of you."

Cecily opened her mouth like she was ready to blast me for saying that, but I held up my hand to forestall her tirade.

"I've known Austin for years. He doesn't lie, and he's always been polite and respectful to everyone he meets. I intend to assume that has continued to be true unless someone shows me irrefutable proof that he acted badly. And this is neither the time nor the place to argue the point. The important thing is that we all work together to find your missing daughter."

Cecily shut her mouth, but she grumbled and muttered continually. I only caught an occasional word, but I knew she was griping because she felt we were taking Austin's part over hers, and she mumbled that she would see us in court if anything happened to her Jade.

I ignored her threats and turned to Austin, who looked so down you'd have thought someone had kicked his puppy. I winked at him, and he tried to smile in return, but there was so much anger in him that it prevented him from smiling.

After a few minutes, Roland and Morey from Dane's detective team trotted over from the parking lot. "Hello, Fin. Austin. Ma'am," said Roland. He held out his hand to Cecily. "I'm Roland Kerwin. And this is my partner, Morey."

Cecily didn't take the hand he extended. In a raspy voice she demanded, "Have you found Jade yet? Are you going to arrest this man?"

Morey looked startled. "Arrest Austin? For what?"

She rolled her eyes. "He's taken my daughter, and who knows what he's done with her. And nobody around here seems to care. They all just keep saying what a nice guy he is…"

"He is a nice guy…" said Morey before Roland could stop him.

Roland put his hand on Morey's arm to prevent him from saying more. Then he spoke calmly to Cecily. "I can see that you're upset. Rest assured that we're doing everything we can to find your daughter and to bring her home safely. In fact, DS Scott requested that we take Austin down to the station to see what he has to say for himself."

Austin looked startled, and he opened his mouth to protest.

I broke in before he could say anything. "I'll call Mr. Gibb's lawyer and have him meet you all at the station. Until then, please refrain from asking him any questions."

I noticed both cops trying to suppress a smile. They knew Austin's counsel would be Newton, and they also knew that it was unlikely that Austin had actually done anything wrong. In fact, it was more probable that after that vicious slap from Cecily, Dane simply wanted him removed from her presence for his own safety.

I took my phone out of the pocket of my cargo shorts and called Newton. As usual when I called, he picked up right away. "Newton, can you meet Austin at the police station? Roland and Morey are taking him in for questioning in the kidnapping and disappearance of Jade Abby, a fifteen-year-old social media influencer."

Newton sucked in a breath. "That's ridiculous. Austin would never do something like that."

"Jade's mother is here with me," I said. "She's very distraught, but I'm taking good care of her." I knew he'd get the sub-text of my words. Austin was not currently in any danger of an actual arrest, but I wanted someone with him at the station, just in case.

"Got it," he said. "I'll go take care of Austin."

Chapter 40
The Return

Once Roland and Morey had departed from the recreation area with Austin, I left Cecily at the table. I asked Noah to open a tab to my account to provide Cecily with anything she wanted until Dane, Tate, and Liam returned.

He scowled at me. "She's accusing my brother of something you and I both know he didn't do. He would never do something like that. She's a terrible person, and you're asking me to be nice to her and serve her free food all afternoon?"

"I'm asking you to serve her free food so she'll stay here where we can keep an eye on her until Liam, Tate, and Dane return with Jade. I don't want Cecily to have an opportunity to contact Jade or anyone else who might be involved in this until we know what's really going on. I know this is hard for you, but right now, it's the best thing you can do for Austin. Think of it as keeping her under surveillance."

His eyes were hard, but he bit his lip and nodded. "Okay. I'll do it."

I headed back to the table where Cecily was weeping softly and staring at her phone. When I told her I was comping her anything she wanted from Ray's Place while we waited for Liam to return, she wasted no time in placing an order for the steak and lobster special with several a la carte sides. She asked for a top shelf margarita, specifying the most expensive tequila we had in the bar. She'd tossed down two of them by the time Noah delivered her dinner, and she asked for another as he carefully positioned the plates in front of her.

"Certainly, Madam," he said, but I could see him gritting his teeth as he walked away.

Cecily ate her meal quickly, not even attempting to savor the subtle flavors of the food. She finished another two margaritas while eating. She asked for dessert and a chocolate martini. And then another chocolate martini.

I rarely drink alcohol, so her rapid consumption startled me. When she asked for the third chocolate martini, Noah raised his eyebrow at me, questioning whether he should keep serving her. I could tell he was as annoyed as I was that she was taking advantage of us, but she didn't seem impaired, so I nodded. I wanted her here when Dane and my friends brought Jade back.

I needn't have worried about her leaving. After a few sips of this latest cocktail, she put her head down on the table and began to snore.

It was getting on toward cocktail hour at Ray's Place, a very busy time for us. I didn't want her sprawled out in the middle of RIO's recreation area. Not only did it not look good for Ray's Place, but it could also be dangerous for her. I texted Stewie for advice.

"'be right there,'" he texted back.

He and Davy left the dive shop and walked across the lawn to the bar. I was surprised to see Davy here, but I didn't say anything.

Stewie paused a moment, staring at Cecily with her head on the table, a trickle of drool forming a small pool under her face. "There but for the grace of God," he said. "And also the support of a very good woman who makes me want to be a better man. Thanks be to the universe. Give me a hand, will you, Davy?"

Stewie and Davy hoisted Cecily to her feet. They each draped one of her arms over their shoulder and half dragged, half walked her to the hammock that was the most secluded and furthest away from the bar. I followed along just in case they needed some additional help, but luckily, even though they had some difficulty, they got her into the hammock without flipping her onto the ground.

We'd no sooner gotten her settled when we heard the roar of an approaching boat. It was Liam's *Enviroman*, on its way back. Liam was in the flying bridge, but I noticed a small, huddled figure sitting on one of the deck benches between Tate and Dane, so I guessed their recovery mission had been successful.

Stewie and I hurried down the dock to greet them. Dane threw a line to Stewie, who wrapped it around a cleat on the dock. When he raised his arm to let Liam know the boat was secure, Liam shut off the engines.

Dane nimbly jumped out onto the dock and held out a hand to help the young woman I assumed was Jade Abby, although the hood of the dark colored sweatshirt she wore hid her face. She stepped onto the dock.

Her green eyes were even more impressive in person than they were in her pictures. "Where's Cecily?" she said, looking at Dane as though accusing him of trying to put something over on her. "I thought you told me she was worried sick."

"I'm sure she's around here somewhere. Fin's been taking very good care of her while we looked for you." He waved a hand in my direction.

For a second, her brilliant green eyes lit up. "You're Fin Fleming?" she asked. "THE Fin Fleming?"

I nodded.

She sneered. "You're wasting your talent in this backwater. You could have really been somebody." She looked me up and down. "But you're a little too old to start now."

I laughed. "Yep. My life is over."

She nodded in agreement. "Too true."

My friends and I laughed while she stared at us curiously, obviously having no idea what we thought was so funny.

When our laughter stopped, I said, "Your mother is resting. Would you like something to eat while you wait for her to wake up?"

"I think you mean until she sobers up, don't you?" she said. "But I am hungry. I haven't had much to eat today."

"Your kidnapper didn't feed you?" I asked.

She laughed. "Nope."

Dane and I exchanged glances. She didn't seem at all like a young woman just rescued from a kidnapping.

"Let me introduce you to the team at Ray's Place. They can bring you whatever you'd like."

She had her cellphone stuck in the pocket of the hoodie, and she pulled it out and began filming. She held the phone away from her as far as her arm could reach and spoke in an excited, breathless voice. "I've just been rescued by a couple of handsome heroes. The famous Liam Lawton—and get this—Tate Crusoe, hot Hollywood producer and best friend of action hero Rafe Cummings. In fact, while I was in captivity, Rafe Cummings himself tried to call me. I wouldn't be at all surprised…"

Dane gently took the phone from her hand. "Plenty of time for that later. Right now we need to find out what happened. Fin, can we use your office?" he said.

I nodded. "All yours. I'll ask Noah to send in some sandwiches and cookies."

I could tell Noah was annoyed when I put in the request. I aways thought he'd been born to be in the hospitality business, and he loved making people happy through the food and drink he served. So obviously, the annoyance was not just because I asked him to deliver some food.

No, Noah was angry because Jade and Cecily had accused his younger brother of kidnapping Jade and holding her captive. Anyone who knew Austin knew it was a crazy story, but still, it must have rankled Noah, especially because it was looking more and more like Jade had made the whole thing up to entertain her followers, without caring who she hurt with her lies.

I hung out near the bar while Noah finished setting up the tray of food. "Here, let me help," I said, picking up a pitcher of iced tea when he was ready to go.

He gave me the side eye, but he didn't say anything. He hoisted the heavy tray of food to his shoulder and walked toward RIO's rear door, with me sloshing along beside him.

Dane and Jade were still standing in the hall outside my office. I could hear them talking as Noah and I hurried toward them. "I don't think you can question me without an adult present," she said. "I'm only fifteen—still a minor."

"I'm not questioning you. I just need to know what happened so we can identify the creep who took you and bring him to justice." Dane stared at her, daring her to keep arguing.

She stared back at him without speaking, her green eyes dark and hard. Noah and I paused a few feet away, unwilling to break into their standoff. From behind them, Davy Jones raced around the corner from the hall that led to the infirmary and the research lab. He wore those stretchy brown shorts all the guys had started wearing along with a blue RIO t-shirt.

He slowed down and turned his upper body and his head away from them as he hurried past. He walked like they were blocking the hall and he was too wide to pass them unless he turned sideways. But he wasn't nearly large enough to need more room, and they weren't blocking him in the spacious corridor. It looked like he'd made the move so his face was toward the wall, but at first, I couldn't imagine why he wouldn't want them to see his face.

Then when Jade spoke, it all became clear. At least to me it did.

"Hey, Austin," said Jade. "Aren't you even going to say hello?"

He stopped but didn't turn to face them. "Sorry. You've got the wrong guy."

Jade narrowed her bright green eyes at him. "I don't think so."

"Don't know you." He shrugged and walked away.

Noah reached out to stop Davy from passing, but I grabbed Noah's arm and held him back. "Let Dane do his thing," I whispered into his ear.

He bit his lip, but after a second he nodded slightly. Without another word, we walked by Jade and Dane to leave the food on the table in the corner of my office.

It was all up to Dane now.

Chapter 41
Mixed Identity

I was at Ray's Place, sitting on a stool near Candy's perch. Worried about Jade's accusations against Austin, my head was in my hands. I'm very bad at inaction. My default mode is to rush into any situation to try to fix it.

Noah was behind the bar, slowly slicing lemons and limes to be ready for the sunset rush. By the third time he'd nicked his thumb, I could tell his mind wasn't on his task either. He was worried about his younger brother, and nobody could blame him.

In this case, there was nothing either of us could do until Dane finished questioning Jade. But at least I could keep Noah from slicing off his fingers. "Go see Doc and get those cuts taken care of. I'll watch the bar until you get back."

He opened his mouth to protest, but Theresa, who'd quietly approached the tiki bar from her office in the main building, spoke up.

"Go on, Noah. We can't be serving bloody fruit in our drinks." She gave him a stern look. "And take some time to yourself. Don't come back until you calm down."

Then she looked at me. "And I appreciate your offer. But no offense, I'll handle this place by myself. Your food service skills stop at pull tabs." She grinned to show she was teasing, but I had to admit she was right.

Noah trotted off across the recreation area to the back door. I called Doc to let her know he was on his way.

"Hmmm," she said. "He has to pass by your office, where I happen to know Dane is talking with that Jade person. Maybe I'll take a walk up that way to make sure Noah doesn't get distracted."

"Thanks," I said. "That's a good idea. You know how protective Noah is about Austin. Especially since they lost Dylan." Dylan Gibb had been the brother between Noah and Austin in age. He'd died a few years ago, and his death had left all his brothers shattered.

Theresa went behind the bar and tied an apron over her t-shirt and cargo shorts. She poured an icy cold lemonade for me, and then threw away the fruit Noah had been slicing, starting over with a bowl of fresh, uncut lemons and limes.

She and I chatted casually, talking about Oliver's upcoming wedding and what we were thinking of wearing. Genevra had told us we could wear anything we wanted. The topic of dresses now totally consumed Theresa and Joely, while I figured I'd just drop by Newton's condo on the morning of the wedding and rummage through the gigantic walk-in closet full of designer duds he had his stylist replenish for me each season. Most of the time I had no need of the fancy clothes the stylist provided, so I usually ignored the whole process.

Theresa pointed out that Genevra would probably not find my lackadaisical plan very reassuring, so we agreed to head over to Newton's after her shift to see what was in the magic closet as soon as Dane cleared up this thing with Austin.

Theresa had excellent taste, and if we picked out my dress together, Theresa would help me choose something Genevra would approve of. I knew there wouldn't be a t-shirt or a bathing suit in the entire collection, but I hoped Theresa would be able to find something comfy and not too frilly that met her standards.

We were still talking about the wedding when Noah returned.

He slid onto the stool next to mine, and Theresa placed an iced tea with lemon in front of him. He smiled his thanks.

"Nothing yet?" I asked him.

He shook his head and stared into his drink, misery and concern etched in every line of his body.

"Look alive, folks," said Theresa. "Here comes DS Scott now. And he looks mighty annoyed." She poured a lemonade to serve Dane when he arrived. He thanked her and picked up his icy mug, and except for Theresa who stayed behind the bar, we all moved to a small square table in the back.

Dane took a long pull of his lemonade. "What a piece of work that woman is. You can't imagine how hard it was to get her to stick to a story and tell the truth. But finally…"

"Complain later. Did she admit Austin had nothing to do with her so-called kidnapping?" Noah was anxious to ensure Jade's information had exonerated his brother.

Dane sighed. "She did. But her name isn't really Jade Abby. It's Catherine Abbandonato…" He looked at me. "That's the name of the woman missing from the guest house. You remember we were on our way there when we ran into Bari mid-ocean."

His expression turned wry. "And it seems Jade is actually older than she let on. She's twenty-five, and she is an internet influencer under the name Jade Abby. Her 'Jade' persona claims to be only fifteen. Catherine says it enhances her 'street cred' that she's supposedly so young and yet she's so sophisticated. And get this. Her eyes are actually brown. She wears colored contacts."

He stopped for another swallow of lemonade. "Apparently her follows and likes were falling, which somehow affects her income. I don't really understand her business. But anyway, she and Cecily hit on the idea of a fake kidnapping, which would engage Jade's followers because they'd be worried about her. The scheme also allowed her to parade around in that tiny bikini, which apparently is also very good for her business. So she rented the room but never went inside, thinking that would set off alarms that she could capitalize on. Meanwhile, she and Cecily were actually staying at the Ritz."

"So why did she have to involve Austin?" Noah asked.

Dane shrugged. "She didn't mean to. She did have a short conversation with him like he said, but she never asked his name. And when she realized how young he is, she says she took off. Later, she met a man who told her his name was Austin Gibb. Catherine confirmed that he was the person who helped her stage the fake kidnapping. And we know she called Davy Austin when she saw him in the hall, making it pretty clear that he gave her Austin's name when they met, even though he denies it. So the real Austin Gibb is off the hook. Davy Jones, on the other hand, has some explaining to do."

I bit my lip. "Do you think Davy is the guy that lured Bari and the other women into swimming in the rip current?"

Dane lifted his shoulders in a tired shrug. "I believe that's true, although it's still unproven at this point. As far as his interactions with Jade, he didn't do anything wrong, he was just stupid. She told him her idea, and he offered to bring her somewhere where she could hideout and be safe while pretending a kidnapper had taken her. He took her there in your submarine, so no one would see them."

I tightened my lips but I didn't say anything. I'd already told Davy I was terminating his employment, and his final day with us was coming up soon. His stupidity would just move his last day up by a few weeks.

Dane waited a moment for me to say something, but when I didn't speak, he continued. "So we'll still be watching the beaches to try to catch the person who's sending people to their deaths, but it will be hard to prove any wrongdoing. If Bari's experience is typical, he never touched her, never threatened her, never tried to force her to do anything. He simply asked her to go swimming, and that's not a crime."

"In this case, it should be," I muttered.

He shrugged. "In this case, you may be right. But anyway, we will be charging Jade—or Catherine, her real name—with a bunch of misdemeanors that won't amount to much. And as soon as we can arrange it, Roland and Morey will escort her and her mother to the airport and stay with them until they've departed from the island. Right now the guys are on their way here with Austin. We never charged him with anything. We didn't even question him. Roland gave him the video game controller Oliver left behind when he was in there a while ago, and Austin passed the time eating cookies and playing games. So no harm done."

"Except I aged about twenty years worrying about my little brother," said Noah. "I won't ever forgive that witch for getting Austin in trouble."

Chapter 42
Bari Meets Austin

NOAH and I left Ray's Place together. I walked onto the dock and the *Tranquility*. I needed the alone time, plus I had some work I wanted to finish. I was always happy to work in the fresh air and sunshine I found on my beloved boat.

I'd been working at the galley table for about an hour when I looked up and saw Genevra and Bari strolling down the dock.

"Permission to come aboard," said Genevra when she reached my slip.

"Permission granted," I said. I rose to help them to step down onto the deck.

When I took Bari's hand to steady her, I said, "How are you doing? All recovered?"

She jumped down and then reached out to pull me into a hug. "I'm fine now, thanks to you. I was pretty much out of energy by the time you reached me. Another few minutes and I'd have been a goner."

"I'm glad I was there," I said when she stepped back.

We sat in the white leather captain's chairs inside the cabin. "So, other than almost drowning on your first day at the beach, how are you enjoying the Cayman Islands?" I asked.

She laughed. "I love it here. It's great to be near my big sister, and I can't wait to start my new job. In fact, is it okay with you if I start tomorrow instead of next week? I've sort of lost my enthusiasm for lying on the beach."

"It's okay with me if you're sure. It may look like we're taking it easy a lot of the time, but I assure you, working at RIO is pretty intense, with lots of long days. Someday you may regret giving up those free days."

"I'm very sure about this," she said. "I can't wait to get started."

Before I could say anything else, I noticed Dane striding down the dock. He asked for permission to come aboard, and he jumped down to the deck as soon as I gave it.

"Where are Jade and Cecily?" I asked.

He grimaced. "Cecily woke up, and since Jade is sticking to her story, I sent them back to their hotel for now. I'll go by later and see if I can shake one of them into telling the truth."

"Who are Jade and Cecily?" asked Genevra. "I don't think I've met them."

Dane sighed. "Jade's an internet influencer. She claimed somebody kidnapped her from RIO's beach and held her captive in a cave. Liam, Tate, and I were able to track her down pretty quickly. The cave she was in was over near the blowholes. There was a stout rope ladder hanging nearby, making it an easy climb to get out of there, and she was just a few steps from the road. Plus she had her phone with her, and the cell coverage was fine. Her story was pretty shaky, but we had to take it seriously until we could prove she was lying. Now that she's told us the whole story, we just need to identify her accomplice."

Genevra shrugged. "You'll get to the bottom of it. We were about to take a late afternoon break. Would you like to join us, or are you still on duty?"

He looked at his watch. "I'm off duty as of right now. I wouldn't mind a cold drink."

Genevra clapped her hands. "Excellent. Because I asked Noah to deliver a pitcher of margaritas and some lemonade, and I think I see him coming now."

I looked up and saw Noah and Austin headed our way with

trays of drinks and snacks. I took the tray of drinks from Noah while he stepped onto the *Tranquility*'s deck and then took the tray of snacks from Austin. Then the two brothers arranged the food nicely on the table and poured drinks. Dane and I asked for lemonade, but the Blackthorne sisters wanted margaritas.

While Austin handed Bari her cocktail, Dane and I watched closely to see if she showed any sign of recognizing Austin. If Jade's story were true—and neither Dane nor I believed it was—it was possible the same man that had lured Bari into the water had been involved in Jade's abduction. We suspected that man was Davy Jones, but still, it would be interesting to see how Bari reacted to Austin.

Bari thanked him when he placed her margarita in front of her, but she didn't call him by name. Nor did she show any sign that she recognized him.

"Bari, this is Noah Gibb," I waved my hand toward the older brother, "and this is Austin Gibb. Guys, this is Bari Blackthorne, my new assistant."

Austin smiled shyly at Bari. "Welcome. Let me know if I can be of any help to you while you're getting acclimated."

"Thanks" she said. "I appreciate it." She beamed her smile.

Noah stacked the trays and held them under his arm. "Ready, Austin?" he said.

Austin tore himself away from staring at Bari, and the two brothers walked down the dock back to the bar.

"He seems nice," Bari said. "I mean, they seem nice." She blushed.

"You hadn't met either of them before?" asked Dane. "Neither one seemed familiar?"

She shrugged. "No, I've never met them before. Why are you asking?"

"Just wondering," Dane said, "if you remembered one of them from the other day at the beach."

She shook her head. "Definitely not. I'd certainly have remembered Austin…or Noah. It wasn't either of them."

"Good." He finished his lemonade. "I've gotta run. I'll see you ladies later." Dane put his empty glass on the table and took off at a trot down the dock.

I followed him onto the dock and whispered a plan in his ear.

"Good idea," he said. "I'll set it up."

I watched him swerve into the dive shop to ask Stewie to help put the plan in motion.

Although Noah had supplied us with an ample quantity of snacks, as the day wore on we started thinking about having something more substantial to eat. I locked my computer in one of the *Tranquility*'s cabinets before we made our way to Ray's Place.

As soon as I walked in, Candy squawked out "Look! It's Fin Fleming." I ducked my head and blushed, but Genevra and Bari broke into fits of giggles. Luckily it was a slack time in the restaurant, and most of the clientele were either RIO employees or regulars who were not impressed by my presence.

Noah smiled a welcome at us and motioned to a four top in the back corner where we weren't likely to be disturbed. Bari and Genevra sat facing the wall, while for a change, I took the seat looking out toward the restaurant.

Austin was working at Ray's Place this evening, and our four top was one of his tables. He hurried over to take our drink orders. Although he was polite and attentive to Genevra and me, it was easy to see that he was completely enamored of Bari. And equally easy to see that she was just as smitten by him.

A few minutes later, Dane, Roland, and Morey came in. Noah sat them a few tables away from us. It looked like they ordered cocktails, but I noticed Roland give Noah the hand signal we'd worked out during another case to signify they wanted non-alcoholic drinks. Noah gave a tiny nod and went to work. The drinks he delivered a few minutes later looked luscious, cold, and fruity. They were adorned with flowers, pretty little umbrellas, and tiny animal figurines. Perfect island mocktails.

A few minutes later, Stewie came out of the dive shop and locked the door. He walked around to where we stashed the rental boats, where he picked up Davy Jones. The two men headed our way.

Noah escorted them to a table two away from ours. There was one empty table between their table and the one where Dane and his team were sitting. Davy took a seat so his back was to the wall, and Stewie sat facing him. Austin had been working behind the bar, but he'd just headed inside to get more ice from the café, so Noah quickly came by to take their drink orders.

It only took a moment for Noah to deliver their drinks. Stewie sipped his soda and Davy took a slug of his beer. Genevra, Bari, and I were laughing at a silly story from their childhood. Something about a teddy bear.

And then it happened. Bari glanced over at the surrounding tables and gave a start. She jumped up, knocking over her chair. Her face was so white and pale it looked like she'd rubbed it in flour. She pointed at Davy. In a harsh voice, she shouted. "That's him. That's the man who took me swimming and left me to drown."

Roland stood. "Are you sure?"

Bari nodded. She was shaking so hard I thought she'd fall down. "That's him. I'll never forget his face." Her reaction was so different from when she'd met Austin there was little question that she recognized Davy as the bad guy.

He put down his mug and started to walk out of Ray's Place. Morey stepped in front of him. "Not so fast, Jones. We'd like to talk to you for a minute."

"Tough. I don't want to talk to you." He tried to push past the policeman to leave the bar.

Just as he passed under the tiki torches, Cecily and Jade were entering Ray's Place.

"Hi, Austin," Jade said to Davy. "Nice to see you."

We all heard it. Again.

Dane, Roland, and Morey took it from there.

Bari had totally freaked out from coming face-to-face with a man who'd tried to lure her to her death, but since Genevra was able to calm her down, we stayed at our table to finish our early dinner.

Austin was always a polite and attentive server, but this

evening his smiles seemed even brighter. While we were waiting for our coffee, Bari excused herself. Genevra and I remained seated at the table, picking at the fresh fruit and cheese on our dessert tray.

I saw Bari coming back toward us. Austin timed his approach perfectly so they met in the middle of the dance floor. They talked for a few minutes, heads close together, and then Bari practically floated to the table.

She tried to play it cool, but she was bursting with excitement. At last, the secret grew too much for her to hold inside. She had to tell her sister, and I had a front row seat.

"Austin asked me to go to dinner with him. Tomorrow. I don't know where yet."

Genevra put a stern expression on her face. "Bari, you're busy tomorrow. It's traditional to have dinner with your boss at least once a week."

Bari's face fell. "Oh, no. I didn't know. What am I gonna do? What if I tell him I can't make it, and he changes his mind and doesn't ask me again?" She was clearly distraught about the idea of missing a chance to spend time with Austin.

Genevra couldn't keep that unyielding face on any longer, and she burst into laughter. "Gotcha, little sis," she said.

Bari narrowed her eyes. "You'll pay for that. Just wait. Your turn will come." Then she smiled and the two sisters slung their arms over each other's shoulders.

Chapter 43
Diving

BEFORE WE'D FINISHED dinner last night, we'd decided we needed to take a diving day. Of course, for me, every day is a diving day, but Genevra and Bari had other responsibilities that they couldn't necessarily fulfill while diving. RIO still expected them both to dive frequently, but it wasn't the total focus of their jobs.

Bari was still a novice diver, plus she'd just gotten over that frightening experience with the rip current, so she was a little skittish. We knew she'd need an easy, shallow site, far from any of the areas that had experienced rip currents, and one with lots of interesting sea life.

With over three hundred dive sites on Grand Cayman, it wasn't hard to find a spot that fit the bill. The hard part was narrowing it down.

We finally settled on Ironshore Garden on the East End. The site isn't too far from RIO's marina, so the trip would be quick. Depending on the weather, the site sometimes experienced a little choppiness or a slight current, but it rarely made the site too difficult for a novice to dive. Plus there's an abundance of sea life, and the caverns and grottos are fascinating.

It was still early when Bari and Genevra came to my office to pick me up. "Let's stop by the dive shop on the way to the *Tranquility*," I said. "There's a few things I need."

"Me too," Bari said. "I need to get setup with rental gear anyway. It will be a while before I can afford to buy my own stuff."

"Let's go then," I said.

Stewie was waiting for us when we arrived at the open dive shop door. "I need some defogging drops, and Bari needs a full setup." I winked at him.

"Last night after you told me you ladies were heading out this morning and Bari needed new gear, I selected a few things I thought she might like." Stewie indicated a small pile of high end dive equipment."

"Oh my gosh. Thank you, but I'm sure I can't afford all that," Bari said. She stared wistfully at the bright pink trim on each piece of equipment.

"Let's see what it comes out to after you select what you like. You may be surprised," I told her. "And if you can't afford it right now, we can put it on hold for you."

Stewie had her try on the black and pink dive skin, and he tested the mask with her to make sure she'd get a good seal. Then he showed her two different styles of fins, and explained how they differed and how they'd affect her diving. Piece by piece, Stewie patiently walked her through the selections until they had amassed a full setup, including a computer, a regulator, and even a pair of dive scissors for her to carry in her new BCD's pocket.

"Thank you for showing me all this stuff, but I think all I can afford today is the mask and fins," she said when he'd finished demonstrating the products.

"Before you decide, let me see what the total comes out to," he told her.

He went to the register and started ringing things in.

Bari was biting her lip nervously.

"OK, by my calculation, the total comes to $3.12. That's CI," he said with a laugh.

"Impossible," she said. "You must have missed a decimal point or two."

"Relax. The total's right. You forgot about your employee discount, and the new employee welcome gift certificate I set up," I said. "This can all be yours today. If you don't have the cash right now, we can arrange for you to pay later."

Genevra, Stewie, and I were smiling at her stunned expression.

"I don't know how to thank you guys," she said. "I'm overwhelmed."

"Forget the thanks. Let's go diving," I said.

We brought our tanks and gear to the *Tranquility* and stowed it carefully. Genevra showed Bari how to clean the film off her new mask with toothpaste while I piloted the boat to Ironshore Gardens.

Genevra used the long handled gaffe to grab the mooring ball when we arrived and tied the boat off carefully.

Bari watched every move she made. "I want to be sure I know what to do when it's my turn," she said.

Once I'd shut down the engines, we all geared up. It took Bari a few minutes longer than us because the gear was all new to her, but she did everything right. We did buddy checks, and then we were good to go.

Genevra went in first, stepping off the dive platform in the *Tranquility*'s stern. When she popped up and gave the okay sign, it was Bari's turn. I went in last, once we were sure Bari was comfortable with her new gear.

We dropped down to about thirty feet, which placed us just above the coral, pausing a moment to admire the stunning elkhorn corals and huge barrel sponges. We pointed out the stands of fire coral to Bari, making sure she knew not to touch it.

Then we dropped over the top of the coral down to the sandy bottom, at about fifty-five feet. I peered under one particularly dark overhang and saw a sleeping nurse shark. I pointed it out to Bari and her eyes grew wide. It was her first shark sighting. Since nurse sharks are usually pretty placid, it was a good one to get her used to the idea of swimming with sharks.

We swam into a few of the tunnels which were open to the surface, admiring the abundant sea life, including a couple of barracuda who glared at us but otherwise left us alone—just as they usually do.

We swam up through a chimney that led back to the top of the coral, where we saw a small fairy basslet, a couple of purple tangs, a bluehead wrasse, a mutton snapper, and a spotted moray eel. Two large grouper watched us curiously from their hiding place under a magnificent staghorn coral that reached nearly to the surface.

Too soon the dive was over and we swam back to the mooring line. The coral started at right around thirty feet, so we stayed over the reef at fifteen feet for our safety stop instead of hanging under the boat. That way we could still get a pretty good view of the sea life while we waited to complete our off-gassing.

When the stop was over, we sent Genevra up the ladder first, so she could help Bari with her gear once she was aboard. As soon as Bari had cleared the dive platform, I kicked over to the ladder and ended my own dive.

It was still early, and although we probably could have done another dive at the same site and seen an entirely different array of life, Genevra had scheduled a fitting for her wedding dress at eleven, and we wanted to make sure she was back on time.

She and Bari sat in the sunshine on the deck while I climbed up to the flying bridge to take us back to RIO. It had been a great dive, and I could see that Bari had the makings of a very fine diver as well as a super assistant. I was happy we'd added her to the team.

Dane Scott was waiting for us on the dock. He helped Genevra tie up the *Tranquility*, then he said, "I have something I wanted to talk to you about. It's regarding Davy Jones."

We all walked to a nearby picnic table and sat down. "So what's up?" I asked.

"We know from Bari's identification that he's the guy who tried to lure her to her doom. And we found a witness from the drowning near cemetery beach who remembered seeing him talking to the victim there. We're going to try to see if we can get manslaughter and attempted murder charges to stick."

I breathed a sigh of relief. The nightmare would soon be over.

Chapter 44
A Wedding

THE NEXT WEEK flew by even though Liam and I were tiptoeing around each other. At night, we each slept in our own house, and we didn't eat dinner together. We still drove to work together, but we rarely spoke during the drive.

Liam never mentioned the note and the engagement ring I'd left next to his coffee maker, although I knew he must have seen it since he made coffee every day. Since we were barely speaking to each other, we couldn't seem to break out of this standoff. But today was Genevra and Oliver's wedding day, and I hoped the happy occasion would help Liam and me to talk through our problems.

They'd wanted a simple wedding that would let them get on with their lives quickly. No long engagement. With Genevra's superb organization skills, they'd had everything ready to go in an almost unbelievably short time.

They were holding the wedding at sunset on the back lawn at RIO, with the reception immediately following. Ray's Place was doing the catering. We'd shut down everything at RIO for the day, including the aquarium and the gift shop so that all RIO employees could attend.

Even the *Omega* was running with a skeleton crew tonight. With the exception of a couple of volunteers left aboard to keep watch, Vincent Pollilo, the *Omega*'s captain, had given his entire crew the evening off to attend the wedding, and by mid-afternoon the ship's tenders were busy ferrying everyone to shore for the festivities.

Genevra and I were watching the preparations through the window in her office. Along with her sister Bari, Joely Wentworth, and Theresa Simmons, who were the other members of Genevra's wedding entourage, we'd retreated to await the perfect moment for the bride's entrance.

We were all ready for the event. Earlier, we'd dressed in my suite at Newton's penthouse condo, where I'd stayed last night. As usual for important events, Newton had sent in a team of stylists to do our hair and makeup and to handle any last minute wardrobe issues.

Once our appearances were perfect, we rode in the limo he'd hired to bring us here to RIO. Since RIO wasn't open today, there wasn't anybody in the entry or the halls, making it easy for us to cross the sunny atrium without anyone seeing us. All the wedding guests were outside, enjoying the late day sun along with a cocktail or two from the open bar.

Theresa, who in addition to being my best friend was also RIO's VP of food services, was fretting about the dinner. And the cake. The cocktails. The ice supply. The napkins...the list went on and on.

"What's up with you?" I asked her. "You can put on an event of this size with one hand tied behind your back, and you know it."

She grinned. "I can indeed. But this is not just any event. This is the event of the year—the wedding of Miss Genevra Blackthorne to Oliver Russo-Fleming. And if I had my usual team working, I wouldn't be worried a bit."

Theresa shot me a look. "But as you well know, everyone on my team is a guest at this event, so I had to borrow people from other venues. And who knows how well they've been trained?" We'd borrowed the catering staff for tonight's event from local restaurants, including Stefan Gibb's place, Nelson's.

Genevra laughed. "Theresa, you borrowed those people from the best restaurants on the island, not some fast food joint. The service and the food will be impeccable. If I'm not worried, you shouldn't be either."

Bari walked in from where she'd been keeping watch in the hall. Her blonde hair hung loose across her shoulders, and her icy blue column dress exactly matched her eyes. She smiled when she saw her sister in her gown. "Stewie asked me to let you know it's time," she said.

Genevra nodded. Her face glowed. Genevra is a lovely woman, but right now she transcended simple beauty. She was magnificent.

"But wait," I said. "I forgot to give you your 'something borrowed'. It's still in my office." I scurried down the hall and around the corner, stopping short when I rushed through my office door.

"Christophe!" I said. "I thought you weren't coming to the wedding." Genevra and Christophe Poisson, the world famous freediver, were close friends. He always said he was in love with her, and she always scoffed at his words.

"You're in love with the idea of unrequited love," she'd say to him, but I knew that wasn't true at all.

Christophe and I had spent hours together every day for months while he was training me for a deep free dive exhibition. Between dives, we'd talked about everything, including his love for Genevra. He'd said back then that meeting her was like a bolt from heaven, but sadly for him, the same stroke of lightning had not hit Genevra. She liked Christophe a lot, but she never took his declarations of love seriously. She'd already been in love with Oliver by the time they met.

Christophe smiled sadly. "I wasn't going to come, but then I thought about Genevra's happiness and how important it is to me. I couldn't let her think I don't care when I care so deeply." He sighed. "So here I am."

"That's great," I said. "She'll be happy to see you."

"Do you have a minute?" he said. "Can we talk?"

I looked at the clock on the wall. "Not really. But as soon as the ceremony's over I'll find you and we can talk then, okay?"

He nodded. "Oui. No rush."

I grabbed the pearl, sapphire, and blue topaz station bracelet that I'd planned to use as the something borrowed and the something blue Genevra would carry. "I've gotta hurry, but I'll see you soon." I raced back down the hall to Genevra's office.

When I got back, Theresa and Bari were waiting outside the office door, while Genevra and Joely were looking out the window and chatting. I rushed over to Genevra and fastened the delicate bracelet on her even more delicate wrist.

She lifted her hand to see the bracelet up close. "It's perfect. Thank you." She lifted her skirt a few inches and carefully stepped over to give me a hug.

Bari stood in the doorway and cleared her throat. "Ladies, it's time," she said.

She checked us over to make sure none of us was experiencing a wardrobe malfunction. She needn't have worried. The whole bridal party looked amazing.

Joely, with her perfectly cut dark brown bob and piercing blue eyes, wore a floor-length navy-blue tuxedo dress that emphasized her thin but athletic frame. Theresa's pink lace mini dress showed off her long legs and perfect skin, while Bari's dress echoed the design of Genevra's gown in many ways, except it didn't have the same lace overlay that adorned Genevra's gown and the color wasn't white. Instead, it was icy blue silk, tea length, with long split sleeves. The color looked fabulous with her blonde hair and blue eyes.

I wore a long sea blue halter-neck dress with a collar of sparkling sequins. The cut-in neckline and low back showed off my strong shoulders and swimmer's back. The dress skimmed loosely along my body and the silk rustled enticingly whenever I moved. My shoulder length brown hair was loose in semi-controlled waves, and I was even wearing a little bit of makeup.

Usually I hate dressing up or fussing with my hair, but today I felt very relaxed and comfy. I was surprised to realize I loved the dress I had on. I felt beautiful in it.

Once she'd finished inspecting us, Bari walked us all out to the hall leading to the door to RIO's back lawn. She lined us up in the order we were to walk along the path to where Oliver was waiting. First would come Joely and Theresa. Then Bari and me. Last would be Genevra, who Liam was supposed to escort down the aisle.

I looked around for him.

No Liam.

I realized I hadn't seen him all day. Neither had anyone else in the bridal party.

I gritted my teeth. "Don't worry. I'll track him down."

I rushed back to my office to grab my cellphone. Christophe was no longer there, but I did find a text from Liam on my phone.

"Called out of town. You know the drill."

I was shocked and extremely angry. I couldn't believe he'd decided that whatever he was doing was more important than this wedding. He and Genevra were very good friends, and they had been for years. He and Oliver were buddies, and soon to be brothers. He'd promised to be Oliver's best man. He'd seemed delighted by the idea of walking Genevra down the aisle.

I was supposed to be his fiancée, and this was a big day for me and my family.

He blew us all off with a text message.

Not only did he blow the day off, but he didn't even call to let me know personally. He sent a text. I checked the time I'd received the message. It had only come in five minutes ago.

It was bad enough that he totally dissed me by standing me up at the last minute on such an important day, but he hadn't even taken a moment to call Genevra and tell her directly.

I'd bet Oliver was wondering what had happened to his best man. Fortunately, Newton was there to step into the breach. He was standing up front next to Oliver, so I guessed Liam had somehow let one of them know about his absence.

I was worried about how Genevra would take it that Liam was skipping out on her wedding, especially considering the important role he'd taken on and how long they'd been friends. How could he do this to her? Given how Liam had been taking off for months at a time with no warning and no communication while he was gone, I considered myself lucky to have received so much as a text this time.

And how could I ever explain it to her? I'd sworn to keep quiet about Liam's clandestine role, and even that role was really no excuse for his rudeness. If it was so urgent for him to be gone, he could have stayed for the ceremony and then departed.

I realized I would not be at all comfortable with Liam continuing in this covert role if we were to get married. This was not the kind of marriage I wanted to have, nor a life I'd want to live.

But first things first. We had a wedding to complete. Who could I ask to escort Genevra in Liam's place?

Christophe? No, that would be cruel considering how he felt about her. Newton was already standing in front of the improvised altar next to Oliver, his son, so I assumed he'd been drafted as a replacement best man. No way could I drag him away from that to walk Genevra down the aisle at the last minute.

Then I had a flash of inspiration. It wouldn't help me explain Liam's absence, but it would enable the wedding to go on as planned. And if nothing else, the wedding photos would be even more memorable than they already would have been.

"Need you in my office ASAP," I texted.

Less than a minute later, Rafe rushed in, Penny on his heels. She had a pink bow in her hair and looked adorable. I knelt down to pat her while Rafe caught his breath. "What's the matter?" he panted.

I stood back up and quickly explained the problem, but without giving a reason for Liam's absence. "He was called away," was all I said.

"Family situation?" he asked.

I shrugged. "He left in such a rush I didn't get the details. I'm sure he'll have a good explanation when he gets back."

Rafe was no dummy, and he knew that Liam frequently disappeared without notice. He also knew that I was always angry and upset when it happened, especially when Liam didn't communicate with me while he was gone.

"Of course I'll do it," he said. "I'm honored that you thought of me."

Although the wedding was small and outdoors, it was formal dress, so Rafe wore his own tux. And as always, he looked fabulous. I pinned the white rose boutonniere I'd put aside for Liam to Rafe's lapel.

Then I went back into Genevra's office to explain the substitution to her.

She took it in stride. She'd worked for Liam for several years before I'd met her, and she must have grown used to his unexplained absences. She assumed Liam had been the one to ask Rafe to step in, and she remarked about what a thoughtful gesture it was.

I gritted my teeth and tried to smile as though I too thought it was perfectly okay for Liam to take off without telling anyone just a few minutes before her wedding. And I never told her he hadn't bothered to find a stand-in before he left.

I took a deep breath to relax. If Genevra was okay with him leaving like this, then so was I. At least for now.

"Ready?" I asked.

She nodded.

Rafe walked over and kissed her cheek. "You're the most beautiful bride I've ever seen. Thanks for letting me be a part of your day."

We all lined up at the back door again, and I sent a text to Chaun. He was acting as the wedding emcee today, so he announced that the guests should take their seats. Once everybody had found a seat, he signaled to the band to start the processional music.

Since all RIO's best photographers were either guests or participants, we'd hired an outside photographer for the event, although it killed me to do it. She'd photographed us earlier at Newton's as we got ready and then taken a lot of shots on the limo ride to RIO. But once we were all dressed and waiting in Genevra's office, she'd gone outside to capture scenes of the decorations and the guests.

The photographer had it easy today. The venue, the wedding participants, even the guests, were all super attractive.

When we started the processional, she was stationed right outside the door, snapping pictures of us as we came through. I heard a slight gasp from her when she realized that Rafe Cummings, major Hollywood heartthrob, was escorting the bride, but she took it in stride. At least she wouldn't have to worry about how the shots with him in them came out.

I knew from experience that it was impossible to take a bad photo of Rafe, and generous soul that he is, he stood out of the limelight and gently positioned Genevra so she would be the main focus and look her best in every frame.

We'd set up white folding chairs along the entire length of the crushed shell path so people would have a good view of Genevra as she passed them by and then have comfortable seating for the ceremony to follow.

As a group, we walked slowly down the meandering path toward the small sandy beach between the dock and the patio at Ray's Place.

When he caught sight of Theresa, Gus Simmons smiled with such love in his eyes that it made me want to cry. Beside him, Newton winked at Joely and wiggled his eyebrows, making her laugh.

When we'd first walked out the door, Bari had seemed nervous, but she straightened up and put a huge smile on her face when she saw Austin standing alone in the crowd.

Everyone in the wedding party had someone special here today, and it made me sad that on this day of love, among a crowd consisting of all my family and friends, there wasn't a single soul who connected with me like that. Nobody was here to appreciate my appearance.

But this was Genevra's day, not mine, so I kept my head up and smiled at everyone we passed. Today was all about Genevra.

Naturally, Genevra and Rafe were last in the procession, and Penny walked slowly and solemnly by Rafe's side with no leash involved. I don't know how he'd managed to train her like that so quickly, but her behavior was impeccable. I felt a glow of pride that my newly adopted dog was so smart.

Everyone stood up as they made their entrance and walked down the path. There were audible oohs and aahs as she passed.

Genevra is a lovely woman in general, but on this day, she was exquisite—the epitome of a beautiful bride. It was well worth a look to see her today of all days. She looked incredible in her simple, classic ivory lace dress with understated makeup. Nothing flashy or overdone. Just simple, quiet elegance.

Her auburn hair was piled on her head in loose curls. She carried a small bouquet of white roses with yellow and purple flowers set off with lots of greenery to match her eyes. Her tea length ivory silk gown draped softly down her body. The long sleeves split just past her shoulders and rejoined at her wrists, leaving the length of her arms bare and showing off their toned muscles. She moved gracefully, like she was floating on a cloud.

She was perfection.

From the look on his face, I could tell Oliver thought so too.

Years ago, Stewie had been ordained in some whacky church. He swore he was legally authorized to perform weddings and other ceremonies, so we always let him officiate at our most solemn rituals. But for those rites that truly matter—like a wedding—we usually also had a more traditional officiant on hand to be sure we had all the T's crossed and the I's dotted.

We'd dragged the podium from the conference room to fill in as an altar on the beach. Oliver and Newton stood side-by-side in front of it, awaiting Genevra's arrival. Oliver's face was glowing with love and happiness.

Stewie stood behind Oliver and Newton, looking almost elegant in a tux of his own. He'd even gotten his hair cut for the occasion, although I suspected that was Doc's influence rather than his own idea.

Of course, Stewie wouldn't be Stewie without a Hawaiian print somewhere in his apparel, but he hadn't worn his usual garishly printed baggy shirt with his tux. Instead, he sported a brightly colored cummerbund adorned with pink flamingos, yellow pineapples, and purple parrots.

Normally when asked to perform a service like this, Stewie came up with some zany process calling on ancient gods, druids, or spirits of the universe, but today he was playing it straight. "Dearly beloved…" he started. He quietly and efficiently took Genevra and Oliver through a traditional, non-denominational litany.

"I now pronounce you husband and wife," he said. "But before you kiss the bride, young Oliver, you need to go through the ceremony again one more time." He stepped aside and let the Marriage Officer, who was a Cayman government official, perform the legal requirements. Just in case.

And then the party really began.

Stefan Gibb—Noah and Austin's older brother—was coordinating the catering. He owned a nearby bar, Nelson's, which was a favorite with locals and tourists alike, so we were in good hands. The bar at Ray's Place was staying open all night for the wedding, with bartenders borrowed from Nelson's and several other venues working hard to keep up with the demand for drinks. We'd set out a massive buffet and circulating waitstaff walked among the crowd offering champagne and tasty bite-sized morsels while we waited for the formal, sit-down dinner service.

The band was playing a terrific mix of music from every genre and decade, so there was something for everyone to enjoy. When the band took a break, a local DJ immediately took their place so the music never stopped.

Oliver and Genevra led off the dancing, and soon everyone had joined in. I noticed Austin and Bari were dancing together practically every song, although she did dance a few times with Noah and once I even saw her with Stewie.

Dane and Maddy danced several times early on, but then later I saw them sitting at a large round table with Doc and Stewie. A few minutes later, Newton and Joely joined them. Everyone at the table smiled, and the odd grouping seemed very civilized.

Rafe, Tate, Chaun, and Benjamin were sitting together, enjoying bottled beer from an icy bucket in the center of their table. Plates of chicken wings, french fries, mozzarella sticks, and jalapeño poppers rounded out their feast. Tate leaned back in his chair, raising the front legs off the ground. He balanced easily.

I noticed Chaun try to emulate the move, but the only reason he didn't fall completely over backwards was because Benjamin and Rafe each had a hand on the chair back. Chaun seemed completely unaware of their support. I smiled at this sign of their friendship and regard for one another.

Everybody seemed to be having a great time, dining, dancing, drinking, and catching up with old friends.

After dinner, Christophe and I were sitting in the back of the bar in Ray's Place, watching the merrymakers around us. We both had our elbows on the bar, holding up our heads as we watched the happy gathering. Christophe was despondent that the wedding meant he had definitely lost Genevra forever, and it was making the sexy Frenchman extremely morose. I was trying to cheer him up, but I wasn't having much success since I was feeling so low myself.

Stewie and Doc danced by the front of the bar. Stewie was clutching a rose in his teeth, and when he passed in front of us, he lowered Doc into a deep dip. She laughed, and their faces glowed. It was good to see them so happy. In fact, everyone in attendance seemed happy.

Except us.

Christophe signaled to the bartender for another glass of red wine for each of us. "What is bothering you, Cherie? And where is Liam? He should be here with you, non?"

I sighed. "He was called away."

Christophe sipped his wine. "He is often called away, is he not?"

"Yes, he is," I said. "And I never know when it's going to happen, or how long he'll be gone. Most of the time I don't even know where in the world he is. He never calls or even sends texts. I don't like it." I cringed at the whiny sound of my own voice.

He nodded sagely. "Is that why you are so sad tonight?"

I nodded back.

"You need to tell him how unhappy this habit of his makes you." Christophe took another sip of wine.

"I did. But it doesn't seem to have changed anything. I love him, but I can't live like that. Never knowing if he'll be there when I get home. Not knowing if he's alive or dead. I hate it."

I took a tiny sip of my own wine. "How about you? Why are you sitting here in the dark with me instead of out there charming all the beautiful ladies?"

"I have lost my one true love," he said dramatically. "And so now I am drinking wine with a different beautiful woman, one who is funny, smart, strong, and brave. And for that, I count myself lucky."

I laughed along with him. "You shouldn't be hiding out back here with me. You're a sexy, smart, exotic man, and there are tons of women here who would love to spend time with you. You should mingle."

"Non. Je suis désolée," he said dramatically.

No. I am desolate, I translated mentally.

He stared into his red wine. "I'll never find someone else to love the way I love Genevra. And no one will ever love me the way Genevra loves your brother." He raised his glass and drained it. "The lucky S-O-B."

"Don't say that, Christophe. Someday you'll look up from your wine, your eyes will meet hers, and you'll be totally in love. When that happens, you'll be asking me 'Genevra who?'"

He laughed and raised his glass to let Stefan know he was ready for another refill. While he waited, he stared pensively at the wood-grain of the bar, tracing the patterns with his finger.

"I want to come back to RIO full time. I'm getting older. I don't like traveling any more, and I especially don't like all the paperwork involved in the franchise thing you have me doing. Can't I come back and just run the freediving school here, the way I used to?"

His melted chocolate brown eyes held a depth of loneliness and sadness that I could only guess at.

"Of course you can come back. Benjamin has taken on a lot of new responsibilities, so he doesn't have as much time to run the freediving school. I'll ask him to find another way to handle the franchise paperwork, and you can teach here the way you used to instead of traveling around recruiting instructors and setting up new schools. You're famous, so we'll probably still want to use you in the advertising for all the schools. I can't guarantee that you may not have to travel from time to time, but this can be your home base. We're lucky to have you on our team."

He smiled like the sunrise. "Oui. This will be my home base." He emptied his glass again. "But now it is late. We should go." We slid off our stools and departed.

Chapter 45
Little Cayman

THE NEXT MORNING, my new husband turned to me with love in his eyes and a smile on his lips. "You're the most beautiful bride there's ever been in the whole history of the world. And I'm the luckiest man that ever lived. Thank you for agreeing to become my wife. I never thought it would happen."

We were lying in a two-person hammock on the beach at the Paradise Villas Resort on Little Cayman. I was dreamily remembering our wedding. It had been perfect.

When we'd cornered the Marriage Officer in the wee hours after Genevra's and Oliver's wedding, he'd been reluctant to perform our spur of the moment ceremony. "I like it better when people plan ahead. That way I know they're serious," he'd said.

But eventually, we'd managed to convince him that we were very serious and that we had given the marriage a great deal of thought.

Or at the very least, some thought.

"This is highly irregular," he said. "I probably shouldn't be doing this. Do you even have a ring?"

My husband-to-be pulled a ring from the pocket of his tux. It was a thick band of hammered silver set with small stones in varying shades of blue. I loved it immediately.

"The gems match the colors I see in your eyes," he said, "Each of its gems has a different color, and there's a color for every one of your moods."

He took my hand. "I bought this ring the first day we met, and I've carried it with me every day since then, hoping that someday this would happen. Thank you for making my dream come true."

If I hadn't already promised to marry him, his romantic words alone might have been enough to convince me. They certainly convinced the Marriage Officer, who quickly performed the required rite in RIO's vaulted glass atrium in front of the aquarium admission ticket kiosk. There were no witnesses.

It had been very late, practically morning, and most of the guests were gone. Oliver and Genevra had left hours ago, rushing off aboard Oliver's boat the *Flemingo* in a hail of soap bubbles that glistened in the moonlight. They'd looked so happy it brought a lump to my throat.

Meanwhile, my husband and I strolled casually through the last few revelers at the party, right down the dock to the *Tranquility* and hopped aboard. We were gone before anyone even had a chance to miss us.

We putted along Seven Mile Beach, enjoying the lights and the music drifting across the water from the many open air bars and restaurants. We headed toward Rum Point to pick up a few things for our impromptu honeymoon. I also needed to make sure that I'd left plenty of seed and water for Chico and Henrietta, even though I planned to text Chaun later and ask him to take care of my pets while I was away.

We stopped to do a dive at Rum Point, my favorite dive site. I tied up on the mooring, which was wide open at this time of night. Or rather, this early in the morning.

We slithered into our dive skins and then did our pre-dive checkouts. When we were good to go, we did simultaneous giant stride entries off the rear dive platform and sank beneath the waves.

We held hands as we descended, following the sand chute path on the way to the drop off. I pointed out Suzie Q glaring at me with her dark enigmatic eyes as we passed over her.

I smiled.

I couldn't help it. I'd never been this happy.

We reached the wall and swam over the drop off, sinking down to about 100 feet. We were swimming against the current, checking out all the nooks and crannies for interesting sea life. As usual, the resident green turtle swam by, warily watching us out of the side of his eye while he pretended we couldn't see him.

Even this early, the immense grouper I often saw here was out, waiting patiently in line to get his teeth cleaned at the cleaning station. The shrimp were busy with a green moray eel who was ahead of him in the queue.

At the turnaround point of the dive, we let ourselves drift up along the wall, admiring the majestic staghorn corals swaying gently in the current. We swam through a small group of purple tangs and passed by a trio of regal queen angelfish. Just before we reached the top of the wall, I pointed out the tiny spotted drum flittering gracefully back and forth in his little grotto, his long ribbon-like fins making lovely patterns as he moved.

As we crested the wall at fifty feet, two spotted eagle rays swam right in front of us, passing no more than three feet away. They both stopped for a second or two to look at us, and my face broke into a huge smile.

Spotted eagle rays are omens of good luck, and the fact that we'd seen two—and that they'd chosen to stop and look directly at us—felt like we'd received the ocean's blessing on our marriage. Suddenly, I knew beyond a shadow of a doubt that we'd done the right thing.

A triangle of squid hovered ahead of us along the sand path, fluttering like colorful angels of the sea. Another good sign. And the bevy of garden eels bowed back into their burrows as we passed over their heads. I honestly felt like all my favorites were here, guests at my first dive as a married woman. I was thrilled.

And so happy. Never had I felt such joy.

At the end of the dive, we hovered at the mooring line at fifteen feet for three minutes, smiling down at the beauty beneath us. Once we'd finished our stop, we climbed the *Tranquility*'s ladder and headed for Little Cayman, where we'd planned to spend a few days. With a late night phone call to the owner, we'd already rented an oceanfront cottage at Paradise Villas.

After I'd moored the boat, the three of us went ashore to our hotel.

"Welcome Mr. and Mrs. Cummings," said the lady checking us in. "And this must be little Penny. She's just as cute as you told me she was." She handed Rafe the key to open our new life together.

I couldn't believe how loving him had crept up on me. Working together almost every day for the last few years, we'd built a rock-solid friendship. We'd also been building a rock-solid love, and I had barely noticed it happening until Rafe tracked me down in my office after Oliver and Genevra's wedding. He'd poured out his heart to me, and my own heart answered. We belonged together.

Chapter 46
Final Dive

WE SLEPT most of our first day as a married couple, and after a quick dinner at the Hungry Iguana, we strolled back to our cabin. We sat on the sand watching the sun rise. We'd been talking and making plans for our future. As the sun hinted at morning, we took Penny for a long walk along the beach, then gave her an early breakfast. We only had a few days to stay here, and we wanted to dive Bloody Bay Wall as many times as we could during our short honeymoon.

I piloted the *Tranquility* out to our chosen site. Rafe was sitting on the bow, head tilted back and a small, contented smile on his famous face.

After we'd moored the boat, Rafe and I geared up for our dive. Once we were ready, we stepped off the dive platform and descended along the mooring line. The wall started at about twenty feet of depth, and we paused a moment, hanging over the deep blue. Even with the astonishing visibility here in the crystalline waters of Little Cayman, I couldn't see the bottom.

Small wonder. It was about 6,000 feet away. We were diving at Mixing Bowl, a terrific site on Little Cayman's world famous Bloody Bay Wall.

The name Bloody Bay Wall sounds like the place must have

been the site of some horrific massacre, but in reality, the name arose because of the vibrant red tones of the coral reef.

The site was spectacular. We dropped down to about one hundred feet and then slowly worked our way up the wall, mesmerized by the stunning corals, which were immense as well as brightly colored.

Hundreds of huge sea fans in a stunning array of red, pink, purple, and orange waved slowly in the mild current. We peered closely at the branches, and the sight of a couple of tiny sea horses who made their homes in the shelter of the giant gorgonians was our reward.

A spotted moray eel made his home in a small but very secluded cavern in the coral. He stuck his head out into the gentle current, working his jaws up and down to force water over his gills so he could breathe. Two groupers joined us as we rose along the wall, and they stayed with us looking for treats or pats until we left the safety of the wall where they made their home.

On the reef top, huge barrel sponges provided shelter for a multitude of small reef creatures, like neighbors in an underwater condominium complex. As we were peering into a large orange barrel sponge, a green sea turtle stopped next to Rafe to see what we were looking at.

When he saw there was nothing special going on, he took off. We turned to watch him swimming along the reef until we lost sight of him in the purple haze when he was about 300 feet away.

As we turned to smile at each other, I saw a spotted eagle ray coming along the wall toward Rafe. I flapped my hands in the sign we used for rays at the same moment he held his hand to his head in the sign for shark. Both creatures swam right past us without a second look.

We headed east and rose up to the sandy flat area. Here we saw the usual array of reef fish, including parrotfish, purple tangs, queen triggerfish, rock beauties, sergeant majors, and a few yellow snappers.

As we passed over a sandy spot, we saw the tell-tale outline of a stingray's wings buried below us in the sand. Only the eyes and the faint outline of her wings gave her hiding place away. We left her alone, of course, but she swiveled her eyes to watch us as we swam off.

Rafe reached over and took my hand. I could see his endearing smile stretched around his regulator's mouthpiece. Even with the mask and regulator in the way, I could see how happy he looked. His face positively glowed with joy.

I knew my own face was glowing too.

We reached the mooring line, and when I looked up, a shaft of sunlight penetrated the crystalline water, leaving us bathed in its golden glow.

I looked at Rafe with wonder. Ever since we'd taken our wedding vows, the universe had been sending us its good wishes. Eagle rays pausing to issue a benediction. Sea turtles swimming alongside us. A grouper wanting a pat. Rays of sunshine lighting up our dive, letting us know we'd done the right thing.

Rafe was looking back at me with love and wonder in his eyes, and I could tell by the look of peace on his face that he felt the same way. We were together, and the universe and everything in it seemed to be telling us we belonged together.

We climbed the ladder onto the *Tranquility* and doffed our gear. As soon as everything was secure, Rafe took my hand and squeezed it. "Let's go back to the villa and get Penny. It's only right we should all be together as we start our new lives."

A Sneak Peek at In Deep

If you're new to The Fin Fleming Scuba Diving Mystery Series, here's an excerpt from In Deep, the first book in the series.

Chapter 1
Freedive Training

It was just after dawn on the day of the first accident, and the scorching Cayman Islands' sun was already warm on my shoulders. Before starting to load my gear onto the *Maddy*, my stepfather's dive boat, I pulled on an old silver dive skin left over from one of the annual documentaries filmed by the Dr. Madelyn Anderson Russo Institute for Ocean Exploration. My name—Finola Fleming—was emblazoned in fluorescent pink letters down the right leg.

I was still in the first month of my new job and trying hard to make a name for myself. After finishing my doctoral coursework in oceanography, I'd rejoined the family business—the ocean exploration institute we call RIO for short—as marketing director and principal underwater photographer, work I love. Mostly because it requires me to dive every day.

My stepfather, Ray Russo, and his lifelong dive buddy, Gus Simmons, were sitting in the twin captain's chairs waiting for me to finish loading up. Today, they were training for a deep apnea dive that we wanted to include in this year's RIO documentary. My assignment was to film some of the training.

I tucked my dive bag under the bench along the side of the 36-foot Munson dive boat that had been custom made for Ray back when he was a champion freediver and a world-renowned treasure hunter. Despite years of hard use in every ocean on earth, his boat still gleamed like new. Ray made sure of it.

"All set, Ray," I said when I'd put my tanks and photography equipment away.

Ray gave me a devilish grin. "Is that all you're bringing, Fin? You sure you don't need any more stuff?"

"Maybe another camera, a change of dive skin, some lip gloss?" added Gus.

Ray finished. "Women never travel light, do they? What is all that stuff?"

Gus chuckled. "I don't know, Boss. But there sure is an awful lot of it."

"Don't need it...," said Ray.

"Don't want it," finished Gus.

Ray and Gus both laughed, and I laughed along with them.

After a lifetime of friendship, the two men were so close they often completed each other's sentences, and to watch them dive together was like watching a single organism perform. I had been diving with them since I was a little kid, and they had trained me and taken care of me all that time. My heart swelled with love for them.

We moored the boat on the rim of a flat reef that dropped off into a vertical wall that went more than two miles down. Ray used a small portable winch to lower a heavy metal plate on a guide rope marked in ten meter increments. They would use the rope as a visual scale while they practiced.

Apnea diving can be tricky. Although it's more common in scuba diving, freedivers are susceptible to narcosis whether from the effects of nitrogen build up as for scuba divers or excess carbon dioxide is still unclear. Either way, it helps to have the rope as a guide. Narcosis, also known as rapture of the deep, can mess with your mind, making you forget which way is up.

"Ready?" Gus asked.

Ray nodded. "All set. Let's suit up."

Ray and Gus wouldn't be using any gear except a small face

mask and an aluminum nose plug while they made a series of progressively deeper breathhold dives. No scuba tanks full of life sustaining air; no fins for propulsion. Nothing but their frail bodies against the cruel ocean depths while training to freedive to 330 feet.

Down that deep, it's dark. It's cold. And it's lonely.

Not to mention treacherous.

Since Ray and Gus would be in the water all day, they pulled on thick neoprene wetsuits for warmth. Before stepping off the *Maddy*'s platform, they strapped dive computers to their wrists to track their depth. The powerful computers were just a little bulkier than a regular wristwatch, but they were technical marvels. My stepfather loved technology almost as much as he loved diving.

I entered the water to videotape their first dives. After filming their entries and exits, I'd have accomplished my assignment for the day, and I planned to spend the rest of my time working on the storyboard for a new promotional video I was planning for RIO.

"Let's start easy. Just 132 feet," Ray said.

Gus nodded. "You go first."

"One of us is up when the other one is down, right?" Ray said, repeating the safety rule for apnea divers. Although I wasn't a breathhold diver myself, I knew the rule's purpose was to make sure if the diver underwater ran into a problem, the diver keeping watch on the surface could come to the rescue.

In theory, at least, that's the way it works.

While Ray floated on his back, calming his mind and body, sipping air in preparation for his dive, I sank beneath the waves to get in position for filming. When he was ready, he made a head-first descent, using his powerful arms and bare feet to propel himself straight down. He was sleek, fast, and focused. A perfect visual for film.

At sixty feet, the ocean took over the work. Ray went still and relied on his body's own negative buoyancy to pull him down. I followed him until at 132 feet, his dive computer beeped. He turned and headed for the surface, kicking hard to break the ocean's hold on him. Shortly after he passed sixty feet, positive buoyancy propelled him to the surface with no further effort on his part. I followed him up, still filming.

He broke the surface and removed his mask. "I am okay," he said, while making the diver's traditional hand on head sign. This was the required protocol in competition, and the custom looked good on video. Ray was always well aware of the impression he made on camera.

For fifteen minutes after Ray surfaced, Gus studied him with care to ensure he wasn't suffering any ill effects from the dive. This was an important part of the after-dive procedure. The prolonged lack of oxygen sometimes makes divers forget how to breathe when they surface after deep apnea dives.

Once Ray's breathing normalized, Gus prepared for his own descent. I filmed him too, and like Ray's, his dive was perfect. Easy, even for Gus, who wasn't as experienced as Ray. But then again, these 132-foot dives had been a mere warm-up.

The human body needs time to adapt to freediving, and divers sometimes worked for months or even years to increase their tolerance by just a few feet. Soon Gus would be fighting to master every additional foot of depth, but for Ray, reaching the goal was a simple matter of reacclimating himself to the sport he'd once dominated.

Their next dives went to 140 feet. At these depths, divers were no longer visible to watchers on the surface. The designated safety diver above relied on the dive's elapsed time to decide whether to intervene. I climbed back aboard the boat to work on my video's storyboard while Gus and Ray kept diving.

By noon they'd progressed to 230 feet. Although Ray had gone much deeper on past dives, this was close to the maximum depth Gus had ever achieved. "One more dive before we break for lunch?" Gus said.

"Sure thing. I'm starving," Ray said. "I'm going to 260 feet on this dive." He inhaled several times and then disappeared under the water.

I checked my watch when he surfaced. Ray had been underwater for over three and a half minutes, still well under his personal best time.

Ray removed his mask. "I'm okay. In fact, I'm fine, and I'm more than ready to eat. No sense in waiting any longer than we need to for lunch since we're all starving. Fin can keep an eye on me. Why don't you dive now, Gus?"

"Okay, if you say so. I'm gonna try for 260 feet too."

"You sure? We're not competing here."

Gus grinned. "We're always competing, my man. And if an old guy like you can do it, I can do it too." He floated on his back for a moment, then swiveled beneath the water.

As we waited for Gus to surface, seconds slid into minutes. I checked the timer on my dive computer. He'd now been under water for three minutes. For Gus, that was a long time.

Gus wasn't approaching world record times yet, but then again, he was not a world class breathhold diver. I could tell from how uneasy Ray was that we both knew he should have surfaced by now, or at least we should have been able to see him making his way back from the shadowy depths.

At three minutes and fifteen seconds of downtime, Ray peered through his mask into the water for any sign of his best friend. I put my camera away and lifted my scuba tank over my shoulders.

Just in case.

Three minutes and thirty seconds.

Still no sign of Gus. I could hear Ray's fearful panting even from my spot on the boat.

At three minutes and forty-five seconds, I saw growing alarm in Ray's deep brown eyes. His breathing was rapid and shallow, and his panic over Gus prevented him from catching his breath. He wasn't wearing tanks, and he couldn't freedive now even to save his friend. He wouldn't get past thirty feet before running out of air.

I donned my fins and stepped into the water. This was a problem. A very big problem.

"Save him," he said. "Please." His voice was raspy, breathless, and full of terror.

I put my scuba regulator in my mouth and sank below the

surface. While I descended, I turned in slow circles searching in all directions for any sign of Gus.

At first, I saw nothing.

At 100 feet, I spotted him, his foot tangled in the guide rope below me. He was very still, not even trying to swim for the surface.

I swam as hard as I could. I reached him at 130 feet of depth. He was unconscious.

I grabbed him and stuck my primary regulator into his mouth, switching to my spare for my own use. I clasped his torso with one arm, using the other to hold the regulator in his mouth in case he began breathing on his own. I began the long trek back to the surface, ascending as fast as I could and ignoring all safety stops.

The alarms on my dive computer went crazy at my rapid ascent. I didn't care. I had to save Gus, no matter the cost to my own health. My heart was pounding with fear and exertion.

Knowing every second could mean life or death for Gus, it felt like forever before we emerged from the water. Ray pulled Gus's limp body onto the *Maddy*'s dive platform.

I scrambled aboard and dragged the emergency oxygen tank over to where Gus lay immobile. I clapped the mask over his face and started the flow.

Meanwhile, Ray grabbed the radio and called RIO. "I need help. Get an ambulance and oxygen to the dock. Gus had an accident." Heedless of the tears running down his face, he gave our location and then began CPR, working to save his friend's life. "Please, God," he whispered, over and over again as he pumped.

I noticed the depth on Gus's dive watch, which showed he'd been down to 330 feet. I pointed it out to Ray and asked, "Why would he go down that far?"

Ray shook his head but didn't break his CPR rhythm. I was sure we were both thinking about the French freediving champion who'd blacked out and suffered lung barotrauma because the judges had set the guide rope a mere ten meters deeper than he'd planned. Gus had gone so much further than an extra ten meters. Still, that injured diver had been able to resume his freediving career soon after the accident. I prayed Gus would be as lucky.

Despite my desperate prayers, I was surprised when after a few minutes, Gus expelled a belly full of sea water, gasped, and at last, began breathing on his own.

Ray's sigh of relief was audible, and tears streamed down his face. He rolled Gus onto his left side to prevent him from choking. The color slowly returned to Gus's lips and cheeks, and his eyes fluttered open. He tried to sit up, coughing, and spitting blood.

Ray put a hand on his shoulder. "Just relax. Take a few minutes before you exert yourself."

Gus coughed again and nodded before he lay back down. After a few minutes, his breathing steadied and once more, he tried to sit up. This time Ray piled several life preservers behind him to support his back.

"That diver tried to kill me," Gus said. "I'm lucky I made it."

Ray and I looked at each other over his head. "What diver?" Ray asked. "What happened down there?"

Gus took a deep breath and shuddered. "I was swimming hard but feeling good. I knew I could make it. Ears and sinuses were clear. I was going so fast I didn't have time to notice anything until I saw this other diver at around two-hundred-forty feet."

"There was no other diver down there, Gus,'" said Ray. "Fin and I were both on the surface. There are no boats nearby, and we didn't see any bubbles from a scuba diver."

"There was another diver," Gus said, spitting another mouthful of frothy blood into the cup I held for him. "Came out of nowhere. With a rebreather and a scooter. That's why you didn't know the diver was there."

"I think you might have been narc'ed, Gus." I said as I poured the cup's contents overboard.

"Freedivers don't get narc'ed," he retorted.

"I'm afraid they do. The latest research shows it's possible whenever you go below eighty-five feet. You were down pretty far, and even though we don't know for sure during freediving if it's caused by nitrogen, carbon dioxide or…"

"Let's not worry about narcosis now," Ray said. "The important thing is you're safe."

"I wasn't narc'ed. It was real." Gus could be stubborn. "As soon as I turned to go to the surface, the diver put a rope around my right foot and held me there. I tried to get away, but the more I struggled the tighter it got. I bet I have a mark on my ankle from the rope." He reached feebly for his leg.

"I'll get it." Ray rolled up the wetsuit leg. A red welt encircled Gus's right ankle. Ray's gaze met mine over our patient.

I shook my head slightly. "Your leg was tangled in the guide rope when I found you."

Gus tightened his lips and waved his hand in a dismissive gesture. "I wasn't hallucinating. That diver held me down there until I stopped struggling. By then it was too late. My lungs were ready to burst. I didn't have enough air to get back to the surface. Whoever was down there tried to kill me. I'd have been a goner if you hadn't come for me."

"Of course I'd come for you." I wiped another trickle of blood from his lips. Bleeding lungs were a common complication of freediving, but the condition usually healed quickly without causing permanent damage. Even so, it was important to have a doctor evaluate Gus right away. I looked at Ray. "You stay with him. I'll drive the boat back to RIO."

He nodded. "Radio ahead that we're on our way in. Theresa will want to know he's awake."

I climbed the ladder to the flying bridge and started the engines. As soon as we were underway, I grabbed the radio to let the RIO team know we were heading to port. Their answer was nearly drowned out by Gus's wife sobbing in the background, and the sound broke my heart.

I raised my voice so she could hear me. "Theresa, he's awake, and he seems fine. We'll be there in ten minutes. Maybe less."

Cheers and applause greeted my words. Theresa shouted, "Thank you."

Theresa and I had met when she started dating Gus a few years ago. I always say she's my best friend, but the truth is, she's my only friend. You can blame my unorthodox childhood for my lack of friends, but I wouldn't have changed a thing about my life.

As a kid, I'd spent most of my time at sea on the *Omega*, RIO's research vessel. That's why I call my mother Maddy instead of Mom, because that's what everyone around me called her. Educated aboard ship by private tutors, I never went to a regular school until college. I was shy, gawky, and isolated, and to make matters worse, I was always visible on TV and the internet because of RIO's popular annual documentaries. Not a recipe for popularity, but I had experiences unmatched in any other environment. And now I had Theresa as a friend. On balance, it was all good.

I pulled the *Maddy* up to the dock at RIO headquarters where the entire staff was gathered on shore to assist Gus. He was popular with the team, and there was no shortage of people wanting to help.

Even before they'd secured the boat, Doc, the EMTs, my mother, and Theresa all jumped aboard. The medics started preparing Gus for transport to RIO's infirmary. Theresa tried not to get in the way while still holding onto him as tightly as she could. Tears rolled down her face.

My mother went straight to Ray and wrapped her arms around him. "You're safe," she murmured. "I am so lucky." They stood together watching the medics strap Gus to a portable gurney.

A trickle of blood seeped from Gus's mouth, and he grasped Theresa's hand. "Can't breathe," he said, clutching his chest with his other hand.

Doc listened through her stethoscope. "Possible heart attack," she said. "Take him to Grand Cayman Hospital instead of sickbay." RIO's infirmary was the best in the islands for diving related injuries, cuts, scrapes, stings, and barotrauma, but we weren't well equipped for other types of medical emergencies. The medical staff lifted the gurney onto the dock and sped off toward the nearby parking lot to rush Gus away.

Doc put her hand on Theresa's arm. "C'mon, Theresa. You can ride in the ambulance with me." The two women hurried after the medics.

The rest of us stayed at RIO, willing Gus to make a full recovery. We couldn't focus on anything except Gus, so we closed RIO's aquarium and all our public areas. The entire staff gathered in the cafeteria, waiting for news.

Later that afternoon, Doc came through the main entrance. She stood at the front of the room so we could all hear her. "I can't give you a lot of details, but I can say Gus will be fine. He did have a heart attack and he sustained some serious lung damage from the dive, but in time, I expect him to make a full recovery. He'll have to stay out of the water for at least six months, maybe more." The crowd broke into cheers at the welcome news.

Chapter 2
Dive on Rum Point

A LITTLE PAST sunrise a few days later—the day of the second accident—I was snorkeling alone in the warm waters at Rum Point on the north side of Grand Cayman. Daily diving was part of my job, and I was still trying to calm down after the drama of Gus's near drowning.

Through my waterproof bone conduction headphones, I was enjoying the sweeping sounds of Ravel's *Une Barque sur l'ocean*. The rolling notes echoing the sunlight dancing through the clear seawater were tailor made for the moment. I aimed my video camera at the pile of sand where a stingray's hooded eyes and the telltale outline of his wings were the only hints to his presence.

I took a breath through my snorkel and dove, adjusting my camera to zoom in on the distinctive white scar above the stingray's eyes. As a kid, I'd named this stingray Harry because of the fictional wizard who bore a similar scar.

We were both a lot older now than when we'd first crossed paths. Recently, I'd taken hundreds of still photos and hours of video of Harry for a short film I was working on for RIO.

Since my playlist would end with the Ravel piece, I knew it was time to finish my dive and get ready for work. I surfaced and took one more breath through my snorkel, gently kicking a few times to bring me closer to Harry's position on the bottom. But when I dove back down, he rose, dipped his wings to brush off the sand, and glided away. Harry never let me get too close, although after all this time he must have known I was neither predator nor prey.

As usual, I was enthralled by the elegance of his gliding motion, and I followed his path with my camera's lens until he dropped behind a large orange brain coral. I lost sight of him just as my lungs signaled an urgent need to breathe. I hated leaving his mysterious watery world, but I couldn't stay any longer. I headed for the surface, while my gaze lingered on the clouds of slowly drifting sand indicating Harry was re-burying himself on the ocean bottom.

The top of my head had barely emerged from the water when something big and fast hit me hard, lifting my body fully out of the sea before I fell back. On the way down, I saw ribbons of blood swirling around me. Then, there was nothing but darkness.

Links to my Books

Shop my online store

Shop the Series Page on Amazon

Also by Sharon Ward

In Deep

Sunken Death

Dark Tide

Killer Storm

Hidden Depths

Sea Stars

Or see the entire series Fin Fleming series by following the link on the previous page.

If you enjoyed Rip Current, you can continue reading about the adventures of Fin and the gang by following any of the links on the previous page.

Also, nothing (except actually buying or reading the book) helps an author more than a positive review, so please give Rip Current (and me!) a boost by leaving a review. Here's the link:

Rip Current

And if you'd like to subscribe to my totally random and very rarely published newsletter, you can sign up here.

Acknowledgments

As always, I have to thank the members of my writing group, Kate Hohl, Andrea Clark, Mary Beth Gale and Stephanie Scott Snyder. They are all great writers and great friends, and I couldn't do this without you.

Nick Sullivan and Chris Niles at TropicalAuthors.com, and all the other Tropical Authors. If you like my books, you'll probably like theirs too.

Hallie Ephron, world's greatest writing instructor. Thank you.

Teri Hoitt, Trish Hoitt, and Patti Hoitt. Great sisters-in-law saddled with my brothers for husbands. Bob, Dave, and Ed. Just kidding. You're great brothers too.

My beautiful daughter Erin, and her amazing children Taylor and Cam, and husband Scott.

For everybody listed above, I appreciate your support

Thank you to my readers. You make me very happy.

And Jack, the world's best husband.

About the Author

Sharon Ward is the author of the Fin Fleming Scuba Diving Mystery Series, which includes *In Deep, Sunken Death, Dark Tide, Killer Storm, Hidden Depths, Sea Stars,* and *Rip Current.* The eighth book in the series, *Sea Monsters* is coming soon.

Sharon Ward was a marketing executive at prominent software companies Oracle and Microsoft before becoming a writer. She was a PADI certified divemaster who has hundreds of dives under her weight belt. Sharon is a member of Sisters in Crime, MWA, ITW, Grub Street, the Authors Guild, and the Cape Cod Writers Center. She lives in Massachusetts with her husband Jack and their miniature long-haired dachshund Molly, who is the actual head of the Ward household.

Made in United States
North Haven, CT
03 May 2025

68532608R00176